BOLETO

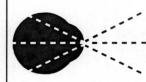 This Large Print Book carries the
Seal of Approval of N.A.V.H.

BOLETO

ALYSON HAGY

KENNEBEC LARGE PRINT
A part of Gale, Cengage Learning

GALE
CENGAGE Learning·

Detroit • New York • San Francisco • New Haven, Conn • Waterville, Maine • London

GALE
CENGAGE Learning·

LIBRARY OF CONGRESS CATALOGING-IN-PUBLICATION DATA

Hagy, Alyson Carol.
  Boleto / by Alyson Hagy.
    pages ; cm. — (Kennebec Large Print superior collection)
    ISBN 978-1-4104-5796-7 (softcover) — ISBN 1-4104-5796-6 (softcover)
  1. Horse trainers—Fiction. 2. Human-animal relationships—Fiction.
3. Absaroka Range (Mont. and Wyo.)—Fiction. 4. California,
Southern—Fiction. 5. Polo—Fiction. I. Title.
PS3558.A32346B65 2013
813'.54—dc23   2013003936

Published in 2013 by arrangement with Graywolf Press.

For my dad and my friend Jane Dominick,
who both love their horses

PART I

She was a gift, though he did not think of her that way for a long time. He paid twelve hundred dollars for her, money that came straight from his single account at Cabin Valley Bank. She was halter broke, and trailer broke, and she had been wormed for the spring. Someone had taken a rasp to her feet. He had seen her dam, Sally's Quick Ticket, win more than one prize in cutting horse competitions. He had no knowledge of her sire. The man who bred her kept good horses at his ranch outside of Cody, on the South Fork of the Shoshone River. The man did not use his horses much, but he had an experienced manager, someone who knew how to care for foals and weanlings. When the man chose to sell some of his animals, the manager, a careful fellow by the name of Campion, asked around. Campion did not go in for the commotion of stock sales. He had four horses he needed to sell, and the prettiest one was a quarter horse filly that was barely two years old. She was nicely balanced. There was a decent chance she had inherited her mother's speed. Was it true what he had heard? Campion asked on the telephone. Was he still in the market?

He knew twelve hundred dollars was a bargain for a strong-legged filly with papers. He knew that even before he saw her.

His name was William Testerman, and he was twenty-three years old. There were days he felt older. And days he felt as lost as a blind pup. His parents had raised him in a way that allowed him to take account of the weaknesses he might find within himself. His older brothers, Everett and Chad, had managed to cover the bases on the family ranch. It was a small place, just ninety deeded acres set along one side of Little Kettle Creek. The town of Lost Cabin, Wyoming, had grown right up to the edge of the ranch, and the town was growing still. It was his father's joke to refer to the hay meadows and corrals he owned as the Lost Cabin Municipal Golf Course.

Town is eating its way right past us, his father said. When I was a kid, you couldn't pay people to live in this part of the state. Too cold. Too much isolation. Now every-body in America thinks they're in love with fresh air and loneliness.

Will knew the Testerman Ranch was not going to become a golf course, but it would remain forever small, even if the grazing permits in the Rampart Range west of town were renewed at a reasonable price. There was some work for him on the place. His father had an ongoing contract with the feedlot in Powell. But he could not see himself in those fields or along those well-strung fence lines, not in the years ahead.

His mother was a schoolteacher in town. He believed he owed some of his restlessness to her. She had taken on full-time work when he was old enough to go to school, and the two of them had driven to and from Lost Cabin for many years. It was a short drive, but in those minutes together — often in the blue cold of a winter morning — they would talk about their days, about who they were. His mother had traveled some when she was young. She was also a great reader of books.

She would say to him, Who are you today, Will Testerman?

And he would say, if he wished to disappoint her, Today I hate arithmetic.

More often he would say a thing to entertain her or to warm up the teacher in her. He would say, Today I am a minuteman from Massachusetts, or, Today I am the man from over there in France who discovered germs. It wasn't hard to please his mother or to make her laugh. This was true even after a difficult day, one that left a grayish color around her lips. She only wanted to talk to him. She only wanted him to know how big the world was.

He had lived away from home for a while. He had wrangled horses on the Black Bell Ranch nearly every summer since he turned sixteen. They liked him at the Black Bell, which was an old-style guest ranch in the Absaroka Mountains east of Yellowstone. They said he could have a job there whenever he wanted. After high school, he spent a few months driving vans for a California firm that shipped horses up and down the West Coast. The job had been a serious change of pace, but he had quickly found its limits. He spent two semesters taking classes at the community college in Casper. It was a chore that pleased his mother more than it pleased him. The best was a stint in Texas. That lasted almost a year. He had worked for a big-money outfit in Texas, and there had been a great deal to learn — about people and about what he himself had best stay away from.

His brothers liked to pretend he hadn't

done anything of value in Texas. They told friends Will had tied colored ribbons into the manes of horses that sold for the price of a Denver Broncos tight end. They said he babysat rich girls. The friends wanted to hear more about the girls, so he shared the kind of stories that made him out to be the fool. He knew his place around his brothers. They were welcome to laugh at him. He had gone to Texas, which neither Chad nor Everett had done, and he had watched men and women down there do their jobs the way they liked to do them, and he had learned. He was not stubborn in the way of his brothers. He did not mind starting at the bottom of a thing and climbing up.

He acquired the filly sooner than he planned. He thought he knew why that had happened. He had the money, first of all. He had been careful that winter. He took every small job that was offered except those that might have kept him away from home at night. This meant he did not go into the Garnet Field, where the natural gas outfits were drilling wells faster than a rabbit had babies. Chad, who had gone to college to be a geologist, was in the Garnet Field. Chad made good money. He lived with a girl in a nice apartment in town. Everett was still very much at home, and he managed the comings and goings of the family cattle when he was done with his shifts driving truck for Cabin Valley Beverage. Will had not wanted to keep those kinds of hours. Their mother had been sick. There had been six weeks of chemotherapy in Riverton, and six more weeks of radiation after that. The doctors hoped the cancer was gone. They had caught it early. Will had made it his business to stay close to his mother, to drive her where she needed to be driven, and to sit in the house while she lay down in her bedroom. He tended to her. It wasn't a problem. But seeing his mother on her feet again, hearing her joke about her hair and how it was growing back in funny gray curls, opened the gate for him.

There was also the business with his neighbor, Annie Atwood. Annie had disappeared the previous summer while she was running near Flat Top Mountain. There was no good explanation for what had happened to her. Will had been questioned by the police more than once because he was Annie's friend. He had plowed her driveway during the winter with the ranch's plow, and he had known her all his life. Annie's disappearance had torn up a lot of people in town. It had raised hard questions, and people had said things in their distress that were difficult to take back. He didn't think it was wrong for him to plan on leaving Lost Cabin for a while, at least until the air around town tasted less sour in his mouth.

He told Campion he would drive up to the ranch on the South Fork of the Shoshone on Monday.

You bringing a trailer?

You think I should?

I guess I do. Or I wouldn't have mentioned it.

She got the build?

I guess I think so. Or I wouldn't have called. I know every man has his own way of seeing a horse, but I'd bet money I know how you'll see this one.

He went to the bank that afternoon. When he took the cashier's check from the teller, his hands felt steady and warm.

The drive to Cody took three hours. He didn't play the radio. The empty trailer rattled in the wind behind him. It made better music than the radio. And he liked to think when he drove. He worked over the edges of his plan in his mind. It was a good plan. Simple. It didn't involve anyone else or their money. He could get out quick if he needed to. Getting out quick was something he had learned to value in Texas.

He stopped to check his tires in Mee-teetse. The truck he was driving, a five-year-old Dodge, had briefly belonged to his brother Everett. Everett had not been satisfied with it, so Will took on the payments. The Dodge was a good match with his Bruton trailer. He had put new tires on the truck at Christmas, but he found that it paid to check the pressure in those tires after an hour on the road. The Greybull River crossed under the highway at Meeteetse. He pulled over just past the bridge. When he stepped out into the unsettled morning with the pressure gauge cold in his hand, the air pushing down through the valley of the Greybull ran icy along the edges of his jaw. It was late spring in Wyoming. The river was as crumpled and brown as a paper bag. It would probably be another six weeks before the water ran clear. He wondered what it would be like to own good muddy ranch land along the Greybull River, whether that kind of thing would ever again be possible for a man his age.

He watched the big shoulder of Carter Mountain as he headed north toward Cody. The morning light was breaking itself into plates and shards against the mountain's rim. The light was golden, and brittle. It colored the snowbound meadows above tree line the color of old bone. He had always loved watching the high mountains of the north, the way they changed with every shift of the sun, the way they never looked like the same country twice.

When he got to the Saber Ranch, Campion was waiting. Mr. Hassan, the owner, came out from New York only during the summer and hunting season. Campion managed the place on his own. Mr. Hassan had gotten rid of all his cows, Campion said. It was down to just horses now.

I got fifteen head, Campion said, if you don't count my own two. Need to go down to less than ten. Mr. Hassan has decided he wants to bring in some mules. And the wife has got in mind new horses for the kids.

Mr. Hassan plan to take pack trips with his mules?

Don't know. Mules don't do much good for me unless I use them regular. And I don't care to ride them. I know a outfitter that might lease them if I ask. Mules can be solid on a hunt as long as you don't get in close with a bear.

Will took in a deep breath of the place. It was a prime location. You could smell the smoky granite of the Shoshone River's bed from the main house, and you could smell the sweet moisture of the spruce trees. He

17

had seen a pair of ravens perched on the buck rail fence when he turned off the county road. He always thought of ravens as a good sign.

You probably don't want any coffee, do you? Campion asked.

Will shook his head. It was still cold at the Saber. The sun wouldn't be on the main house or the barns until noon. He kept his jacket zipped. He made sure he had his gloves.

Let's get to it, then, Campion said. You're a man who likes his business.

There were several horses in the corrals, most of them in blankets. Campion pointed out a high-earning champion mare. She had a new foal by her side. And he pointed out his own paint gelding, which was being doctored for a split hoof. He told Will he had kept the filly inside so she would stay clean.

How's she run with the other horses? Will asked. He wanted to make sure he went through all the right questions.

Good, Campion said. She's been with her mother, who didn't get in foal last year. Sally don't spoil her babies. She noses them out when she needs to. This one weaned well enough, and she keeps her place.

Shy?

18

Not like you mean. I couldn't say if she's got the mind for toughing it out in competition. I couldn't make any promises there. But she don't give in to the others without making some noise.

The barn was a two-winged affair, part of it as old as the Saber Ranch itself, part of it as new and imposing as Mr. Hassan's Wall Street money. Campion took him in through a small door that led into a concrete-floored washing stall. There was a cat sitting in the corner of the stall, a tabby licking its scabs. Campion ignored it.

You take a elk this year? Campion asked. The newspaper said the herd down your way was big and healthy.

Will saw tenseness in the way Campion stood on the concrete, and he realized Campion was delaying the moment. Campion lived alone on the Saber Ranch. He was a tall man, and thin, and if he ever had a family, he seemed to have lost it. It occurred to Will that Campion, as lonely as he was, might regard the showing of a horse as a kind of striptease, a ritual to be savored. He thought maybe Campion was afraid that he, Will, would rush things.

I got a spike bull in the Ramparts in December, he told Campion. It wasn't a great shot, but it was good enough. I hauled the quarters out in two trips. We don't have the trouble you have up here with drought. Or with wolves.

The drought is as bad as the wolves, Campion said. It was hard to get into the backcountry this year. The snow come at the wrong time.

Will pushed his tongue in among his teeth while he glanced at Campion. I got lucky, if you want to know the truth, he continued. Missed a bull with a big rack the year before.

Campion hooked his fingers deep into his vest pockets. He looked like he was working his way through Will's story in his head, cataloging it. The story seemed to satisfy him.

She's down at the end, Campion said. Why don't you wait here, and I'll get her. We'll take her to the arena.

He didn't want to wait, but he did. He watched the tabby cat while Campion strode away from him. The cat watched him back with its slant green eyes.

He heard the sounds of a horse stirring in sawdust and straw. He heard Campion working at the latch of a stall door. The barn, which was cold and dully lit, seemed to be empty except for the one horse he had come to see. There were no birds up in the rafters. No sleeping dogs. Even the green-eyed tabby acted like she was part of something temporary. He reminded himself of his promise. This was a business proposition. If he was to buy this horse, it would be a decision based on business.

Campion led her up the aisle with his hand tight on the lead rope, right up at her throat. This caused the filly to carry her head too high and to stretch out her nose in a way that made her look like she had a weak front end. He couldn't see the lines of her legs. The light was too dim. And he couldn't see her shoulders or flanks because she wore a blanket, a heavy plaid sheet that was checked with gray and blue. But he could see her head, wide at the brow and nicely tapered above the nostrils. She had a tiny patch of white on her forehead. It looked like the triangle of a man's pocket handkerchief. Her eyes, he saw, were rotated back toward Campion and his heavy hand. She was shouldering in on Campion, too. She wasn't at all relaxed.

I'm gonna take this little girl to the arena, Campion said.

Can you stop her right there? he asked. I don't need to see her in the arena. I can get to know her here.

His request frustrated Campion. He could see that in the way Campion dug his square chin back toward his collarbone. Campion probably had it all set up — how he wanted to stand the filly in the better light of the arena, how he wanted to trot her out in the good footing there. Campion was not ready to have another man take charge.

But he was the buyer, the one with money. They both knew it was usual to let the one with money take charge.

He did not make a move toward her. He stood silently in the center of the aisle until Campion loosened his fingers on the lead rope and the filly began to lower her head. She kept her eyes on Campion, who was off to her side. He was the one who made her feel vulnerable. But she had brought her lovely ears forward at the first sound of Will's voice, and she kept them there. She had, he noted, perfect quarter horse ears. They were set evenly on either side of her smoothly rounded poll, and they were shaped like tears, like a pair of shadow-filled tears drawn by a child's hand. They were not too large. He was thankful for that. Large ears belonged on geldings, in his opinion.

He watched the way she distributed her weight on her feet. He watched her draw in air with her nostrils as she searched for his scent. Her left ear rotated back toward

Campion as he took a step away from her. Her large eyes, which were edged in the same unmarred black skin as her muzzle, also remained on the manager.

She's halter broke pretty good, Campion said. Did I tell you that?

He didn't answer. He wanted to see how the filly settled herself. She was young yet. He knew that. There was a lot she hadn't seen. What would matter was how she put herself forward.

She had a good head. There was nothing goat nosed or weak chinned about her. Her jaw was a fine crescent that transitioned into a neat, clean mouth. Her throat arced gracefully away from her jaw into a long, but not too long, neck. She'd fill out more in the neck as she aged, but he could already tell she'd never be too thick there. And she'd never be spindly either. He was surprised by the hue of her neck and face. She was one of the deepest blood bays he'd laid eyes on in a long time. He realized he had never asked Campion what color she was. The question hadn't even come to mind. Color wasn't important to him. But her color — if she kept it — would make her one to remember. Oxblood to old copper, that's how he would describe it. Whatever it was, it contrasted perfectly with her black legs and mane.

You want to see how she moves?

He shook his head. Not yet. You could learn a lot about a horse from what it told you when it was standing on its own piece of ground.

He moved around her to her left, slowly. Campion remained on her left side, both hands on the woven lead rope, so he moved wide of Campion, staying close to the row of stalls that ran along the barn aisle. The filly watched him as he moved. She brought her head down a few degrees and tucked her nose in toward Campion's gripping hand so she could follow the stranger. Will knew he was doing her a favor by staying on her left side, with Campion. She had probably always been handled from the left — it was the kind of thing he'd have to change if he took her — and she probably hadn't spent much time around more than one human being. He'd have to change that, too.

She was watchful but not skittish. She shifted her weight onto her hind legs when he was blocked from her view by Campion. She stayed ready. But he walked clear of her hindquarters, he didn't challenge her in any way, and he came back up the other side of the barn aisle close to the wall. She did not have a weak front end. He could see that now. She was small, not much more than fifteen hands. She looked a little short in the back, though it was hard to tell with the blanket. He let her watch him. He didn't touch her at all.

She'll let you handle her feet pretty good, Campion said.

He nodded. We'll get to that, he said. He listened to his voice drift down toward the ground. He had quieted his voice quite a bit, unlike Campion. He had made his words float toward the other man because when he was talking now he was talking to the filly.

He made his second approach from her left side, again. He eased himself next to Campion and reached for the lead rope, which the other man gave to him. Then he just stood by her side. And she stood there, watching. As Campion moved off toward the washing stall, well in front of both the filly and Will, the filly relaxed a little. She kept her weight on all four feet, squarely, and she didn't bunch up at all when he began to speak to her. He still did not touch her. He just talked for a while, telling her who he was and where he came from and how he liked the way she looked, the way she behaved with caution and smarts. He squared his shoulders with her shoulders as he talked. He kept his hands low on the lead rope, down near his waist. He talked. She listened as hard as she thought she ought to listen. Before long they had somehow managed to move closer together without appearing to move at all. Her blanketed shoulder began to brush against his upper arm. That was fine, he told her. It was all fine. They didn't need to do a thing all morning but stand there together and talk.

It made Campion restless. Will knew he would soon have to include the other man, even though the whole interaction, the whole business, had nothing to do with him.

Is she sound? he asked Campion. It was a dumb question, but he didn't want to draw the manager into anything complicated.

I wouldn't have hauled you up here otherwise, Campion said. He was irritated. His lower lip was working at the longish gray hairs of his mustache. The talk that was happening in his barn was not the talk he had imagined.

You feed her supplements? She gaining any weight?

Campion went into an explanation of his feeding regimen, what he changed in the summer, what he changed in the winter, where he bought his hay. Will listened politely. It was important information, though it was nothing that would make a difference from this point on.

She'll let you handle her feet, Campion repeated.

I'd like to take the blanket off her, Will said, if that's okay.

Campion made a quick move forward to help. The filly drew her head up just as quickly and dropped her weight into her rump. She chittered sideways like a crab. That's all right, he said to Campion, not moving an inch himself. I can do it. It's the best way. Thank you.

Campion withdrew. The manager of the Saber Ranch was gonna have to be reassured, Will told himself. Mr. Campion was going to have to be soothed and plumped up.

He kept the lead rope in his left hand, and he kept that hand loose and relaxed by his waist. The filly could step away from him anytime she wanted. She could step up, back, or sideways, and he would let the rope go, and it wouldn't bother him. He used his right hand to work the blanket hooks free — first the ones around her girth, then the pair of hooks at her chest, right at the place where the hair of her remarkable coat fanned itself into a set of complicated cowlicks. He was sorry he had his gloves on. He needed to slip those off. And he needed to reassure the filly that he wasn't going to do anything sudden or threatening down near the base of her neck. He shushed to her. He worked his talk into a soothing tune as he pressed his right glove into the back pocket of his jeans and left it there, then began to roll the heavy, dusty winter blanket off her withers. When he saw she was shaking, he stopped. He wondered how the hell Campion had gotten the blanket on her in the first place.

She don't know what to think of you, Campion said.

I don't know what to think of her, either, Will said, his voice no more than a murmur. So we're even.

He took his time. It was another thing he had inherited from his mother — the ability to be patient. He eased the edge of the blanket off the filly's shoulders. He waited. He allowed himself to touch her with his right hand while he waited; he put his hand on the large, sloping muscle of her shoulder, and he stroked her. She was very warm. Her skin was as soft and thin as chamois. That was a sign of good breeding and good health. Campion was on the mark there. He knew how to take care of a horse.

The filly decided to let him do what he wanted. He could feel the decision take root within her. She continued to inhale his scent with long, slow breaths through her nostrils, and she continued to watch him, but she had made up her mind about him — for the moment.

She's got the look, like I told you, Campion said. I come out of the rodeos, like you. I haven't messed much with racehorses or what those polo people ride. But I've seen enough to know the look. She's the type.

He thought Campion was right about that. People would pay a lot of money for a well-trained horse, but they would pay even more for a horse that looked like something special. The filly's dam had won a lot of money as a cutting horse. But her daughter had a more precise appeal. He had seen Sally's Quick Ticket. She was a tough, handsome mare. But if he were to describe the two animals to someone like his mother, he would say Sally was like an artist's drawing done with a soft pencil. The filly was like a portrait lined out in ink.

You'll get a good deal if you buy her, Campion said. Mr. Hassan hasn't even seen her in the flesh. He don't know what he has in her.

Will wished Campion wouldn't talk so much. His talk was leading him to say things he shouldn't say.

He pushed the blanket onto her hindquarters, then he pushed it again until it slid right off her croup, onto the ground. She didn't startle much. It would not have mattered to him if she had. He took a considerable look at her ankles, her knees, the angle of her pasterns and the shape of her feet. This was business. This was his money. Chances were, it would all go wrong at some point over the next weeks and months, and if it did, the bad news would come from her feet and legs. He had seen plenty of good-looking horses in his day. Most of them were just that — all looks.

You want to trot her out? Campion asked. Get her into the arena?

I'm just gonna walk her up and down in here for a minute, he said.

She let him take his post again by her shoulder, and she let him lead her forward. Like most young horses, she was as confident as a banker moving forward. She stepped right out. He let the feel of her walk work its way into his own walk, he let his hips swing with hers. She underreached with her back feet, but that wasn't unusual in a horse that hadn't been trained to use its body. He liked the way her short back appeared to work in her favor. A short back might help with quickness. He would have to let Campion jog her out for him just to be sure, but he was fairly certain she would move well at speed. It would be more than a year before he had the answers to some of his questions. He could look all he wanted, but the proof would come in the training and the riding. If he bought her, they would be in on the gamble together. They would be rolling the dice every day.

He stopped. Because she was confident, the filly kept right on walking. She walked forward two or three steps, and he let the lead rope slide through the fingers of his now-bare hands. Then she stopped. And she tilted her neat and pretty head back toward him, just slightly. He could just see the querying pinpoint of light in her large brown eye. He could see the sparking question there.

He stopped in Cody and bought a hamburger. He had let Campion fix him a cup of coffee, and he had listened to Campion talk about the Saber Ranch, how much it was worth, how much the operation took out of him every summer, even though he loved it so. But he had told Campion he couldn't stay for a meal. And he couldn't. He wasn't truly hungry even now. The urge to get on home was strong.

He had set up the trailer so the filly would have plenty of room. She loaded readily enough. Young horses often did. They were willing to try a thing because they did not yet realize how hard it was to change a decision once you made it. But the filly got fussy when she saw she was enclosed in the trailer alone, and she continued her complaints as he eased his rig down the Saber Ranch's long driveway and across the river. This was the hard part, he told himself. The filly was a herd animal. He was taking her away from the herd, the only security she had ever known.

He pulled into the Wal-Mart in Cody, where there was plenty of room to park, and he walked to the nearest place he could buy a hamburger. He did not go back to the trailer to talk to the filly. He saved that until after he had bought his meal, though he couldn't say why he had done such a thing — it wasn't like him to be distant with animals or people, either one. He wondered if he was drawn to make a cold move toward the filly in order to counter the hot, instinctive move he had made in buying her. He wondered if he was somehow trying to protect himself.

After he got his hamburger, he walked slowly back toward his silver Dodge truck and his trailer. The food smelled good, even in its cheap white bag. He had bought the same brand of hamburger for his mother after her radiation sessions in Riverton. She had insisted on the meal, though she had rarely been able to eat it. The food had rested on her lap until it went limp and cold. His mother had her appetite back now, or so she said. He looked to the west, his own stomach gurgling, hoping there wouldn't be any big changes in the weather. He was glad to see the sky was still the quiet blue color of mountain violets. When he looked back over at his trailer, he could see the tapered shape of the filly's head. It was a black and swaying silhouette.

Hello there, filly, he said when he got to the trailer. You okay with the ride?

It looked like she was. He had hung a hay net for her, and Campion had given her water from a bucket before they left the Saber Ranch. They had decided not to wrap her feet for the journey. The rubber mats in the trailer were good, and wrapping her feet would have been a hard lesson to teach on short notice. Will had put one of his own travel blankets on her, however, a red one.

She was fine wearing the blanket. It was a thing she was used to.

He leaned against the outside of his Bruton trailer and watched her. She paid attention to him at first, but then she didn't. There were plenty of other things to hear and smell, even in a parking lot in Cody, Wyoming. She tested the length of the tiedown rope. She nickered into the afternoon air but got no answer, not even from him. He realized after a few minutes that watching her — even for just a short time — might soon become as basic to him as breathing. And he realized he hadn't breathed much, not really, over the past few months. His mother's cancer had worried him. It worried him still. There was also his ongoing quarrel with his father. His father thought he was too much of a dreamer, that he took chances on things a person could not touch or see, that he did not place enough value in the normal, unpleasant things a man had to do in his life. That was not a false judgment. He did not always put himself forward as normal. And he had been known to smash himself up among his dreams.

He lifted one of his hands and slipped it through the bars of the trailer so the filly could smell him again if she wanted. But she did not move closer to him or to his hand. He told himself that was okay. He understood. Reluctance was, on some days, going to be a high hurdle for them both.

He pulled over to water the filly before they rolled through the town of Thermopolis. He filled a bucket from his travel tank, and he unlatched the side door of the trailer, and he got into the trailer with her. The temperature had dropped considerably. The sky now looked like a cold gray field that had been plowed by a raging giant. The filly was agitated by the stop. She wanted to be out of the trailer. But he couldn't do that. He held up the bucket. She wouldn't drink, not at first. So he began to tell her a story.

He told her an easy story — the one about Hawk. Hawk was his big-boned Appaloosa gelding. Hawk was one of the important horses in his life that had not died or been sold off. The filly would like Hawk. He was sure about that, and that was what he told her. Hawk was waiting for her at his parents' ranch.

I found him at the Kaycee rodeo, he said. I was taken in by the leopard spots on his big Appaloosa ass. Wait until you see those spots. There's no way in the world you can look past them.

The first time he saw Hawk, he told her, he could tell something was wrong. The gelding was lop eared, and his blue roan coat was starting to wash out to gray, and he looked tired, somehow ill used.

It didn't take me long to solve the puzzle, he said. Hawk belonged to two brothers I met, a pair of sawed-off plugs of muscle from Casper who thought they were bull riders. They didn't care about Hawk. They didn't need him except to say they had him. They lent him to friends who wanted to fill out the draws in calf roping or whatever. And they were willing to swap him for a saddle and some alfalfa hay and all the cash money I had in my pockets. I had plenty of cash. The rodeo had gone good for me. Hawk was too old, anyway, that's what the brothers told me. He was used up. But Hawk wasn't that old — any fool could tell that by looking at his teeth. He just wasn't being fed right. And he hadn't been shod worth a damn. His feet were a mess.

You should have seen his feet, he told the filly. They were a tragedy. And you need to be smart about a Appaloosa in that regard. Hawk has got a little crookedness in one of his forefeet, for instance. You have to be smart.

The filly had turned away from him while

he talked. She had worked herself diagonally across the open part of the trailer, taking up as much room as she could manage. But she wasn't ignoring him, not entirely. After he finished talking, she brought her black nose up and extended it toward the bucket of water. He held the bucket. She exhaled onto the cold surface of the water, splashing. She brushed her muzzle against the plastic rim of the bucket, but she didn't drink. That was all right. She didn't need to drink.

You've got some attitude, he said to her. You'll need that with Hawk. But you won't be able to fool him about nothing, so don't even try. That's the best advice I can give to you. Follow his lead. Don't mess with his business.

The filly had relaxed some. He was glad to see it. He emptied the water bucket onto the cheatgrass at the side of the road and checked his watch. In two more hours they would be home.

He couldn't help but read the country for signs of posterity and struggle as he passed through it. This was his father's habit, and it had become his own. He saw large bands of pronghorn along the road west of Shoshoni, does mostly, their beige coats motley from the long winter, their ribs beginning to spread in pregnancy. He saw a For Sale sign at the entrance to the Flying M Ranch. That was no surprise. The market for Simmental bulls had been luckless.

He saw a golden eagle feeding on a mashed jackrabbit at the side of the road. The eagle stooped over its meal in the posture of a rude teenager.

He watched storm clouds calve, like icebergs from a glacier, off the south end of the Wind River Mountains.

He noticed that someone with a familiar brand of enthusiasm had released a herd of crossbred steers onto the pastures that had once belonged to the bad-tempered sheepman Nathan Rone. He wondered if the new operator would pay attention to the spread of locoweed and leafy spurge.

He counted the horses in Smiley O'Malley's overgrazed pasture. Ten, twelve, twenty. Smiley was running more than two dozen horses in a space that was barely suitable for half that many. Except none of Smiley's horses had the strength to run. Their chests were sunken and their hips were as sharp as shovel blades. Their bellies were distended from malnutrition and worms. They barely looked like horses. They looked like creatures the Devil might spur from Hell if he were inclined to inspire desperation. He wondered why Smiley O'Malley didn't shoot the horses if he couldn't take care of them. Better yet, why didn't Will Testerman, or some other good citizen, stop and shoot them? Who would blame him for putting such animals out of their misery?

Someone would, of course. People in Wyoming knew how to cut deep with a certain kind of blame. It wasn't considered neighborly to direct a man toward his faults. And you were never welcome to comment on someone else's livestock or children.

He noticed there were two new-model diesel Fords in the swept driveway at the Wexler place. Cheryl Wexler taught school with his mother. He had heard Cheryl was a genius at saving her pennies. He would ask his mother about the trucks. He was sure the question would inspire his mother to laugh one of her high, wispy laughs. It's all about the do-re-mi, she would say. Cheryl Wexler's husband has a foul mouth and no inclination to get out of his easy chair unless it's to work his shifts for the railroad. That's just about all Cheryl has got to keep her going right now, his mother would say, that shiny do-re-mi.

They arrived at the Testerman Ranch in late

afternoon. No one was at the house. The weather had finally uncorked itself when they were driving along Beaver Rim. They had done the last thirty miles in icy rain and hail, but it hadn't been too bad, and he was glad to see that the fields around Lost Cabin had also been doused with rain. There was mist rising from the banks of Little Kettle Creek. It might rain again. He decided to take the filly straight into the barn.

She began to make noise before he even set the parking brake on the pickup. There were other horses at the Testerman Ranch, and she could smell them.

He unlatched the rear gate of the trailer and snubbed it open. The surface of the ranch yard was slick. He could feel the weight of new mud clinging to the soles of his boots. Hawk, who was alone in one of the corrals, came to the corner of his fence. His broad back was wet and steaming from the rain. His ears were erect.

Will went in through the side door of the trailer and unknotted the tie-down rope attached to the filly's halter. She was ready to go. She was ready to back out of the trailer without a second look, but that's not how he wanted to do it. She was more likely to hurt herself moving backward. He talked to her, and he planted himself to the inside of her left shoulder as if he were a pivot, and he tried to convince her to ease herself around him until she faced the rear of the trailer. She did all right. She didn't have much sense about how to balance herself inside the tight space of a trailer, and she came close to banging the top of her head on the trailer's ceiling as she got sight of her escape route, but she did all right. He let her make her own awkward steps to the ground.

She put her head up high like a parade horse, and her nostrils began to pulse like the valves of a working heart. There was sweat on her neck just above the edge of the blanket. He could smell it. It smelled of salt and worry. Her eyes tried to roll in all directions at once — she was looking everywhere for danger — and he could see the unspoiled whites of her eyes for the first time. He moved her away from the trailer in case she spooked.

Hawk hung his large gray-and-white-flecked head over the fence. He was interested but not captivated. He had seen it all before.

The filly didn't seem to notice Hawk. She got herself fixated on the bull. It occurred to Will later that the filly had never seen a bull before, and she had certainly never seen the kind favored by his father. The animal corralled next to Hawk was as long as his mother's four-door sedan and weighed twice as much. It was the color of fresh brick, with a white anvil face topped by dirty curls and a blunt pair of horns. The Hereford bull probably wouldn't have bothered the filly much if it hadn't begun to walk. Nothing walked like a stubby-legged, big-balled Hereford bull.

He took tighter hold of the filly, and he hoped the bull wouldn't bellow. But it did. It filled its giant pair of lungs like they were a set of bagpipes.

At one point all four of the filly's feet left the ground. And at one point she stepped on him. If she hadn't been brand-new, he would have let the rope go and recaptured her later. But she didn't have any points of reference. Neither did he. He couldn't be sure what she might do to herself if he let go. The bull didn't bellow for long. It was too lazy. It had made its goddamn point.

By the time he worked the filly down to a simple walk around the open center of the ranch yard, they were both breathing like thrown steers. Their legs were muddy to the knees. Hawk had retreated to the far side of his corral, unimpressed. He began to bang at the feed trough, which was his way of saying he was hungry.

You can see how it is around here, Will said to the filly, laughing even though the foot she had stepped on hurt like hell. Welcome to the Testerman outfit. Everybody's got their rules. Everybody's got something to say. And nobody's anxious to let you get to the front of the line.

His father was the first one home. He came into the barn. Skim, the irritable cuss of a cow dog, came with him. Skim was too old and stoved up for ranch work. He now spent his days at the print shop with Will's father.

I see you're back all right, his father said.

Yes, sir.

This your new horse?

It is. She's green as a tree leaf. She wonders where she is.

She'll get over that, his father said, taking a quick look at the filly in her stall. Mind if I ask what you paid for her?

He did mind. Because he knew his father was asking the question only to make his kind of point. It didn't matter what he said, what the price of the filly might have been. The money he had shelled out would always be too much for his father.

I got her for a good price, he said. Twelve

hundred. And she's got her papers.

Is that so?

Yes, sir.

Then you got your work cut out for you, his father said. I guess you know that. I heard Bent Stallworth was auctioning mustangs in Riverton for less than two hundred dollars apiece. But I guess you know best.

He understood that it was not his role to respond to such remarks. His mother sometimes called his father a badger, a badger in his dark hole, and the comparison was meant to say something about his father's moods. But Will didn't see it. His father might have the cornered fighting sense of a badger, but there was nothing ambling about the man, there was nothing about him that cared to survey open territory. He was committed to a thin, practiced diet of low expectations.

She won't get in the way of nothing, he said to his father. You know I'll see to that.

His father nodded before he rubbed one of his ink-smeared hands across his mouth. He looked more tired than usual. The two jobs he was trying to hold down were catching up with him. And cattle prices were not what they could be. He nodded again before he turned on his heel and left the barn, with Skim limping along in black-and-white obedience behind him. His father had not even bothered to take a decent look at the filly.

His mother and Everett came to the barn later. He had unhitched the trailer, and he had unpacked his travel gear, but he had not otherwise left the filly. She remained restless in her new stall, circling and circling in the fresh straw. She paused on occasion, every muscle in her body aquiver, to call out. Will knew she was calling for her mother. And for the other young horses on the Saber Ranch that had been her companions. The sounds she made were rushed and searching and broken in pitch. They were met with silence. She arched her neck and snorted when he brought Hawk into the barn, but since she didn't know Hawk yet, the gelding's presence was of no comfort. Will decided to leave Trampas and Bison, his father's two box-headed geldings, in the round pen. They could be outside for one night. The weather had cleared. And he knew that those two, with their hardened natures, would only make things worse for the filly.

His mother was enthusiastic. She was less interested in livestock than the men in her family were. This made it possible for her to talk about the animals that came and went on the ranch with some sincerity.

She's pretty, isn't she, Everett? She's as pretty a girl as we've had here in a long time. This was what their mother said after watching the filly churn through her circles in the locked stall.

Everett agreed. Nobody's ever said my brother don't have an eye for horses.

Did she make the trip all right? their mother asked.

I believe so, Will said. You're seeing what I'm seeing. This part is a lot harder than the trip.

She'll get used to us, his mother said. An animal knows how to adapt. Tell me again what you want to do with her.

He wants to make money, Everett said, interrupting. You know that's what he'll say — that it's a investment to make money.

Will didn't respond to his brother except to step closer to the filly's stall so he could make the kind of sound that might eventually help him quiet her. His family had all manner of things they believed about him — where he was weak and where he was strong and where he was likely to break away from them to cut his own path. His words wouldn't change what they believed.

You can let Will speak for himself, their

46

mother said to Everett, raising what was left of her eyebrows into a pair of straight lines.

I'd like to train her up, Will said. I'm not too specific yet. But I'd like to teach her what she needs to know from the ground up. That's all it is.

Everett made a rough sound in his throat. He was a big man, capable, a man who wanted nothing more than to run a smart, modern beef operation. But he didn't have enough land at his disposal, and he didn't have the capital to expand like he wanted, and he — like his father — had to hold down at least one town job to plug the hole in his income that came with ranching.

That's not all it is, Everett said. You don't spend twelve hundred dollars for a horse so it'll end up as a pet for some Jackson Hole lawyer. You got plans.

Will was sorry Everett knew how much the filly had cost. He must have learned that fact from their father.

It's his money, their mother said. She had never uttered a word to her husband or her older sons about the way Will had cared for her during her sickness. It was not her style. She hadn't asked for the care, but Will had given it.

It *is* his money, Everett said, licking at his words for their mother's benefit. To tell you the truth, I like how he's going for a big payoff this time. I like how he's hanging it out there.

What are you saying?

Everett's saying he thinks I've grown a new set of balls, Will said. And he laughed in a way that shifted the target away from his older brother.

Well, have you?

Yes, ma'am, he said. I believe I have. I want to go someplace with this one.

Right to the bank, Everett said, patting the pocket in his jeans where he kept his wallet. Right to the goddamn bank.

Maybe so, he said. He looked directly at his mother through the dusty, stirred-up air of the barn. She was smaller than she had ever been. And there was a brittle appearance to her bones and to her hair. He had noticed that. She moved as if more than her breast had been scorched. But most of her had not changed. She was still asking him, Who are you today, Will Testerman? Who will you be today? She still had her beaming, teacherish eyes.

The first pony he ever had was named Spot, and his family found him sleeping in Spot's stall the morning after Christmas, despite the fact that it snowed sideways throughout the night. He had wrapped himself in saddle pads and the heavy canvas tarpaulin his father used on hunting trips. When they found him, his blond hair was a pincushion of straw. He was four and a half years old. Spot was so fat and so splay footed, no one dared guess how old he was. He still had his wolf teeth in the back of his mouth, and he was docile enough that Will could finger the useless stubs of those teeth whenever he wanted. The teeth didn't bother Spot because he never wore a bridle. Any kid in the world could ride Spot bareback with a bosal and reins. The old pony pretty much operated on verbal commands.

He earned the money for his second pony by clearing all the irrigation ditches on the ranch with a shovel and by helping some of the teachers at his mother's school with yard chores when they asked. He bought the pony, a swaybacked pinto mare, at auction. He signaled his intentions to the auctioneer on his own, but his father had to sign the bill of sale. He was eight years old. He named that pony Queenie for the way she held her head. Queenie threw him out of the saddle many times. She never got used to dogs or birds bursting into sight from the deep brush of the fields. But she was strong enough to keep up with his brothers' horses, and that was what mattered at the time.

He had slept in the stall with Queenie only once. Her belly had gotten tight and swollen, and it was clear to everyone she had colic. He stayed with her to monitor the situation. He was supposed to run to the house and call the veterinarian if Queenie lay down. But the pony stayed on her feet all night, which was more than he could do. The bad twist in her bowel somehow untwisted itself. He resold her at auction when he was twelve and replaced her with a roping horse bred by a retired bronc rider who lived on the Bighorn River. He was sorry to see Queenie go.

He wasn't going to stay up all night with the filly. There was no reason to. She was not a baby. He let himself into her stall, and he checked again to make sure there weren't any loose boards or sharp edges. She had water. And he had already given her fresh flakes of hay, which she'd barely touched. He left the stall and mixed up a small portion of pellets and grain in a coffee can and brought the can back into the stall. He spread the feed in her trough. A secure horse would have nickered at him the moment he took the lid off the grain barrel. A secure horse would have tried to nudge past him to get to the trough, but the filly wasn't there yet. She moved closer to the door of the stall when he left, but she stepped away again when he returned. He thought she looked all wrong cinched into the baggy fabric of the red travel blanket. And the halter he had put on her at the Saber Ranch looked all wrong, too. The halter was made of thick black nylon webbing and was the kind of thing meant to look functional on a functional horse like Hawk.

He removed the blanket, and he did it quickly. He also removed the halter. He thought of his hands as tools as he worked, as lightweight wrenches and pliers. The filly tossed her head with indignation. And she scuttled away from him, into the back corner of the stall, when he stripped her of the blanket. Her eyes glittered. He could hear the mistrust in the air that rushed from her contracted lungs.

You don't know what I'm up to, do you? he said.

His voice had no effect on her, not now. The only thing the filly cared about was where he stood and what he planned to do with those ungentle hands.

I don't know what I'm up to, either. Not always.

He paused a moment to think about what he wanted to say. He could smell the sweet, burst kernels of the grain he had left for her. And he could smell her, the blend of heated blood and skin and hair that would soon become more definable to him than any name he might choose to give her. What he needed to say now was not part of the rituals they were about to embark upon together. The rituals would begin tomorrow. What he needed to say now was just between the two of them.

I will always be good to you, he said. That's all I really need to promise.

And he left her stall. He shut the door to the feed room, and he turned off the lights in the barn. He spoke to Hawk as he walked down the dark, tunneled aisle. Hawk was hoping for his own portion of grain. Hawk was always hungry. But he said nothing more to the filly.

It was spring in Wyoming — the shortest, meanest season on God's green earth. He woke to three inches of sloppy, wet snow. He knew the weather had turned as soon as he opened his eyes. The square of his bedroom window held the muted light of falling snow as if it were silver water in a basin. The house was silent all around him. He rose from the low frame he had constructed for his bed and went to bring his father's horses in from the cold.

Skim, the old cow dog, lay on his side near the pellet stove. He didn't even raise his head.

The air was thick and chilled. It hadn't yet been torn into currents by the wind. If they were lucky the wind would stay down and ice wouldn't begin to coat the roads. The snow might be gone by nine o'clock. He was glad, not for the first time, that they had no newborn calves on the ranch this year. Weather like this was dangerous for lambs and calves.

The ranch yard resembled a rumpled white tablecloth. Each step he took left a muddy tear in the snow.

Trampas and Bison were squeezed against the lee side of the round pen like a pair of old men huddled at the door of a closed café. He didn't need to do anything more than open the gate to get them headed into the barn. Their bony backs were mapped with continents of moisture. Their tangled forelocks were beaded with water. But they were no worse for wear. They trotted toward their respective stalls.

He paused to listen while invisible geese called out to one another as their flock crossed the dense sky above the barn. The cries of the birds were hurried and attentive. The geese were flying low, but not so low that he could hear the buffeting strokes of their long, angular wings. He wondered if they had set down in his father's fields during the worst of the storm. They probably had. He had always admired the brave way geese moved together in poor weather. He zipped his heavy jacket up to his neck as their passage faded into the fog.

The filly was awake. Her ears were a pair of black flames atop her head, flickering. Trampas didn't seem to notice there was a new horse in the barn. But Bison did. The blaze-faced chestnut made a point of approaching the filly's stall and pinning his ears and showing the filly his clacking yellow teeth. Bison made a run at the newcomer. She broke to the back of her stall. Will hollered the old bastard off, which didn't take much, and guided him into his own stall. Bison was a bully with young horses, which was all he could get away with. The filly would be able to handle him before long.

First lesson, he thought. Even before he fed them. He went to the filly. She had a mixed opinion about his approach, he could tell that. She was hungry and she was on the defensive, but he was the only one she knew. He stood just inside the gate of the stall. And he talked to her. That's all he did. No halter. No task-oriented hands. He just talked. He explained the ranch and the weather. He explained the Hereford bull and how Bison had the cranky temperament you often saw in a gelding that was part of a small herd. He talked about how most of their days together would go at a slow and steady pace.

She listened to him, her breath coming from her nostrils in huffs that were visible in the wintry air. He saw again how beautiful she was, how well shaped below the brow. The stakes were higher this time, he might as well admit it. He could not afford a total fuck-up. His mother said that a good person knew how to make something out of the salt and sand around him. A good person did not fear change. He talked to the filly with the kind of rhythmic certainty that he wished were the truth of his life. Horses preferred certainty. The skin around the filly's eyes began to smooth out, and she lowered the set of her tail. That was another thing about her. She knew how to carry her tail. It would be a lovely black flag when she was running at speed.

Second lesson. She would not always be first. He fed Hawk his hay and grain, and he scratched Hawk between the eyes just the way the Appaloosa liked. Hawk was a jokester. He fed Trampas and Bison next, and he dried them each with a towel while they ate. He also checked their feet and legs. His father was a stickler about that. He did not like a horse to come into his barn unless you knew the status of its feet and legs. Then he fed the filly.

Third lesson. He would come and he would go. She would have to learn to take care of herself. He wouldn't release her into a field with the others horses, not yet, but those days were coming. He could have put her in a stall next to Hawk, but he hadn't. The stall next to her was empty. And Bison, the S.O.B., was across the aisle. She would have to get used to a personality like Bison's.

I got chores to do, he said to the whole audience.

Then he slipped out into the iron light of morning.

On snowy days, it was hard for him not to think of Annie Atwood and how she had disappeared from the world without a trace. He had usually spoken to Annie on snowy days when he was clearing her short driveway. He had not quite been in love with her. She was older, and she was married, but they had developed an understanding that involved a kind of affection. Annie had trusted him with her house and her dog. Annie had lent him good movies to watch. They had laughed together, and last summer, he had halfway taught her how to rope and ride. He missed her. Not knowing whether she was dead or alive made it hard for him to sort through the shelved portion of his feelings, though he knew it was impractical for him to imagine he would ever see her again.

He walked toward the house, where he could see brackets of light around the curtains that hung in the front windows. Someone else in the family was awake. And the robins were trying to start their day from the branches of the cottonwood tree that stood to the west of the porch. He heard a few hesitant notes of birdsong, rising notes, plucking. The robins had made it as far north as the ranch just that very week, and here they were, stranded on one last peninsula of winter. Bad luck for them. His mother would toss them some seed from the porch before the end of the day. They would be all right. You didn't show up in a place like Lost Cabin, Wyoming, unless you could handle being stranded.

He didn't have much to say in the mornings. His parents and his brother were always in a hurry, and he was not. He walked into the kitchen, got his mother's car keys, and left without a word. He started his mother's car for her, just to get it good and warm. It was parked in the converted machine shed, so he didn't have to sweep it clear of snow.

You'll pick up the feed from Jansen's today? his father said when he returned to the kitchen. His father was stabbing at a bowl of cereal. His gray hair was wet from the shower, but his voice was far from fresh and clean.

Yes, sir.

Call before you leave for there. Give Hugh Jansen the warning he likes. And I need you in the shop today. Sometime before four. I got two big orders to ship.

I can come early.

I don't need you early. I just need you.

Yes, sir.

And if Everett wants a hand, I expect he'll tell you.

I don't need nothing, Everett said, scratching at the back of his neck. Everett was staring at his toast like it was more awake than he was. I can't do much in these mucky conditions.

Have you checked the belts on your mother's car, like I asked? This was another sentence fired at him by his father.

No, sir.

Then you need to pray she don't break down on the way to school today, you hear me?

I'm not going to break down, his mother said, intervening. The car's running fine. It just squeals a little when it gets wet underneath.

He needs to do like I ask. It's not much. I'm not suggesting he run for governor.

His father left with a large thermos of coffee. Skim followed him out the door, tilting away from the stiffness of his bad hips. His father didn't even take a lunch to work with him anymore. It was as though he believed the printing business would steal his lunch from him, as it had stolen so many other things. Everett dragged on a pair of irrigator boots and said he was going to check the cows. Everyone understood he was truly stepping outside to have a cigarette. Everett no longer smoked inside the house.

Will gathered the bowls and coffee cups from the table. It was his job to do the dishes.

Those can wait, son, his mother said. Walk with me. I have projects to carry to the car.

His mother had tried something different with her hair. He noticed some shiny gel clumped at her temples. He didn't say anything. His mother mostly managed a light heart, but she didn't always have a good sense of humor about how she looked. He took the canvas bags she handed to him. They were heavy with her students' projects.

You have to forgive your father somewhat, she said, snapping herself into her quilted winter coat. Bills are on his mind. He's got worries.

I'm sorry about that.

Don't be, she said. It's not your situation. It's ours. And your dad sometimes makes a hard thing harder than it needs to be.

He stepped out of the house ahead of his mother and held the door. The clouds had sunk all the way to the ground like scuttled boats. He couldn't see more than fifty yards in front of him. The yearling calves were bawling at one another from the far side of Little Kettle Creek. Calves weren't as resourceful as geese, he thought. Their crying wasn't going to take them anywhere that mattered.

His mother began to speak to him. I don't like to say it, Will, because I love seeing your face in the morning, but it looks to me like you have plans to go away again. Is that so?

Yes, ma'am. I'll go back to the Black Bell in May. They'll make me corral boss.

I'm not talking about the Black Bell, she said. You know what I mean. That pretty little horse you brought home is not part of any summer job. I mean what comes after.

He walked ahead of his mother to her car. His head was bare. He felt the temperature of the morning as a thick, icy finger at the base of his neck. He knew his mother. She was a schemer, in her way. She was trying to tell him something.

Ma?

Yes.

Is the cancer back? Is that what's eating at Dad all the time?

No. And that's the truth. The damn cancer is not the issue.

Because I can —

No. You're getting out of here. You're not changing another thing in your life because of the cancer. Let it change me, please. It's mine.

Are you sure?

I'm sure, Will. That's what Dr. Pradit says. Let's listen to him for once. I have what I want. Sons, a husband, the kids I teach. Being sick hasn't taken that away. But you need to go on. I can't have you waiting around here for something. Waiting is a waste.

He didn't say anything. He laid the canvas

61

bags in the backseat of his mother's car. The car still smelled new because of how neat his mother kept it.

I'm almost asking for a promise here, Will. I want you to do something for yourself.

Okay.

You're a little different from your brothers. And you're different from me. I put together what I wanted in my life. I don't have regrets that matter. You need to think about your own big picture.

But what if what I want is crazy?

It's not crazy, she said, putting a hand on his shoulder. Risky is not the same as crazy. Failing is not the same as being worthless. Your dad doesn't always see those distinctions, but other people do. You're a hard worker.

He tried to look his mother in the eye. She preferred that.

Aren't you?

Yes, ma'am. I don't have a problem with working hard. But my history ain't all that great. I've busted up before.

His mother made the face that drew her eyebrows together. Her eyebrows had almost grown back, but they, too, were grayer, and thin. Then make that part of the reward, she said, how you don't quit after a bust-up. I don't think this is the time for either one of us to be curling up or cutting back. This is not the moment for limits. Can we agree on that?

Yes, ma'am.

Have you talked to Lacey?

No, ma'am. That's done with.

All right. I understand. I just don't want you to be lonely.

I'm not, he said.

She brought her right hand up and mussed it through his hair. She had to stand on her tiptoes to reach that high. Good, she said. I don't want you to feel like you're alone in any way. Thank you for listening to me. I'm just old enough to enjoy it when my sons indulge me.

Do you think your car is all right? he asked.

The car is fine. It'll get me to my roomful of sugar-fueled fifth graders. How about you wish me the luck I'll need to deal with them?

He found the halter that once belonged to Cedar. It was a fine, hand-stitched halter with brass buckles and rings. It still held the dark color of much-oiled leather, though it was dry to the point of cracking on the noseband. Cedar had been dead a long time. He wasn't sure his father had ever gotten over the death of that mare, even though it hadn't been his fault, even though there wasn't a damn thing any of them could have done. They were moving cattle out of a canyon in the Ramparts. The mare had stepped into some kind of hole and flipped. Her neck had been broken in an instant.

He wiped the dust off the halter with a rag, then rubbed a little oil into the thirsty leather. Cedar had been a large and presumptuous animal. Regal. He would have to adjust the buckles on the halter to make it fit the filly.

His first thought was to release the filly into the round pen, let her get a look at the place. But he changed his mind. He made it his plan to work with her on a lead rope first. She needed to be better on the lead rope. She tossed her head, giving a little sneeze, as he put the new halter on her. Then she tried to crowd him on the way through the stall door. He had to put a stop to that, so he circled her back around, away from the stall door, and stood by her left shoulder, his shoulders square with hers.

You need to take your time, he told her. You're smart. You were trying to anticipate what we were gonna do. But my job is to teach you to anticipate what *I* want you to do. Don't guess too quick. My mother says smart kids in school thrive on being quick.

But it sometimes gets them into trouble.

The filly two-stepped forward and began to exert some pull on the long, double-ply lead rope. He circled her around again.

We don't have to go nowhere right now, he said to her. We just need to listen to each other.

He told her that she would see the Hereford bull again. Everett had fed the bull before he left for his shift making beverage deliveries, but the bull had not been turned out into the field. He told her that Hawk would stay in the barn for the morning, and that Bison and Trampas had been moved to the large corral that was sometimes used for branding. He kept his body and voice relaxed. The filly didn't think much of his tempo. She moved toward the open stall door again. He stopped her and eased her into another circle.

When he thought she had the idea, or at least the shape of the idea, he reached out and closed the stall door. They waited. Then he opened the stall door. They waited some more. She was ready the second he leaned his body forward. She moved right next to him as they stepped into the barn aisle.

He didn't want to do too much with her. Young horses could absorb only so much civilization in a day. You needed to leave plenty of space for their untrained natures.

He stopped and started her only once more along the length of the barn aisle. He liked the way she posed when she stopped, balanced and alert.

The sun was up. It cast a basking light across his father's fields. The swallows that lived in the open eaves of the barn were going about their labors, flitting to and from the bowls of mud and spit that were their new nests. He hadn't seen a cat all morning, but he knew they were around. He allowed the filly to swing her body away from him like a clock pendulum as she took note of the long, reddish shape of the dozing bull. It was all still a surprise to her — where the buildings were, where the fences were, how she might find a path to escape. He wondered what it was like to be inside her head, where her ears and binocular eyes and large nose put together a version of the world that was so different from his own. What did she think of the scent of the yearling cows? Was their smell a good smell to her? And what about the diesel-fuel tank? What did she make of that stink?

He let her prance her way to the gate of the round pen. When she saw yet another unfamiliar threshold, she stiffened to a halt.

The round pen was as secure as a fort,

which was what he and Chad and Everett had used it for when they played cavalry soldiers and Indians as kids. He was too young to remember his father building the pen, but he knew his father had done it, as he did so many other things, the right way. The peeled logs that made up the fencing were no greater than six inches in diameter, and each of them had been sunk into the ground to a depth of at least six feet. No coyote would ever be able to dig its way into the pen. And no unmannered mustang would ever be able to break its way out. The fence was every bit of six feet tall. The pen was thirty feet in diameter. Will had softened its surface with a fresh load of sand even before he drove to the Saber Ranch to look at the filly. He had been feeling optimistic.

I know you've seen one of these before, he said to her. They have one at the Saber. I saw it. I expect you been in it a hundred times, probably with the colts you got weaned with. Today it's nothing but a place for exercise. I'm not asking you to do something you don't already know how to do.

The filly pressed backward on her front feet like a sprinter setting herself into the blocks for a race. He didn't want that to happen. He didn't want her to decide to bolt.

It's nothing, he said, keeping his hands low on the lead line. You can go in there and cut up all you want. But you got to go in.

She had to think about it. And she had to check every angle of the surroundings. But she walked in beside him, more or less shoulder-to-shoulder. He unclipped the lead rope, then latched the round pen gate behind the two of them.

The filly immediately began to use the space. She walked across the pen, her black nose held forward like a probing finger. She made a murmuring sound high in her nostrils, then she actually whinnied. She was still searching for her herd. After a silent moment, she broke into a trot for three steps, stopped, then crow-hopped on her hind feet like a child playing hopscotch. Play. That was just what he wanted to see.

The first real horse that ever throwed me, throwed me right onto the ground of this pen, he said to her. She was one of my dad's auction buys. He thought he might be able to sell her as rodeo stock. She could really buck. She was bug eyed and stocking footed, but she could buck. She had some draft horse in her, I'm sure of that. She had those big Percheron feet. My dad wanted me to try her first, so I did. And she sent me right into the sky. You're not gonna send me into the sky, are you?

The filly wasn't really listening to him, which was all right for now.

You're not gonna throw me onto this dirt, he said to her. You know why?

The filly had stretched her head high on her neck like a giraffe. She was trying to identify a way out of the pen.

It's because I got different plans for you. I'm not even gonna put a saddle on you until you're three years old, I'm not even gonna try to ride you while the two of us are still on this ranch. I bet that's a surprise.

The filly tucked herself into a high-stepping walk. She began to circle just as she had in her stall.

Because here's the deal. I'm taking you with me when I go up to the Black Bell to work my summer job, but I'm not riding you up there, either. Nobody will. I'm gonna work with you, we're gonna work so hard you'll be happy to see the sun set on some days. But there's not gonna be a saddle on you for a long time. There's probably not gonna be a saddle on you until after we get all the way to California.

I haven't told you about that yet, have I?

About California? It's a idea I have, and it involves you and me and a man I know called Don Enrique. Don Enrique is willing to give me a chance. The weather's good in California, he said. I been there. They don't lie about that part. And there's a lot of good horses out there too, some of the best I've ever seen. How'd you like to meet up with some fancy California horses?

She circled away from him with her legs scissoring beneath her. She didn't have the muscle she needed yet. She was too narrow in front, and her quarters weren't built up. She could easily be mistaken for a small Thoroughbred, given the neat lines of her legs and the delicate bones of her head. The prettiest bay Thoroughbred you ever saw.

He allowed himself a smile. He had been talking too much, and it was all for his benefit. She didn't need to hear his talk. He dropped his arms to his side and moved carefully to the middle of the round pen. Then he stayed there, silent, giving the filly a center point when she decided she was ready for one.

The work he did at the print shop was never as hard as his father declared it was going to be. Not from his point of view, anyway. He didn't mind hauling bales of bleached paper, though he didn't care for the taste the paper left in his mouth. He liked to operate the binder. He knew how to stack boxes. He knew how to move pallets to the loading dock and set up for a quick transfer that wouldn't waste a truck driver's time. It was all fine. He didn't have feelings about it one way or another. His father had the feelings.

His father had fallen into the printing business when he was trying to make extra money to expand his herd of cows. Winters were long in Lost Cabin. Jobs were not easy to find. But Sal Tassione had kept his eye on Hank Testerman after they were first introduced at the Moose Lodge, when Hank was a young married man with vinegar in his spit. Sal had run Liberty Printing on a shoestring for a very long time. He was ready for some help.

Sal was old-school, but he wasn't stupid. He saw Liberty through the transition from lead type, which he could set at the speed of a schoolgirl playing jacks, to computers. Hank was his assistant mechanic, his inventory manager, his foreman in all kinds of ways. Hank was no kind of salesman, and he didn't have a taste for bill collecting, but those weren't skills he needed as long as Sal and his exuberance were at the front desk.

After ten years, Sal retired himself to the Pioneer Home, in Thermopolis. He didn't want to work until he died, he said. The job, which had been lofted in Will's father's mind as a temporary, money-raising thing, became an ever-shortening ball and chain.

Did you pick up the feed? he asked Will.

Yes, sir.

Have you moved the wrapped pallets to the back? Did you check the stacks?

Yes, sir.

I need you to see if Roscoe needs help in the offset room. It's been hell in there today. It's been hell everywhere.

Yes, sir. I'll talk to Roscoe. I can stay till after five if you need me.

I might need you, his father said, his eyes scribbled with red. *I'm trapped,* those eyes said. *And I'm mad about it.*

I can stay, he repeated.

But you'd like to go, his father said, smacking one of his stained hands against the stained thigh of his jeans.

Will knew better than to continue the conversation. He went to find Roscoe.

You can tell your mother I'll be home late, his father said, talking at Will's back as he headed for the offset room. The computer has fucked us again.

I'll tell her, Will said. I'm sorry about the

computer.

Fucking late, his father said. Tell her that's what it's come to. Again.

It was just another thing he didn't know how to fix, his father's unhappiness, and he was enough of a bad son that he didn't really want to try. He wasn't going to take over the printing business. Neither was Chad. Everett had worked at Liberty for a short time while Sal was still in charge. That had been a disaster even their father wasn't eager to repeat. So it was rooted deep, the unhappiness. The money was necessary. The business was dying. His father understood only one option: to squeeze the rock until it was dry.

Will made a list of the good things he saw during the short drive back to the ranch. A kayaker purling through the waters of Little Kettle Creek. Extra vehicles at the Book-binders' lambing sheds, which meant the babies were being born. Some new horses, all of them Appaloosas, in a small field north of Lone Eagle Garage. Indian horses, beautifully marked animals. He wondered if George Lone Eagle and the tribe had brought them into town to be sold.

A story about his father came to him. They had been camping in the Beartooth Mountains, just he and his parents. It had been a good trip. They were all still pleased with themselves and with their time together, despite the fatigue that came with living in the high mountains. The road was wet with summer rain. There were motorcyclists in both lanes of the road. Before they knew what had happened, the four-horse trailer began to swing into a slow-motion jackknife. His father drove like a hero. The trailer still went over, but the motorcyclists had a chance to get into the clear, and the truck stayed upright, which was important. But his father knew they might have lost some of the horses. His father was calm as he got out of the truck. His mother was calm, too.

They did not go to the trailer until they found help to slow the traffic ahead of them and behind. The grateful motorcyclists handled the traffic. Then his father opened the rear door to the trailer. There were four horses — Tomahawk, Cedar, Debra Dun, and Frosty. They had been riding in pairs, two up, two back, with partitions between them, and now they were trapped in pairs, left sides down. It was tricky work. Each horse had to be dragged from the trailer by its hind legs, and the horses on the bottom, fat Tomahawk and his father's own trusted mare, Cedar, had to remain still until the horse and the partition above them had been removed. Somehow they got it done, despite the fact that Frosty, in particular, was known to be a jug-eared fool of an animal. Somehow the four horses knew what they had to do, and they did it, against every instinct they must have had. A panicked horse could have ruined everything, could have hurt itself or the other horses or a person. He had wondered about that for a long time, and his father wondered about it still as he told the old story again and again. It was a kind of mystery. What made one horse do the right thing, when another horse, in the same situation, could not?

There was never a good reason to think about what had happened the year before with the girls in Texas. The experience hadn't made him a better man, not by his definition. But it had made him more cautious. The experience had also reminded him that people with money, young people or old, occupied the world in ways he could hardly imagine.

He was a groom for the Passante family. He had worked his way up from stall mucker to the one who trailered the saddle horses, six or eight of them at a time, to the shows. The trainer followed later in her air-conditioned Ford. The Passantes followed even later than that. He had seen Emily Passante, who was no more than sixteen years old, change out of her pajamas and get on a champion mare and take a ribbon at a high-level show without so much as a smile.

At shows he put tack on the horses. The trainer warmed them up in an auxiliary ring until the veins beneath their shining coats filled with blood. The trainer, a straight-mouthed woman named Randal Clague, believed a good warm-up was essential. Saddle horses were all about gaits and rhythms. They needed momentum to perform. Randal Clague and Will both got help from a Mexican fellow who seemed to have worked for the Passante family for many years. The arrangement was fine. Will learned what he needed to learn about shipping and vetting and handling show-ring horses. He got familiar with the paperwork and the rudeness. The pageantry was something he was already used to. It was the same the world over, whether you were working with saddle horses or cutting horses or those tiny ponies that are no bigger than a Great Dane dog. When horse people got together they liked their gossip and their parades.

Emily Passante flirted with him plenty.

She wasn't shy about it, and neither were her friends. They were all slender girls, different versions of the same plucked and posing creature. Some of them loved to ride. For others, it was like tennis or waterskiing — just a thing you did out of family habit. Randal Clague told him to be careful about the girls. They would look to get him in trouble.

And they did. There were mainly two of them — Emily and Alex, her friend from north Texas. They offered to take him to parties. They showed him the vodka they had in their shoulder bags. They talked about men on the circuit — trainers and riders — and what they'd heard about those men, the crude acts they preferred. He was twenty-one years old and interested enough. But he didn't have much money, and the Passantes, or the Passantes' horse operation, gave him the kind of job experience he wanted. He was careful. He was polite with the girls, but he kept his distance. They weren't fixated on him, anyhow. He was just another cowboy, and Texas was chock full of cowboys. The Europeans who came and went, with their sunglasses hooked to the fronts of their shirts, were more interesting. And the South Americans. Older men were also interesting. Alex, in particular, liked to talk about older men. She spoke of them as if they were part of a performance she had scheduled for her future.

There was no mystery to it. They were at a show in Fort Worth, and there was the usual fuss. He and Jorge, the Passantes' Mexican helper, had been on the grounds since Monday. He and Randal exercised the animals, bathed them, thinned their tails and braided their manes. They made adjustments in the feeding schedules. Emily was on track for an association championship. Mr. Passante, a businessman who owned some kind of packaging company, made it clear he wanted no mistakes.

There were none. Emily got her blue ribbons and her division championship medal and her association points. She was satisfied. But her friend Alex had been riding a horse that threw a shoe. She was very angry. She made a point of dismounting just beyond the arena gates with a grand, frozen look on her face. She dropped her riding crop and her gloves onto the ground. She refused to talk to her trainer, and she wanted nothing to do with the hindered horse. Will had seen it a hundred times before.

I can take that horse to a farrier, if you

want, he said to Alex's trainer. I'm done for the day.

The trainer, a wizened little man who wore a Panama hat, looked at Will as if he had acquired the halo of a saint. The trainer was under a great deal of stress. Alex's little sister was an entrant in the next class.

Thank you, the trainer said, grabbing at Will's extended hand. Thank you very much.

Will loosened the girth of the flat and polished saddle that was still on Alex's horse. Such a saddle cost, he knew, more than he earned in a month. He loosened the throatlatch of the bridle, and he made sure the noseband wasn't too snug for the horse's comfort. The horse was a quality animal. He had beautiful gaits. But he'd been the victim of misfortune and was likely to find himself in a new barn, with a new set of expectations, by the end of the week. That was how it was. Horses were among the many things in the world that could be thrown away.

Alex came to him later. She wanted to apologize. He found it a continuous wonder how Texas girls could turn themselves into completely different people when they wanted to. Alex was polite, maybe even a touch hangdog. She was still in her riding britches but wore tiny golden sandals on her feet. Her toenails were painted. She had redone her makeup so that her eyes were perfectly lined in black, like a cat's. Her blond hair hung loose past her shoulders. She seemed to breathe perfume.

I shouldn't have done that, she said. I was being a bitch.

He shrugged. Alex was on his territory now, in the Passantes' rented row of stalls. He didn't have to put up with her.

It's hard to lose all the time, she said.

You don't always lose, he said. It was just a thrown shoe. Bad luck.

I should quit riding, she said, rounding her voice up out of her pouting mouth. It's not my thing. I need to do something different — something I'm good at.

You'll be in college soon, won't you? They were next to the empty stall where Randal Clague stored all the gear and tack. He had been organizing the travel wraps when Alex arrived.

She laughed a cooing laugh. I'm already in college. I'm older than Emily by almost two years. Why do you always pretend to forget that?

He shrugged again. But the shrug didn't help fill the warm, hollow shape that was beginning to stretch itself inside his body.

She was standing close to him, leaning against the door to the stall. He was tired, and he didn't feel like being manipulated by anyone else for the rest of the day. His main goal was to stay polite. He reminded himself of that.

You don't have to be afraid of me all the time, she said. You did me a favor. You acted like a gentleman.

He walked around her into the empty stall. He needed to store the travel wraps. And he didn't want to have to look directly at Alex anymore.

She followed him into the stall.

I hope you're not here for another favor, he said. He tried to talk like he was dismissive, like he was pushing her away. He didn't much like Alex. She was spoiled. But he was tired, and he was somewhat angry with her, and he could hear it in his own words now — the angry arrow of want.

Well, she said. I believe I am.

It was nearly dark outside, and the stall, with its tiers of trunks and bagged feed, was as snug and crowded as a closet. She came toward him, but he didn't wait. He didn't wait one second. They rammed their bodies together. It was a game to her. So he made it a game, too. He bit at her mouth, and he bit harder when she reached for his balls, when she tried to show how bold she was. He cornered her in the back of the stall. He tore at the zipper of her tight britches. He yanked her britches down.

Go on, she said, her voice low and stabbing. Do it if you can.

He wasn't surprised to feel how baby smooth she was between her legs, how hairless and wet, and he wasn't surprised by the lashing words she used next, crude words, to egg him on.

See if you're big enough to fuck me.

See if you can make my pussy work.

She was a dirty girl, in her way. She thought she had to talk like that. He got his own jeans undone. There was no mystery to it. She widened herself and bit at him and scratched at his neck and back. He had liniment on his hands from working with the travel wraps, and he knew Alex would feel where he'd funneled into her with his fingers, that she would burn inside there from the liniment, but he didn't care.

They drove at it, fierce.

The Passantes caught them — Mr. Passante, Emily, and Mrs. Passante, with her pair of rat-sized dogs. They had come to look in on the horses after dinner at a restaurant.

He expected to be fired, to be tossed out

on his ass. He didn't expect the beating. Mr. Passante came at him like a rabid animal. He didn't know much about Mr. Passante. He didn't know how to read the man's purplish mask of rage. It was not his usual mask, the one that had transformed Mr. Passante from a poor Mexican boy into a successful businessman who told everyone he was Italian American. This was another face entirely. The daughter Emily was jealous. That was all her squealing meant. And the mother merely added to the squealing with her own kind of expected noise. Only later did he come to think that the beating from Mr. Passante, the fists and kicks and furious blows from the stirrup irons, might have been more about Alex than Emily. He had been inside Alex. That was territory Mr. Passante might have considered his own.

He got out of Texas. He lost two weeks' pay, but he thought he'd done well to get his personal belongings and his truck, all of which Jorge gathered for him. He met Jorge at a strip mall not far from the Passantes' farm. Jorge did not smile at the sight of Will's blackened eyes or the stitches sewn into his face.

It's all right, Will said to the other man. I made a mistake. I paid what I owed. And you have brought me my things. *Gracias.*

The Mexican lifted his hands. He didn't want any credit.

I made a mistake, he said again. Don't tell Emily or them people you ever saw me again, okay? There's nothing more to it.

Jorge nodded.

You take care of yourself, he said to Jorge. Keep a eye on those fine horses. Then he shook the man's hand. Then he checked the gas gauge and the oil gauge on the truck's faded dashboard. It was more than twenty road hours from where he was to his parents' home in Lost Cabin, Wyoming.

He felt something slide off him when he left Texas.

While he was teaching the filly to work on a long line, he told her stories about his great-grandmother. They were in the round pen. The sand made a whispering sound around the filly's hooves as she walked from right to left. He could hear Trampas and Bison banging at the boards in the large paddock. They were like widows, those two. They believed in their superiority. It would be a favor to his father if he rode Trampas and Bison later in the day, just to give them a job. The clouds overhead were the color of a sun-pitted bucket. A crow had landed on the gate so that it could pry mites from its breast feathers with its beak. He recognized the crow. It had a patch of white on one wing and a reputation for staining Everett's truck with crow shit.

If he rode the geldings, he wouldn't need to go any farther than Solemn Butte Canal. That was all it would take. For now, he was teaching the filly to pay attention to her gait, and to her balance. She was a good student, but she would reach her limit before long.

My great-grandmother was what they called a strong woman, he said to the filly after he clucked her into an extended walk. He held the long line in his left hand and a slender whip tipped with a white flag in his right. I never met her. I was born too late. But Chad remembers her. He says she was something else — like a character out of a book. She was my mother's grandmother. Her name was Mary Patricia O'Donnell. She has been dead a long time, but she still gets talked about. My mother says she don't take after Grandma Mary Pat, not at all, and I get the idea she's glad about that.

My great-grandmother started off in Canada, where she was poor, he said. Poor and Irish. There wasn't much in Canada, so the family dropped down into the Dakotas and somehow got their feet under them. My great-grandmother got married, and she hit the jackpot there because she married a man who worked hard, who didn't drink, who was Irish, and who knew how to build up a farm. There was a few good years on the Red River in North Dakota. Children. High yields with the crops. The right politics for farmers. They weren't rich, but they had a bunkhouse full of hired hands, and they raised almost everything they needed on the land they owned. My great-grandmother was famous for her wood chopping and her fruit pies. Things were so good that two of my great-grandfather's brothers, some of the O'Donnells, left their farms and started a bank in Fargo. They took care of their friends' money. Or that was what they said.

He asked the filly to slow her walk by slowing the movement of the whip in his right hand. The whip was held low, with its flag brushing the ground. It was aimed at a point just behind the filly's hocks. The filly slowed when the flag slowed. She watched the flag carefully.

I guess those brothers fell into some kind of trap of greed or overconfidence, he said. There was land speculators everywhere in those days. They would lie to you about anything. And farmers asked for loans against their harvests, and some people started playing the stock markets in New

York and Chicago. That's how my mother tells it. The O'Donnell brothers made mistakes. Then they added to the mistakes by cutting some corners. Before it was all over, they faced a long time in prison.

Except that the brother who had stayed on his farm on the Red River couldn't let it happen. He'd kept his hat on. He wasn't in no kind of debt, and he had twelve men working for him. It didn't matter. His loyalty was hard as a diamond inside of him. Can you imagine that now? he asked the filly. You think most families would act like that now? That brother, my great-grandfather, sold everything he had to save his family. The notes were paid off. The law was satisfied. The O'Donnells had their freedom, even if they had lost their reputations.

He stopped the filly on his signal, then he used the whip to ask her to line up her feet, to stand squarely. After a pause, he asked her to turn and begin a slow walk, right to left. He made all of these requests without words. The filly was learning to keep her chin down, and she was learning to bend herself around her own shoulder with some grace.

My great-grandmother wasn't gonna stay on the Red River and work for some other farmer, he told the filly. She knew her husband had done the right thing. But it felt terrible to her, the way she and her children had lost what they had. She told her husband they had to pack up and leave North Dakota, and they did.

It's not necessarily a happy story, he continued. Chad says my great-grandmother was stingy and mean and always trying to do difficult things — like hanging gates or repairing washouts in the road — by herself. She didn't have a speck of patience. My mother says it was a fight for my great-grandmother to keep from hating people each and every day. She had five children, but they got no praise from her. One was killed in World War Two, and there was a daughter who ran away and was never heard from again. The others made it through. My great-grandfather was a shell of a man after he auctioned off his farm. He didn't have the heart to start over. So they lived in little towns, and my great-grandmother did laundry and took in sewing and raised chickens and sold herself to the ugly tasks town people didn't like to do. She could break a chicken's neck with one hand. She tore the end off one of her fingers while she was on a ladder, washing windows for a rich family, he told the filly. Chad says you could see the sharp end of the bone under the skin in her hand if you looked for it.

He clucked the filly into an extended walk. She was beginning to fight the restraint of the long line, he could see that.

Nothing was easy in those days, he said. People didn't have much, and they went under all the time. America was a place that tested you. My mother's mother finished high school and ended up a secretary in Rapid City. She married my grandfather, and he had some business sense. They set up a store in Newcastle, Wyoming, for the tourists going in and out of the Black Hills. The family history is kind of basic after that. Small ranchers and town people. We ain't done much in the way of dramatics. So we keep going back to my great-grandmother. She never set foot in a church once she left the Red River, not until her own funeral. She had no use for God because God didn't come to the aid of good men. That's how she told it. But she hung on until she was ninety and blind, allowing what was inside her to boil down to pure spite, if my mother is to be believed. She even lived with my parents for a few months near the end. They were the only ones who would take her in.

He stopped the filly. There was sweat on

her neck and between her legs. He dropped the long line and the whip.

It's interesting to me, he said, approaching the filly, signaling a gentle release from their business. My great-grandmother was the kind of person you can say lived a hard life. And she didn't bring that hardness down on herself at all. She wasn't a bad woman, or a criminal in any way. It's a puzzle, don't you think? What does a person really get after a lot of honest work? Who gets happiness at the end of the line, and who don't?

His brother Chad came by the ranch after living in his truck for three days. Chad's company handled seismographic measurements for natural gas speculators. He'd been in the Garnet Field, trying to make sure the work was done right.

The sand out there's so bad, I've ruined two pairs of goggles, he told Will. The CD player in my truck can't even play music anymore. I feel like I been stationed in Iraq.

You making a living? Will asked.

Everybody's making a living, Chad said. I'd just like to keep my eyeballs and my sanity if possible. Hannah won't get near me until I've showered. I have to take all my clothes off outside the door before she'll let me in.

And that's new? Will asked, joshing.

Go to hell, his brother said, punching at Will's shoulder. I came to see your new horse.

Chad was considered the smart one in the family. He was the oldest, and he carried himself like the authority bequeathed to him was no big deal. He'd never had any problem admiring his youngest brother. He liked horses himself, and he liked working with cattle and skiing in the Rampart Mountains and hunting and doing all the things that would keep him happy in Lost Cabin, Wyoming, for the rest of his life.

What do you call her? he asked.

Nothing yet. She don't have a real name.

You planning to give her one?

I don't know. Maybe. Nothing permanent. Whoever buys her will name her something permanent.

So that's your plan? You're going to sell her?

Yeah. When she's ready. I'm not rushing at it this time. This is gonna be different.

You think you can get a lot?

Hope so. It depends on how she turns out. And what people think of her.

She looks good. She's not real big, though.

She don't need to be big for what we're doing. Just fast. And quick. And fearless in a certain kind of way. I'm almost afraid to talk about the whole thing. I know rodeo horses and saddle horses. Polo horses are a reach for me. She's put together good for a two-year-old, but I don't even know how she'll work under saddle yet. Everything I say is a guess.

I think you've made Everett nervous this time. He's afraid you might break out, get some kind of leg up on things. He thinks you're gonna stick him with all the work that has to be done around here.

Everett wants me out of the way.

He might say he does, Chad said, but he really doesn't. Everett acts like he's trapped in a box canyon on issues that are important to him. If he was a bull, he'd charge you three times a day. But he isn't ready to see you branching out as an entrepreneur. He likes it better when you fuck up.

He'd better stay quiet about it, then.

He will. He's kind of scared of you. The big money is in California, right?

There's money all over. There's big money right here in Lost Cabin for certain things.

You know what I mean. I mean the kind of money that rolls in and knocks you flat. The kind that buys because it wants to buy.

They got that in California, yes. Some of it comes in from the south, up from Mexico and Argentina. They get crazy over their horses in Argentina.

So you're heading back out there?

That's what I'm telling myself. We got a long way to go, this filly and me. We don't know our ass from our elbow yet. So it won't be tomorrow.

You think part of it is getting away from here? You think that's how it sets up for you — you need to leave?

Might be. I can't quite say. I haven't thought through that part. I just want to do something I haven't seen done before.

Does Ma know?

She'd say good-bye to me tomorrow. She wants me to believe she's one hundred percent well.

Maybe she is.

Then why don't I feel as good about the cancer as she does?

Because you're a worrier, and she's a worrier, and she's taught you too good. She knows me and Everett have figured out how to feed at the trough of our own needs. She's afraid you're holding back.

Well, I guess I get to decide about that. I've got ten weeks of work at the Black Bell, maybe a little longer. If Ma's still good, then

I'll aim for California. Assuming Don Enrique will have me.

Has Dad said much?

He says I paid too much for this horse, which is what he always says. Otherwise, he don't care.

He cares, Chad said. I been out of the house long enough to be able to read that road sign.

Well, if he gives a damn, he's got a funny way of showing it. It don't matter. I'm never gonna be the one to give him the boost he's looking for. I'm just not. That's your job.

Right. And I'm fucking good at it, Chad said with a torn laugh. College boy who knows just enough to ruin field trucks for an out-of-state gas company. Don't worry. Dad knows how to lay into me. But you're right. Let him feed his own bad moods, whatever they are. We're sons. We got the right to make our own love and trouble.

Amen, Will said, wishing he knew how to laugh the ways Chad did.

You're not going to let them rip you off, are you? Chad asked. Big money sometimes comes attached to small minds. I see that in the gas fields at least once a week.

I don't plan on getting ripped off.

Good.

I just want to sell a really nice horse.

That's the way to say it. I like your style. Not that you care what I think.

I care.

The hell you do, Chad said, swiping at Will with his fist once again. You are your own muddy river. Don't start pretending you're some kind of regular cowboy asshole while you're standing right here in front of me. I used to change your britches, remember? I've wiped up your shit. You are not completely regular. It's never been easy to turn your head.

Thanks, big brother.

I'm just saying. You are your own kind of crazy flood. Don't forget it.

There was one story he did not tell the filly. It was the story of Caliban. Caliban had been a durable gelding, a reclaimed mustang with a portion of quarter horse blood in his veins. He had come to the Testermans as part of a barter deal when Simon Painter and his brother, Jace, got into money trouble with their ranch. The Painters owed Hank Testerman for the service of a bull and for a cash loan meant to help the brothers pay the fees on a federal lease in the Rampart Range. The Painters owed money to a lot of people. But Hank Testerman was willing to take some of his payment in livestock. He asked for two weaned heifers. He found the mustang, unshod and grazing without a halter, in his creek meadow instead.

The unexpected arrival, who was as black as the inside of a tractor tire, had been cut late and had the thick, top-heavy neck of a stud. His mane and tail were ropes of bramble. He featured the ankles of a plow horse, and there was a goggled quality to his eyes that kept him from being considered handsome. The white blaze on his face was the shape of a pulled tooth. After a stint of cursing, Hank decided to keep the animal as an I.O.U. There was no question who would take care of him. Chad was at college. Everett was a decent manager of cows, but he had no touch with horses. Will was given the task. He was fifteen years old.

I don't care what you do with him, his father said. Just don't hurt him in some way that'll give Simon cause to back out of our deal. He owes me more than a thousand dollars. Is that S.O.B. right there worth a thousand dollars?

No, Will said.

Could he ever be worth that?

Will took the question seriously. Only if he comes into being a polished mount, he said. It would take awhile.

Don't you do Simon Painter's work for

him, then, his father said. Mess with the horse how you want, keep him healthy, but don't you do any work for free. I want the cash that's owed me, and I plan to get it.

It was his mother who came up with the name after the black horse threw Will from the saddle. They were in the round pen. The situation had been going well until the black horse changed his mind about the atmosphere.

That one's stronger than he knows he is, his mother said as she watched the animal stand over her flustered son. He seems a little sorry about that fact.

Caliban. The beast and the mystery. They understood each other from the get-go. It wasn't always perfect between them, but they were somehow matched up, two young males stumbling their way from morning to night.

The Painter brothers were sucked deeper into their whirlpool of trouble. They stopped returning phone calls. Hank Testerman wanted to know if the long-haired mustang he had somehow acquired could be taught to carry hunters into the mountains during elk season. Better yet, David DePew was looking to rent good packhorses. Could the sorry bastard be taught to carry a load? A packhorse could earn them as much as five hundred dollars.

There's some things he's ready for, Will said. He'd make a mount for a heavy man, one who knows how to maintain a horse's interest. But he don't have the seasoning to carry a load in a string. He don't think of himself as a follower.

Maybe he needs to stop thinking, his father said, disgusted.

As it turned out, there was time for seasoning. The Painter brothers made no move to reclaim their horse. Will used the gelding on the family hunting trek when all four of them, the brothers and father, rode into the national forest south of Owl's Head Peak and brought back two elk, one bull and one cow, and a whole Thanksgiving dinner's worth of tales. The black horse hadn't done anything of note, but he hadn't embarrassed himself either. He hadn't been unnerved by the heavy scent of butchered meat. He hadn't tried to walk himself home, like Chad's horse, Tattoo, had when the electric fence went down in the middle of the night. Will took Caliban with him to the Black Bell Ranch the following summer when he began his first job there as a dude string wrangler. The ranch manager, Shea Petrie, tried to buy the horse at the end of the summer, but Will didn't have the legal standing to sell him. He didn't think he would have made the sale even if he could have.

He ain't a finished horse, he told Shea Petrie. Me and him got lots to figure out. He needs to learn to keep his lid on during foul weather, for one thing. But I'll ask the Painters what they're thinking. Maybe next year.

Simon Painter signed the horse over to Hank Testerman in October. The Painter brothers had lost everything they'd ever pretended to own. It turned out Jace had a problem with gambling. The brothers moved into separate houses in town, one with their mother, the other with their married sister. They no longer spoke to each other, and the ranch was sold to a sportscaster from Connecticut. Will's father told him it was time to cash in on the horse.

I'd like to wait until spring, he said to his father. He's a solid saddle horse now, as long as you don't ask him to do nothing fancy. Six more months of sweat and agility work, and I might be able to sell him as a horse you can rope off of. That'd really punch up the price.

The accident occurred on another hunting trip. Chad had drawn a permit for an antlered elk in the Green River drainage. It was difficult country, mostly unknown to the family, but Chad thought it was a rare opportunity to get a trophy bull, and he talked his brothers into going with him. The weather was operatic, but that was something they had prepared for. The wild card was the girlfriend Chad decided to bring along. She was nice enough, but she knew as much about hunting and horses as a bowl of spaghetti did. She needed to be looked after.

Later, there was plenty of blame to spread around. Chad had lent his best horse to the girl, so he was riding a mare that was known to lose her nerve at times. Will, using his father's steady horse, Cedar, was riding drag and was too far from events to have any influence. Caliban, who had been taught to carry panniers, was loaded with two bear-proof coolers filled with food. He was tied between a pair of sullen mules, Rosie and Rooster. The brothers were never able to re-create events in an agreed-upon way. Did the narrow trail somehow break off under Chad's horse, or did the mare just make a mistake? Why didn't the pigging string between Rosie and Caliban snap when the mule began to fall? Was Rosie's load off balance or too heavy? Had that been an issue? Had Rooster crowded Caliban and made it impossible for him to back away? The girlfriend screamed when the animals began to scramble. There was no doubt about that. And the girlfriend absorbed all of Chad's attention just when the pack animals needed it most. Everett, who was riding point, said later that it looked like stuffed animals being tossed out the window of a car. Rosie and Caliban were gone — more than a hundred feet down the slope, through scree and scrub brush and cornices of fresh white snow.

Will didn't rush. He knew enough to make sure Chad and his girlfriend were safe. And he knew enough to take both his guns down the hill with him, the pistol and the rifle. Rosie was on her feet. Everett, who had pulled up around a bend and had a good view of the situation, called out to say he could see Rosie. Caliban was off the radar.

There was nothing like it, putting down an animal you knew. He had done it when his mother's English setter got too old, but he'd planned his approach to that ordeal. He had taken the dog out into a field where it had once flushed its share of pheasant, and he had shot the dog while it was trying to quarter the field for birds. He buried the dog on the spot. His mother hadn't wanted to see the body. What he remembered most about the burial was how his mouth kept filling up with unwanted spit. He had to spit about a hundred times while he dug. This time, he had to pick his way down into the canyon, but his mind was not in planning mode. This was triage. Rosie's load had torn loose. There were tent stakes and cookware and camp tools all over the ground. The skin was mostly peeled from one of the mule's shoulders, and she wasn't able to put weight on her left front ankle. She was making a braying noise that sounded like she had a spool of fence wire caught behind her teeth.

Caliban was pinned sideways by the bulk of his load, but that wasn't the worst of it. Something — probably a blade of rock — had torn into his insides. His belly was slit open like a change purse. It was leaking. His guts were steaming in the cold air, and there was a blackening gloss of blood on the ground.

Will could have waited for one of his brothers. He could have pretended there was an element of judgment in what he did. But there was not. He cut the panniers loose with his hunting knife. He went to Caliban's thrashing head, for the gelding wanted to get to his feet, it was his only instinct, and he didn't understand why he couldn't stand up. Will said the gelding's name several times. He made sure Caliban knew he was there. He stroked his bony brow. Then he knelt on the gelding's flopping neck in his heavy hunting clothes and he rotated a bullet into the firing chamber of his pistol and he shot the gelding through the up-facing eye. It was the way he'd heard you should do it if you wanted to be sure. You didn't want to shoot them in the forehead, where the bone was thick. You wanted to do it in the eye. To be sure.

He didn't have the heart to look once more into that black eye before he fired.

Everett joined him at the bottom of the hill.

You did good, Everett said. That horse looks like shit. What about the mule?

Will didn't say anything. Everett was just filling the air with words. They both knew the verdict on the mule.

We'll have to carry everything up top ourselves, Everett said.

So?

So, it's more work. What a cluster fuck. That woman of Chad's won't ever want to touch him again.

We got to do something about Rosie, Will said. His head felt tiny and hollow, like it was emptying itself of everything connected to his body.

I got it, Everett said. And he took Will's rifle and shot the mule in the head, aiming at her like she was a target set up against the hill. The mule's bruised lungs emptied with a long groan. The sound was rusty and terrible.

Will stripped Caliban's carcass. He left nothing but the heavy, studded horseshoes — the kind that were supposed to be good on ice. He wasn't willing to summon the indignity it would take to pry the shoes free. The gelding's blood kept puddling onto the ground, even though he was dead. The blood sent vapors into the air. And Will couldn't keep himself from looking at the ruptured blossom of what had once been the upturned eye. He was afraid to lick his lips, afraid he'd get a splattered taste of the hot jelly from that eye. Everett began to carry their belongings back up to where Chad and the girl waited, under a torn sack of falling snow.

Will hadn't known Caliban meant anything more to him than Rosie or the cussed cow dog Skim. There was an unexpected turmoil inside him as he began to lay out the tent stakes so he could repack Rosie's panniers. He found himself tangled in his feelings. He had heard from his Christian rodeo friends that the fights inside you were always the biggest fights. The invisible demons were the ones that had the most power. But he didn't even know what this demon — if that's what it was — might be after. He sensed that Caliban's death was about to fall upon him like a big, flat stone dropped from a scoured sky, and he didn't know why. He would never know why. It just seemed important that he fight to keep the death above him, away from him.

He strapped one of the bear-proof coolers that Caliban had carried across his own back. The cooler was filled with steaks and potatoes and ears of corn, the kind of food hunters celebrated with. Chad would want to turn back for home, Will knew that. They couldn't organize a good hunt without enough pack animals. So it would all end up being a waste. One mule. One good and decent mustang. He grabbed at his knees as he thought about the gelding and the way he loved to lick salt from a person's hands, the way he let the barn cats leap on and off his broad back. He had just killed an animal that had been working hard to make its own history. That thought clenched his guts into the roll of a sour, unsatisfying puke before he staggered up the long hill alone.

■ ■ ■ ■

The day she came up lame was a hard one. He was in town with Everett, overseeing the transfer of some dry cows to the auction lot, and the horses got after each other. His mother heard the ruckus from the house. Trampas, who was universally considered to have the gumption of a basking toad, jumped two fences to get himself into the same paddock as the filly. Then he went after her. Or somebody went after somebody. It was impossible to say. His mother had left her work at the kitchen table and walked down to the corrals to find the fur flying.

Trampas kept trying to corner her, his mother said. He was biting and carrying on. Hawk stayed clear. But your filly had to run as much as she could until I got in there and grabbed Trampas's halter. The old criminal. What did he think he was up to, anyway? his mother asked. He's not a stud. She wasn't eating his feed. I've never seen him work that hard for anything.

There were no obvious cuts or bruises, but there was no doubt about it. The filly was favoring her left front.

He tried not to overreact. He had learned

a few tricks in Texas for dealing with injured performance horses. Most of those tricks involved drugs he didn't have and wasn't prepared to use, but Randal Clague, the trainer he had worked for in Texas, was also a big proponent of ice and massage. Will applied ice along the filly's left leg even before he identified any heat in the joints or any swelling. He gave her a mild analgesic. It was nothing like what the saddle-horse people or racing-horse people pumped into their animals, but it was a start. He stayed in the barn for hours, waiting to see the unlucky signs of a bone chip or a badly injured tendon.

The filly continued to favor her leg, although she did not go off her feed, and there was no consistent evidence of swelling.

You could call Art Slocum, his father said.

I was thinking of Brett Easter, over in Riverton, Will said. You used him when Cedar was in foal.

Brett's good, his father said. Expensive as hell. You should save yourself some money.

And Art is cheap but crazy, Everett said, adding his straw to the camel's back.

Art is his own kind of man, their father said. I don't care for his attitude about almost anything, but that don't mean he don't have what it takes to treat a crippled horse.

She's not crippled, Will said, his face burning.

You know what I mean, his father said. If you got money to pay him, he can be here in ten minutes.

No one seemed to know the sum of Art Slocum's history. He had arrived in Lost Cabin four or five years before and set up a veterinary practice with money that appeared to come from his own pocket. There was already a good vet in town, and there were big practices in Riverton and Dubois that specialized in large animals. Art Slocum lived alone. He didn't even seem to keep a dog. If you called his office, he was the one who answered the phone. He didn't advertise. He didn't try to soften up potential clients by judging at the 4-H fairs. He didn't seem to care whether he practiced medicine or not.

Except word got out. Lizbeth Patrous, one of those women who made it her life's work to adopt wild horses from the Bureau of Land Management, called Dr. Slocum thinking she could get something for nothing from the new veterinarian. The other vets were tired of her wheedling. Art Slocum came out and tended to her herd. He even managed to boss Lizbeth around in a way that left her happy. But he didn't cut her any slack. He told me I'm keeping too many fertile mares, Lizbeth said without a trace of her usual truculence. I've decided he's right. I need to neuter some of them, as much as it breaks my heart. It's best for the older ones.

Then Slocum did some work for the Painter brothers while they were still in the pink. They liked his brusque manner, his low prices, his utter lack of indecision when it came to doctoring a horse. He might be a little cold in the veins, Jace Painter told Hank Testerman, but he can really stitch up a colt.

The Painter brothers seemed to think Art Slocum came from Iowa, that he had made a pile of money working with big commercial hog operations there. Somebody else claimed Art had trained harness horses in Arkansas. It didn't matter. He was cheap. He didn't try to sell you a dozen kinds of medicine. He came when you called.

Art Slocum arrived in a fragile-looking Toyota truck that featured a homemade cap painted in the colors of desert camouflage. It was said he kept his truck like that so he could pretend he was invisible. Art did not go in for the fashionable collection of medical gear most veterinarians toted in their big diesel rigs. There was nothing fashionable about him.

Will led him to the filly's stall. The vet watched the horse for a moment, spoke to her, took note of her demeanor. He placed one of his large, gnarled hands against her muzzle when she lifted her head to him.

What do you think? the vet asked.

I'm hoping it's just a bad bruise or a muscle pull, Will said. I don't know what I think. I been trying some heat and massage.

Massage? You believe in that foolishness? Art asked, showing his worn teeth. Art Slocum had teeth that might have come from Iowa. They looked like they'd ground themselves down on yellow corn for years and years.

I believe in whatever works, Will said. I'll try anything once.

Did it work?

The massage? I don't know. She seemed to like it.

I suspect she did, the vet said. She appears to prefer attention. She's no wallflower.

She's pretty aware of things, Will said.

That too, Art said. Why don't you take her out of the stall so we can find out if I know anything or not?

Art was like that. He practiced veterinary medicine like it was nothing more than conversation. He wore work clothes the color of faded concrete. His cuffs were threadbare, and his sleeves were always clean, though his hands sometimes appeared to have recently emerged from the insides of a gasoline engine. He was white haired, with a bad haircut, a hard, protruding belly, and legs no bigger around than a kitchen table's.

He watched the filly as Will attached a lead line to her halter and led her from the stall.

You want to hear any of my guesses? Art asked.

Will shrugged.

Maybe not, Slocum said. You're serious about this horse, I can tell that. She's not one of your father's throwaways.

Art Slocum was like that, too. He tended to insult men close to his own age. He could be merciless about it.

You giving her analgesic? he asked.

Will nodded.

Then let me try my magic. You won't tell on me, will you?

No, sir. Will smiled a tight kind of smile. He had wondered if it would come to this. Art Slocum liked to play the eccentric

111

whenever he could. The magic will stay between us, he told the vet.

As it should, the older man said, tucking the rolled cuffs of his sleeves above his elbows.

It would have been called faith healing if horses could be accused of having faith. Art Slocum was good enough at the regular business — with needles and scalpels and worming tubes. But this was what people loved to gossip about: his hands. He could tell you where and why your animal was hurt with the laying on of his hands. And he could sometimes fix it.

Walk her out for me, he said to Will. Just up the aisle.

Will moved forward with the filly.

Stop her there, Art said. And he approached her left side with his large hands spread open like baseball mitts. He ran them up and down her neck, then up and down the perfect angle of her shoulder, keeping his hands an inch above her skin, never touching the horse directly. He looked like a dowser, Will thought. Like a man who was searching for a hidden river.

She's got a tear right in there, Art said, pointing to the front of the filly's shoulder. I can feel it, and so can she. Watch her foot.

Will watched the filly lift her left foot like

she was being tickled by a deerfly whenever Art Slocum ran his hands in the air above the point of injury. She moved the foot like she was some kind of puppet.

It's not bad, Art Slocum said. It'll heal on its own in a while. You want me to take a stab at it anyhow?

Will nodded. He'd seen Art do this only once before, on a bucking horse at the county fairgrounds. Ned Shepperson, who ran the fairgrounds, swore by Art when it came to keeping his rodeo stock healthy. He just didn't want to talk about how Art did whatever he did. He didn't want to have to say he believed in it.

Art kept his hands spread. He closed his eyes. He didn't say anything, and he didn't appear to do anything, not really, but he kept his hands in place over the filly's supposed injury for about two minutes. His hands hovered like knuckled wings.

Try her now, the vet said.

Will walked the filly forward a few steps. She moved so well, he walked her forward some more, all the way to the end of the barn.

She feels better, don't she? the vet said.

Looks like it, Will said.

So I've fooled another one, the vet said, laughing behind his ground-down teeth. You

113

keep giving her the analgesic and don't work her for another day or two. Keep her up. She'll be fine.

Do you want to tell me how you did that? Will asked.

Do you want to know?

I think so. I don't think it's true that you're just a damn witch doctor.

Is that what they say? Are you parroting your father?

Will didn't take the bait.

It's an ancient Chinese thing, Art Slocum said, clearly joking. You could say I got it from a genie in a bottle I found by the side of the highway, or you could say I got it from an old uncle of mine who shod horses for more than fifty years. My uncle was a tight-lipped, teetotaling Methodist from Indiana. About as Chinese as anyone I ever knew. The old vet laughed aloud again. Give me your hand, he said.

Will hesitated. It was hard not to think of Art Slocum as a prankster.

Come on, the old vet said, hold out your hand.

Will did it. Art placed his own hand in the air above Will's bare palm, not touching, staying about an inch away. He kept his hand there until the heat spreading into Will's own fingers made them tingle.

I warmed you up, didn't I? Art Slocum said as he broke off, dropping his hand down next to his hip. I learned how to do it from my uncle. Maybe it's a family curse, maybe not. But I can feel that living heat in everything I get close to, and I can feel where that heat has gotten disrupted or torn. It don't make me magic. It's just a tool. I try to use it well. I wish I could say it was as therapeutic with women as it is with animals.

How much do I owe you? Will asked, still looking at his tingling, outstretched hand.

How much do you have in your pocket?

I have a hundred dollars, Will said. I hoped that would be enough.

You hoped that was what it would be worth, the vet said, looking up into the cobwebs that hung from the rafters of the Testerman barn. Is it?

Yes, sir.

She's a good-looking horse. Is she valuable?

She is to me.

Then I'll take everything you've got in your pocket, Art Slocum said. I've always enjoyed robbing a man when it involves a good-looking horse.

Everett followed him into the barn one

morning a few days after Art Slocum had worked on the filly. Everett's breath was acrid with the smoke of a cigarette.

How's your horse? he asked.

She looks okay, Will said. Like nothing happened. I guess we dodged the bullet.

I could take care of her, you know, Everett said. If you don't want to take her to the Black Bell. You won't have much time for her up there. And she looks kind of delicate to me.

She's not delicate, Will said. She's just young. Why would you want to mess with her? Don't you think the heifers and cows will keep you busy?

I'm just offering, Everett said. Trying to be a good brother.

It took Will a moment to put the pieces together. He could see how the idea made sense to Everett. But it didn't make sense for him and what he wanted.

I appreciate it, Everett. I really do. But my guess is, you'd need to charge me for hay and grain and maybe for handling my horse a little. That would only be fair. Shea Petrie at the Black Bell don't have to charge me for those things. He's got room. So I can make it work up there. Can I ask you a question, though? Are things really that tight?

116

He watched Everett swing his thick, bare hands in front of him. Every now and again the hands smacked together like the blades of a posthole digger.

Things is always tight, Everett said. You know how Dad is. If I can get just a little more money together, we could go for another bull. I got my eye on just the right one.

Have you thought about renting stalls to somebody else with horses? We're close enough to town.

You know how Dad is about that, too. He don't like other people's business in our business.

Okay, Will said. But you're gonna have empty stalls in this barn all summer. What about penning a bull or two for somebody else? What if Bent Stallworth has some over-flow?

Everett twisted his mouth to the right side of his face the way he did when he was com-mitted to interior thinking. Will remembered what Chad had said about Everett feeling like he was always trapped in some canyon.

The next thing I hear from you, Everett said, carping, you'll be saying we need to rent this barn to one of those hippies who raises llamas.

I didn't say that, Will said, making sure he

didn't show any smile. You know how Ma feels about llamas. One look at them and she starts to spit worse than they do.

Yeah, Everett said, starting to smile on his own. That's true.

But you could pen bulls, Will said. It's a idea.

Sure, Everett said, bulls.

Will walked himself into the grain room. He had never had an easy relationship with Everett. Their tastes were too different, too contrary.

Can I bring up another question? Everett asked. Since I got you here.

Sure, Will said, shouting from the grain room.

You seen Lacey Henderson lately?

Will paused. He wanted to make sure his brother wasn't trying to push him down a steep slope. No, he said. She's with Travis Bonham. Or that's what I heard. You know something different?

I don't, Everett said. But I know she's still got her looks.

No surprise there, Will said, stepping back into the barn aisle. I thought you were going out with Catarina or whatever her name is, Bobby Finn's little sister.

We go out sometimes, Everett said, his mouth beginning to twist again.

Not working out so good?

It works until she starts talking wedding gowns. Are the girls better up at the Black Bell and places like that? More fun?

It always sounds better when you talk about girls who ain't from home, Will said. Don't be fooled by that. I've seen some wild at the Black Bell. And I've seen some nice ones down here. You just got to keep your own picture clear, or that's how I figure it.

But you had Lacey Henderson, Everett said. And you let her go. Most people would say that was stupid.

I don't think anybody *has* a person like Lacey Henderson, Will said. That's not how it works.

Well, Catarina Finn acts like she's got to have some man before she turns twenty. I'm not sure I'm up to it.

Then keep that picture clear in your head, Will said. He wondered if women saw the same corkscrewing vulnerability in Everett that he did. He wondered if it tempted them. Bulls, he said to his brother. Then women. Cows. Then women. In that order.

His mother told him there was going to be a service for Annie Atwood.

It's not a funeral, his mother said. It's not going to be all tear pulling and sad. They

119

can't really have a funeral, since there's not a body, but the family wants to do something after all these months. I guess her husband wants to do something, too. He's had a difficult time with the family. Some of them are still suspicious.

I can see why, Will said.

Yes. Annie didn't always have it easy in her marriage, his mother said. We know that. But there's no evidence he did anything. I'll probably go to the service. I've known her parents a long time.

I'm not going.

I'm not saying you should, his mother said. The police were very hard on you. They were hard on other people, too. Annie's husband made sure of that. I can understand why you'd want to keep your distance.

It would be bad luck to go, he said, squeezing his eyes shut for just a blink. I think it would give me the wrong feeling. Like I'm giving up on Annie and whatever happened to her.

You might be right, his mother said, looking down into a curdled cup of coffee. They were in the kitchen, just the two of them. It was the place they often talked.

I'll keep on remembering her my own way, he said, reaching for his hooded jacket. It's my choice.

Do you think we'll ever know?

We have to, he said. His voice was louder, more rampaging, than he'd meant it to be. Nobody deserves to be an empty question, like Annie is now.

He left his mother, and he left the house, and he went outside toward the barn, except that he knew he didn't really want to be in the barn. The wind was wet and slapping. It came from the north, bearing some of the rough grab of the Pacific Ocean. The ranch yard was a jigsaw puzzle of crusted mud. It looked as though every soul who lived in the small town of Lost Cabin had left a trail across it. A pair of mallard ducks were nesting behind the flume of the irrigation ditch. He could hear the ducks directing each other, tasking. Annie Atwood. It was still hard as hell to think about her.

There was the way she flirted with him, for one thing, trying to make him comfortable and uncomfortable at the same time. She wasn't even thirty years old. She worked at the bakery in town, and she spent hours training for the kind of difficult, crazy marathons that people run at high altitudes. She also made jewelry from silver and glass. He had seen the bracelets shine like electric threads on her arms. Her husband was away for weeks at a time, climbing foreign mountains with teams of adventurers. Everybody wondered if Annie got lonely, but when she asked Will to teach her how to rope from a saddle, he didn't analyze her motives. He liked Annie. He knew how to teach a person to rope.

She wasn't a good rider. She said it was hard for her to feel balanced on the back of a horse. He put her on Hawk, but he did that only after Annie had learned to throw a loop from the ground. She was pretty good with a lariat. She told him she practiced in her own backyard, and he believed her.

This all happened early in the summer before his mother found out about her cancer. He was in Lost Cabin after his time in Texas. He had sworn he wouldn't put his tail between his legs, and he didn't. He took every job he could find.

But he was smoldering. He knew it. He felt the kind of hot condensation in his blood that he'd felt during the slow, garbled weeks before his graduation from high school. Texas hadn't thwarted him, not entirely. Yet he needed some kind of intention. A delivery point. Instead, he found himself thinking about Annie Atwood more than he should have. He thought about being in bed with her. She had a small, girlish body and bountiful eyes. He wondered if that was what she was after — wishing she could be touched by him — with the roping lessons and the throaty way she laughed about them.

Annie was the one who asked if he would work with the bad horse. She was impressed with Hawk. And she was impressed with what he said about horses, what he seemed to know, and how he knew it. He wanted to impress her. Some of what he said was blowing smoke. Would he be willing to call the Chathams and talk to them about the Thoroughbred that had spooked their daughter? That was what Annie asked him in her smiling, sweet-voiced way. The Chathams were some kind of cousins of hers. As he thought back on it, he now understood that Annie had been sweet-voiced with everyone.

The Chathams lived on thirty acres of sheltered land south of Riverton, near the reservation. Both parents worked for the government, but it looked like the family had extra money from somewhere. The barn they had built was too nice for the horses they had in it.

The bad horse was a victim of her own good looks. It didn't take him long to see that. She was a young chestnut mare, beautifully marked with four white socks and a near-perfect white diamond between her eyes. Mr. Chatham said the mare had been started on the track in California, then trained under English tack for the show ring. He said she had won many ribbons in confirmation classes and flat classes before he bought her. His daughter, Tia, was an experienced rider. He made the purchase because it seemed like a good deal.

Has she been hard to handle? Will asked.

Neither Mr. Chatham nor Tia wanted to answer the question.

Does she run with you?

I don't even get that far on most days, Tia said. She doesn't like to leave the other horses in the barn, and she doesn't act right in the ring. She's really strong.

She worked like a dream in California, Mr. Chatham said. I think we feed her too much grain.

He started from the beginning. The mare, who had a long, French-sounding name, was terrible in halter, and she was anxious in the cross ties when he hooked her up to groom her. The Chathams didn't have a round pen, so he tried to do a little ground-work with the mare in the white-fenced riding ring. It was tricky. The mare was undisciplined and assertive, and the ring gave her too much room to maneuver. He had to keep a close eye on her.

I'll come twice a week if you want me to, he told the Chathams. I think we ought to go back to square one. I'd like Tia to get the horse out of her stall and groom her every day. Make it a ritual. Make her mind you while you're working. But I'd stay out of the saddle for a while, until she remembers who's in charge. She's a big, strong gal. She's got to be taught how to use that.

Annie called to say the Chathams had loved him. She wondered if this could be a start for him. He wanted a start, didn't he? The Chathams had a lot of horse friends with money.

His father told him he should be careful working with people who were new to Wyoming.

The Chathams have been here for almost five years, Will said. They've built their place up. It's nice.

You know what I mean, his father said. They think they got the time to ride the kind of horses that need to be ridden every day. They like to give everything to their kids. They won't get it done, and then they'll be mad at you for not getting it done for them.

He worked with the chestnut mare for

three weeks. The mare accepted him as dominant, and she began to recall the careful training she had received in California. She remained spooky. He knew it would take significant work to teach her not to take the bit in her teeth when she was under saddle. She still believed she was a racehorse. But he had gotten the upper hand. He asked Mr. Chatham if he could keep the mare at his parents' ranch for the next month. He wouldn't charge more money, but he thought the animal needed to be handled every day.

I'd rather keep her here, Mr. Chatham said. She's Tia's responsibility. Tia needs to work with her, too.

That's the way it was with clients. You could suggest solutions, but you couldn't impose them. He reminded Tia that she should stay out of the saddle. The mare's listening to me real good, he said. But we're in the process of breaking a whole series of bad habits. She'll want to go back to those habits. Our job is to teach her new ones.

Annie was the one who told him. She walked over to the ranch from her house. She was carrying her lariat.

Tia's in the hospital in Denver, she said. She's got a dent in her head.

Will felt something sharp and cold pierce

his stomach.

The girl hadn't even tried to ride the mare, but she had tried to imitate what Will had been doing with groundwork. The riding ring was big and square, and when the mare worked herself into a corner, Tia tried to retrieve her by hand. The mare ran her down. It might or might not have been malicious. No one had seen what had happened. Tia had been on her own.

The horse was too much for her, Will said. I should have told them that.

The horse is dead.

Then I'd say it's a terrible outcome for them both.

Mike Chatham shot the horse, Annie said. He felt like he had to do it.

How bad is Tia? he asked.

Pretty bad. She's in an induced coma. It could go either way.

I tried to explain the limits, he said, angry. I tried to get them to listen to me. Tia's smart. She knew that mare wasn't a toy.

Maybe she was just trying to learn something, Annie said. You can't blame yourself.

Do you feel any blame?

Annie lifted her wet eyes. She was dressed in lightweight running clothes. There was a crease on the left side of her mouth that he had never seen before. The crease trembled.

He wanted to reach out and touch it with the very end of his finger.

No, Annie said. Tia was looking for a good trainer. I found her one. It was an accident. If you live around here long enough, you learn to make peace with accidents.

Her sorrow made her more beautiful to him. So he did it. He raised his hand and touched her face. Her skin was very warm, and damp, like a flower. Her mouth softened as he touched her, just for a moment. He thought of it all — the slenderness of her waist, the way his tongue would work against hers. Then she tightened her mouth the way she knew she ought to, and that was it. He didn't even need to feel the pressure of her hand on his forearm. He understood.

A few weeks later she vanished without a trace during a long training run on Flat Top Mountain. He joined the search teams. Dozens of people combed the mountains and found nothing. He didn't even know what had finally happened with Tia Chatham except that she hadn't died. People didn't talk about Tia. They talked about Annie Atwood. He thought it was an ugly and certain thing, how one bad story swallowed another.

The police got on him about the time he

spent alone with Annie, but he hadn't been the only male friend she had, and there was nothing for the police to find, though he sometimes wished there had been. He would never forget the spill of feeling in her eyes.

For months, he wouldn't work with anyone's horses. He made money at his father's print shop, or by sorting cows at the auction lot. He paid rent to his parents. Then his mother found the hard lump in her breast, and he couldn't imagine a happy ending to any single chapter of his life. That was his delivery point, or so it seemed. He was going to be just another solitary cowboy shuck.

His father was in the living room at the small table he used as a desk. Skim was asleep next to the stove, his legs stretched straight away from his body, in the pose of a dog about to scold a heifer. His father's large and grimy hands were on top of the desk, resting on a scatter of papers, but he wasn't holding a pencil or a pen. Instead, he was looking at his fingers, working them like pincers and pliers to see if they might somehow become more interesting to him.

I could use you at the shop tomorrow, he said.

Okay.

Roscoe's building himself up to ask me for a raise. I don't want you to discuss that kind of foolishness with him. Not a word.

No, sir. I can be there whenever you want.

After three is fine, assuming the goddamn trucks aren't late. Drivers are worthless these days. Less than worthless. They love to take their time.

I'll be there.

Did you sign a summer contract with that manager fellow up at the Black Bell?

No, sir. I know you think I should, but I didn't. I haven't. Shea Petrie's always treated me fair.

His father raised his left hand and worked it into the muscles on the side of his neck, just above his shirt collar. Then he plowed the hand into the gray stubble of his hair. You can't trust the people in that business, he said. Not anymore. They'll get rid of you if their reservations don't fill, or if somebody shows up who'll work for less. Bent Stallworth says it's got just like it is with the Mexicans. Some of those dude ranches are hiring Russians, of all the goddamn things. Russians. They can't even save their piss-poor jobs for Americans.

I'm corral boss this time, he said, looking at his father, seeing how it was true that a man could be described as old in some ways and still kicking in others. His father's hair had turned gray before he was thirty, but the rest of him was sound, at least when it came to muscle and bone. Shea Petrie will stand by me, he continued. We got a history. And seasoned wranglers is hard to come by.

No, they aren't. Every boy from here to Star Valley wants that kind of job. And they'll tell lies to get it.

Are you saying you don't want me to go, because I —

I just think you need to hear some advice.

Advice?

I think you need to be ready for the managers and the tourists to shit on you and shit on you good. Did I ever tell you about the time I tried to get into the army?

No, Will said. This was news to him. He and his father had never had a conversation about the army. The story he'd been told was that there was a high school football injury that spooked the military, and that was that.

Some of us tried to sign up after high school, his father said. Some of us were really hot for it. Eddie Franklin. He wanted the army bad. His mother was mixed blood, and he had all these tough Shoshone uncles.

He wanted to fight. I went along.

And they wouldn't take you?

Oh, they took me. Or they pretended they had. The cartilage in my knee wasn't too good, but I knew how to keep the swelling down before I took the physical and whatnot. I was sure I could survive everything they threw at me. It was only the army. We weren't even fighting anybody anymore.

So what happened?

They pretty much yanked me out of line, his father said. I was packed up. I'd shaved my head to bald, just like Eddie had. There were four of us leaving from the old bus station, and our families were there, looking scared and proud, and the recruiter, a shit-mouthed sergeant named Curnow, put his fat hand on my shoulder and took me out of line.

Why?

He said I'd failed some test somewhere along the line. Turns out that was a big lie. I'd done good on the tests, better than Curnow expected or wanted. So he screwed me because he could. He didn't like my attitude. I hadn't laughed at his bad jokes, not once. And I knew he had the hots for Eddie.

You mean —

No. Not like that. I mean Eddie was prime

military meat. Strong. And just dumb enough to believe what people told him. He rode that bus all the way to basic training and a career fueling helicopters at the ass end of the world. I'd say that was a waste, too. If you take a guy like Eddie into the army, you need to train him up to do some killing. Anyway, I haven't looked at promises from any man, or any woman, the same way since.

What did Ma say? Was she there? Will had the murky idea that his mother had always been part of his father's life.

Hell no, his father said, with a dry snort. I was dating Mariah Cheeseborough then, or I thought I was. Turns out Mariah was praying the army would haul me out of town. She had other plans. She lives up in Powell now, with about six kids, half of them already in jail. Still dresses like she was born in Jackson, though. Your mother hates her.

Really?

Yeah. Your mother doesn't have much respect for shallow character.

The Black Bell has always been straight up with me, Will said. He spoke very carefully, aware that his father had given him the rare gift of his direct recollection. They're too far from Yellowstone to get the cotton candy kind of guest. They need skilled help.

Times are changing, his father said in a dragged-over voice. A low-paid Russian looks good in a cowboy hat.

Can a Russian saddle a whole string of ponies in half an hour? Will framed the question in a way he hoped would make his father laugh.

Hank Testerman lifted his head on his tired neck. His face was puffed around the outer edges of his eyes. The skin below his chin was sagging. You'll get what you deserve if you talk like that, he said, but he didn't crank down the smile that torqued at his lips.

I'll be careful, Will said. Thanks for checking on me.

You did a good job with your mother, his father said. I hope you know that.

It wasn't nothing. It was —

You did a good job. You know, Eddie Franklin never did come back to this town. He ended up in Arizona, I heard. Married a Indian gal from down there and set up a motorcycle repair shop. Never came home.

And that was all his father said. When Will tried to catch his eye, to say something additional, to make the right kind of sound, he couldn't. His father had sealed himself back into the world he wanted to occupy.

Bills. Bids. Accountables. His father was looking at his hands again, trying to shape something with them.

He packed two good saddles and a small bag of clothes. He packed special feed for the filly. He cleaned his rifle and his pistol, and he put them in their cases and stowed them behind the seat of his truck. He took a set of hand-tooled saddlebags that he won in a raffle at the Fort Bridger rodeo. He took cash and the only credit card he had ever owned. He took a radio. He sluiced his trailer clean with cold water from a hose, then he hung two hay nets for the horses, then he checked the brake lights to make sure they were working. Hawk was ready. The filly was as ready as she could be. He would be at the Black Bell Ranch for at least ten weeks. He had time to think about what he might, or might not, want to take with him to California.

He understood that his preparations would be imperfect. He would forget something he needed. He was going to make mistakes.

He had once thought it would be easy for him to remember his brothers' faces whenever he wanted. And he had once believed a person could hold his mother and his father in memory precisely the way he wished to hold them, forever and ever. But it didn't work that way, not when he was on the move. Faces just seemed to fade on him. Most animals did better than he did. A crow, and certain breeds of dog, could remember the details of a human face for years.

The things that never changed for him were the details of home. The furl of light on the tin roof of the barn. The contours of the two-track that ran along the edge of the meadow, all the way to the property line of the ranch. The hard kick the old furnace made when it turned on in the basement of the house. He could always recall the peculiar stink of his mother's lilac blossoms when they thawed out in the spring. He could practically write lyrics to the music the field mice made in his bedroom walls, or the midnight bawling of cows and calves. These were the truths that were fixed inside him. They hung like well-used tools on a workshop wall. People were not fixed. People slipped away like weather over a horizon. You could love a person all you wanted, all that you were capable of, but a person would not settle once you left them behind.

■ ■ ■ ■

He didn't drive to her house until it was very late. He didn't call ahead. There didn't seem to be a reason to call. He only wanted to say good-bye. He had done that with his brothers, and with his brother's girlfriend, Hannah. He would say a few more words to his parents in the morning. They were always up early, and they would not want him to leave without them watching. His mother would insist on waving him down the driveway.

There was no reason to say good-bye to the town where he had lived his entire life. Lost Cabin would be there, changed and unchanging, whether he had anything to do with it or not.

She lived on Custer Street with her mother. The house was small and square and set far back from the curb, beneath the bend of three old cottonwood trees. She had often cursed those cottonwoods, how she had to clean up after them from season to season with a broom or a rake. He had helped her rake leaves once. They had pushed the leaves into piles and jumped into the piles like the children they still were. Their arms and legs had become covered with yellow leaves. Their mouths had filled with the bitter autumn flavor of the cottonwoods. Laughing, they had shaken themselves clean like wet dogs. Her mother didn't own the house, yet the two of them had lived there for so long — since before he had even known Lacey — that he always thought of it as theirs.

The house was dark, but her Honda was parked on the street in its usual place. He remembered what he had said to Everett about Lacey Henderson, how no one would ever really have her, how no one should.

He knocked on the door. He could see through the front windows that someone was awake and watching television. There was that kind of light, blue and wandering, leaking through the windows. It didn't take Lacey long to get to the door.

She looked at him for a moment, her eyes moving up and down, before a smile came to her lips. She pushed her hair out of her eyes. Her hair was down and not in its usual ponytail. Some of the hair clung to her fingers when she pushed at it, like it was alive with its own electricity, like she'd been brushing it.

Will.

Lacey.

She looked him over again as though he

138

needed to be thoroughly assessed. She had always been smart like that. Smart and watchful.

I haven't seen you in a long time. I heard you were working.

I been around, between this and that. I'm headed out to the Black Bell for the summer. Then it'll be California.

So you're leaving again. For California. I bet it's nice in California.

It's crowded, he said.

But you're going anyway.

I am, he said. Yes.

And you came to see me?

I did.

Why'd you come to see me?

It was a question he knew she would ask. She was not the kind of girl who let a fellow get by on a pretend performance.

I've known you a long time, he said. You shouldn't leave good people in the dust.

You didn't leave me, she said. I think it was just the opposite.

Maybe, he said. He'd taken his hat off at some point. He was holding it in his hands. It was his everyday Justin hat, and it was grimy at the crown. She looked back over her shoulder, toward the inside of the house.

Come in for a minute, she said. The baby is sleeping.

He stepped over the threshold of the door on tiptoes. The door led into a tiny mudroom, a place that held a washer and a dryer and snow shovels and brooms. He'd hung his coat in that mudroom many times.

She closed the door behind him, but she did not lead him farther into the house.

How's the baby? he asked.

Growing, she said. Getting bigger every day. She spoke with a practiced weariness in her voice.

You doing all right? he asked.

I think so, she said. Travis wants us to move in with him. He's got a trailer.

Travis Bonham was her current boyfriend, and the father of the baby, so far as anyone knew. Will had played football with Travis. He had been mean, but slow. A lineman.

That what you want?

Her left hand went to her hair again, squeezing at it.

I don't know. My mom thinks I shouldn't.

He thought about the times they had discussed their futures. They had driven into the mountains in his truck and talked about their options as if they were auditioning for roles in a Hollywood movie. As if the movie would always be there and they would always have a chance at a part. He had loved Lacey for a long time. He probably loved her still. That was how he was feeling right that minute, under his shirt, where his heart was beating around a tight and spoiling ache.

You should be true to yourself, he said.

She laughed. It was a loose, honest laugh. That's your motto, she said. That's how you see things. You got to remember how I'm different.

You're not so different, he said.

I am now.

He didn't say a word. He had never lied to her.

Why are you here, Will?

He felt a kind of hot numbness spread across his shoulders. I wanted to see you, he said. There's some things a person shouldn't be allowed to forget.

Is California going to ruin you? Is that why you came to see me? There was a whisper in her voice now, a gentle shush. She had dropped her hands away from her hair.

I don't think so. I been in a rough patch. You probably heard about my Ma.

Yeah. I did. She was always good to me. How is she?

She's better now. That's what she says. I aim to pick up where I left off, whatever that means. I bought a new horse.

You did?

Yes. I got the focus for that now.

She moved closer to him. She was like a shadow, a woman made up of all kinds of shadows. The forgotten light of the television flailed across the walls of the rooms behind her.

Your daddy still a prick?

Sometimes, he said. He looked into the useless bowl of his hat. He's mad at a lot of things.

Well, I don't exactly know from experience, but I hear that's how most daddies are. They like their mad.

Maybe.

You got a decent heart, Will. The decentest I've ever seen. She moved her face under his chin until he could feel her warm breath on his neck. He had always been taller than she was. His arms felt numb now. He didn't know what to do with them. She leaned upward and kissed him in that way she had, a dry and funny pecking at his mouth. It was how she liked to get started.

I didn't come to —

She brushed her mouth across his mouth. Her hands were at his belt buckle, solving.

Sssssh, she whispered, the baby.

There was her mother, too, he thought. Though he knew from experience how soundly the old lady slept in that little house. Lacey's mother had never tried to stop anything between them. And there was Travis, who was pulling a swing shift in the Garnet Field. But Travis wasn't going to stop them either.

He kissed her while she pressed into him. He kissed to earn the feeling back into his hands and arms. But she was the one writing the episode. She got his belt out of the way and she got his zipper down. Her hands were soft and careful. Her breasts were bigger than they had been, and they were very warm, almost hot. He could feel them through his shirt. He thought they must be hot because of the baby. She made a laughing sound far back in her throat when she got him free of his jeans just like she wanted. She had always been that way, eager and laughing.

She was still pretty, even with her tired eyes.

When she dropped to her knees and went to work on him with her mouth, he tried to speak. There were things he wanted to say to her, everlasting things. But the words in his head scattered like dark birds in a field. Lacey was making it easy for him, just as she always had. Lacey. He wondered why she was so good to him, when he wasn't worth a damn thing to her anymore.

He braced himself against the front door as his knees started to loosen, and he watched the nodding bloom of her light-colored head. He closed his eyes. He let his eyes follow the boiling light behind their lids for a minute before he opened them again. She liked you to keep your eyes open. She wanted to see you when she looked up, she wanted to see how you were doing. Always. The young thing that had woven itself between them over the years had never been about denial of any kind. He was sure of that. So he braced himself, and he thought of how Lacey knew him, of the generous ways of old love that never left a body or the mind, and he gave what he could in that cluttered mudroom, a place he had walked through day after plain day, a place that tasted of piled laundry and empty boots and the rising lemony flavors of a woman's electrified hair.

■ ■ ■ ■

PART II

■ ■ ■ ■

He met with Mr. Ward, a member of the family that owned the Black Bell Ranch, and Shea Petrie, the ranch manager, after he unloaded his horses. Shea Petrie walked from his office in the main lodge and stood beside Will's truck while he was backing his trailer into place.

Glad you're here, Testerman, he said. Come see us as soon as you can.

It had been a smooth ride from Lost Cabin. He watered Hawk and the filly in Cody, then put his Dodge truck to the test hauling the loaded trailer over Dead Indian Mountain, with its many switchbacks and steep declines. He could hear the filly scramble on occasion. Hawk was steadier. Hawk had made rough mountain hauls before. He thought to himself that it was no wonder the old-timers had chained heavy logs to their wagons as they tried to manage the descent into Sunlight Basin. You would need a heavy log, maybe two, to keep your loaded wagon from throwing its brakes and going straight downhill on a runaway. The brakes on his modern pickup barely did the job.

Shea Petrie got right down to business.

We've hired you for ten weeks, but we hope you'll consider staying longer if the guests keep signing up. The fall season could be good for us. I've got you at five hundred a week, same as the head cook, because you're just about that valuable. Corral boss. You'll be great at the job, I know it.

We aren't making money like we should, Mr. Ward said. He was a slim, white-haired man who jutted his chin as if he'd been in the military. He worked as a lawyer in Cody, but he'd also been an outfitter at one time, and a corral boss for the Black Bell when he was young. He knew the terrain. He was no fool.

Petrie nodded. He hadn't sat down at his office desk. He was pacing instead, like a man who was on a very short leash. His forehead, which was usually covered by a gray pinch-front hat, was the color of old milk.

I need a tight operation, Mr. Ward said, but one that pleases the guests. We have our reputation. How many guests are return visitors?

More than half, Petrie said. Which is damn good in this economy.

So they're happy, Mr. Ward said, and I want them to stay that way. I don't want them going on the Internet and comparing our amenities with someone else's. I don't want them thinking about comparisons. They need to be soaking up the mountain views and the goddamn fresh air.

You're not the entertainment, Testerman, Petrie said, turning to him.

No, sir.

Not you or anyone under you. You're my quality control out there. Wranglers. Grounds staff. The fishing guide. I want every one of them buckled down. You hear me?

Yes, sir.

And you're the whip on Kenny Braithwaite's ass. I don't know why I have him up here again, but I do. You need to keep your eye on him.

We'll make it worth your while, Mr. Ward said.

But they wouldn't. The tips from the guests might make it worthwhile, but Petrie and Mr. Ward would not offer him extra money. He might get a slap on the back. He might earn their respect. But they would never stuff his pockets with a real bonus. They were tight.

Are there other things I should keep in mind? he asked. He knew that Mr. Ward, in particular, would regard this brief conversation as an ironclad verbal contract.

Efficiency, Mr. Ward said, with no hint of a smile on his rugged, bloodless face. We are first-class yet efficient.

Stay on the staff's asses about customer service, Petrie added. I know you'll do it in a nice way. Margit and I will do the same. It's a long summer. We want it to be a good one.

He shook their firm hands before he left the small, paneled office. They wanted the dream, as always. No rain. No dust. No snow. No insect bites or blisters or bad falls off a horse. Money in the bank. Wide smiles at the cowboy country club. Hats and boots for everybody. And who could blame them? There was no other way to make a living on ranch land this close to Yellowstone Park unless you were so rich you didn't need to make a living at all. The only thing they had to sell was the dream.

He asked Petrie about the old red roan that was in what they called the hospital pasture, a fenced-in place across the river, next to the hay barn. The horse had met him at one of the gates, hoping for company. It bobbed its bony head up and down on its wasted neck. It followed him along the fence line with a tender, stumbling gait that reminded him of a child running to catch a school bus. There weren't many horses on the ranch yet. The dude strings were still on their winter pasture in Cody. There was Hawk and the filly. There were two of Mr. Ward's Morgans and a couple of animals owned by Petrie and his wife, Margit.

He's done for, Petrie said. He's got a parasite in his gut we can't get rid of. We've had to quit trying.

He's thin, Will said, thinking of the horse and the way its whiskered muzzle made it resemble a vagrant man.

I need to take him up one of the draws and shoot him. The Forest Service will let me leave him for the bears if I drop him close enough to the tree line. The bears were out early this spring. They've already been down here trying to eat Margit's pigs.

Have you called the Forest Service? Will asked. He didn't want to be drawn into the situation, but he understood that part of his job at the Black Bell was to finish the things Petrie couldn't bring himself to finish.

I haven't.

I can do it, Will said. I'll do the whole thing, if you want.

No, Petrie said. I promised Margit. We've had him for a long time. She practically learned to ride on him. Morris. His name is Morris, if you can believe that. He was named for a family friend.

Should I keep him on the grain list? Will asked. He knew Margit, and he knew the marriage suffered a long and elastic strain each season the couple managed the guest ranch.

Sure. I need to stop acting like he's going to make it. I keep thinking he'll just not wake up one morning. Or that he'll goddamn disappear, like things do out here. Keep him on the grain list. It's not like he's worth any money. I'll figure it out. I have to. I promised Margit.

His first week back at the Black Bell was an avalanche of chores. He cleaned the tack room. He mended cinches and bridles. He greeted the staff as they arrived one by one in their college-kid cars or their capped pickups. He rode the trails with Hawk and cleared them of downed timber. He wasn't able to reserve much time for the filly. She had to content herself with watching everyone come and go at a pace that would stay fast for the next ten weeks.

When he had a few minutes, he put the filly in her halter and led her up the lane. They passed the chicken coop that remained empty after Margit's failed attempts to provide guests with freshly laid eggs. They passed the pigsty that wriggled with the three piglets destined to become next year's bacon and ham. The filly was dismayed by the pigs. She hated the noises they made and the quick, low-legged way they moved. During Will's first summer at the Black Bell, when he was just sixteen, a mountain lion had come for Margit's pigs in the night. Kenny Braithwaite, who was corral boss at the time, had scared the cat off with a rifle shot into the air. Kenny believed you could be a gentleman with the wildlife. When the cat returned a second night, Shea Petrie killed it with two shots. Then he had it stuffed and put on display in the main lodge.

Will didn't tell the filly about the bears. Bears came down to the ranch early in the summer or late in the fall when they were hungry, on both ends of their hibernation. He carried bear spray whenever he went onto the trails, just as he carried his pistol, but the pistol was on hand as a noisemaker. He was not under the illusion that his gun could stop a grizzly. The best policy was not to surprise a bear in the first place, and that was easy to do when you were with a horse. Horses made noise, and they had good noses, and they were not shy about sharing their opinion when they smelled a bear.

He sometimes allowed the filly to drink from the irrigation ditch as they walked up the lane. It depended on her focus. She was not allowed to eat grass until he decided they had stretched their legs enough, and sometimes she wasn't allowed to eat at all. The choice was his, not hers. But he would talk to her about the birds they saw — osprey, bald eagles, tanagers, warblers of all kinds — and he identified the animal tracks left in the soft soil of the lane. They often flushed white-tailed deer out of the thick timber along the river. Once they had to wait for a fat badger to waddle its way into the underbrush. The badger kept glaring over its shoulder, challenging Will and the filly to follow. Will liked how curious the filly was. She really looked at things, pigs or badgers, wheelbarrows or woodpiles. And if a familiar thing had changed somehow, if it was different, she would notice the change before he did.

She did not care for the neighbor's cows once they were turned out into the large pasture that bordered the Black Bell. They were yearling Angus, square backed and ignorant. They tended to charge the fence as if the filly was a fantastical and threatening creature, as if they didn't see horses a dozen times a day. The filly also didn't care for the pivot irrigator that the neighbor, a wealthy oilman, used to water his pasture. Will made her familiarize herself with the irrigator. He stood in the lane with her as the long silver arm sprayed cold water over the two of them — choosh, choosh, choosh — until the filly understood that the water and the huffing, slow-rolling pivot arm wouldn't hurt her.

He did not take her down the lane after dark. There were elk in the lane at night, and sometimes moose, and the coyotes and wolves were always on the move. He had seen tracks in the sandy soil from all of them. It was enough for the filly, or for any of the horses, to have to hear the hunting songs of the packs from the safety of the corrals.

Kenny Braithwaite could no longer arrive at a place like a normal man. It hadn't always been that way. Kenny had once had a family in Detroit, or that was the story. And he had once held a decent job in Detroit. There

155

was even a rumor that Kenny had been a city policeman. But families and jobs insist on schedules and normality, and those things had fallen away from Kenny. Or they had been pissed away. That was the more general judgment. Kenny Braithwaite had his talents, but alcohol got the best of him. Drinking tended to leave him on a ledge.

This time he was a day late getting to the Black Bell. When he did show up, he was behind the wheel of a two-tone 1986 Cadillac Coupe DeVille. The Cadillac had red leather seats and less than seventy-five thousand miles on the odometer. It was missing a wheel cover on the right rear tire. What the Cadillac did not contain was a good riding saddle. And it wasn't pulling a trailer with a horse. Kenny had sworn to Shea Petrie he would show up to take his position as wrangler with both a saddle and a horse. What he had, instead, was a garbage bag full of freshly washed clothes and a backseat covered in empty beer cans.

Will was in the corrals. He was sorting through the string of dude horses, making notes for the farrier who was scheduled to shoe the horses later in the week. Will had struck a deal with Shea Petrie. Kenny would occupy the role of head wrangler. It was a step down for Kenny, a demotion from corral boss, but it was all Shea Petrie was willing to trust Kenny with now. Kenny would make the decisions he could make. But Will would be the one in charge.

Willy Boy! Kenny shouted. It's good to see you.

Will nodded from under the brim of his straw hat. Braithwaite always looked sober from a distance.

You like my chariot?

Will grinned. He had not given Cadillacs or any kind of road sedan the time of day until he spent his year in Texas. Some of the cowboys down there had worked to change his attitude. The Texas cowboys liked the comfort of a car when it came to driving to bars and honky-tonks. They claimed a girl would more easily go with a man into the backseat of a car. The bucket seats of a truck weren't so attractive to girls.

I do, Kenny. You better keep your eye on it. I might take it from you.

You're welcome to try. See anything good in that bunch of horses?

A little, Will said. They're mostly fat and sound.

Then let me park this thing away from all the riffraff. I got some advice for you. That spotted mare there, I remember her. She's more evil than she looks. You'll need my help before you can get the gist of her.

Will nodded. It would be like this all summer. He had worked under Kenny for three years. The man had style. And skill. He also enjoyed talking before the work got done.

Is Petrie around? Braithwaite asked. He used his singsong voice to assemble the question.

You know he is, Will said. He's been waiting.

Good, Braithwaite said, squaring his shoulders against the fine leather of the Cadillac. He needs to learn some patience.

Where's your horse? Will asked.

She's in the pasture of a woman I know in Cody, Braithwaite said.

Do you owe the woman money?

I probably owe her lots of things, Braithwaite said. But I definitely owe her money.

Petrie was planning on you bringing your own horse, Will said.

So was I, Braithwaite said. That's the second thing Petrie and I will talk about. The first topic we will discuss this fine morning, however, is patience.

Shea Petrie had hired a first-class farrier. Will suspected that Mr. Ward didn't know about the extravagance. But sometimes, even Shea Petrie believed in spending money to save money. Oliver Doak was top-of-the-heap. He was driving down from Bozeman, Montana, to shoe all sixty horses at the Black Bell.

Will did not believe in cutting corners with farriers, either. He had handled a lot of horse feet. He could do the basics. But he knew his limits. He had three days to observe Oliver Doak, and he didn't plan on wasting one hour of that time.

Doak was a tall man with a thick and barreled body. He looked too tall to be comfortable cradling hooves on his thighs, but he had been shoeing horses since he was a teenager. He had grown up in Vermont or New Hampshire, one of those eastern states that westerners respect only for their abundant rainfall. Doak had traveled all over the world to study how other tribes cared for their horses. He liked to mull over what he had seen, the habits of the Uzbeks, the considerations of the Mongols. Some of the old-time ranchers didn't care for Oliver Doak's creativity. He was known to quote poetry aloud, whether there was another human being around to hear him or not. He claimed horses had a natural affinity for poems. He had been seen wearing tie-dyed shirts while he worked at his forge, and he sometimes let his red-brown hair get long.

But he never made a fuss on his own behalf. His first concern was always the horse. He was as meticulous with a cheap dude string pony as he was with a senator's cutting horse.

The Black Bell had a concrete-floored shoeing shed set in the middle of the corrals. Oliver Doak was happy to see there was an additional power outlet in the shed. He liked to work to music.

I hope you like Bruce Springsteen, Doak said as he gripped Will's hand. This is shaping up to be a Springsteen type of day.

As corral boss, Will was tasked with bringing the horses to Doak. He would shuttle them in and out of the corrals. He and Doak would also discuss the horses' prospects. There were one or two that Will and Shea Petrie thought might not make it through the summer. Kenny Braithwaite was supposed to be rehanging a pair of gates on the Huff Gulch trail. But Kenny couldn't keep himself away from the shoeing shed. He showed up with his belly perched on the shelf of his belt, the sharp knobs of his knees visible through the denim of his jeans.

It's good to see you again, Ollie, Braithwaite said, leaning against the hitching rail. We haven't spoke since I worked on the Goetz spread, outside of Bozeman. You did a great job for the Goetzes. I'm sure you remember that.

It's been awhile, Oliver Doak said, sucking on a sun-blistered lip. He took a long look at Kenny Braithwaite. Doak's hands had the square, spatula shape hard earned by farriers and stonemasons. The skin on his fingers looked permanently baked. The Goetzes never asked me back, he said. I guess they didn't like the work as much as you did.

You don't say, Kenny said, removing his cowboy hat to reveal a badly trimmed set of sideburns. I'm sorry to hear that.

But Kenny Braithwaite wasn't fooling anybody. He hadn't lasted more than a few weeks at the Goetzes' Lazy L 2, if he had ever worked there at all. The management of that operation did not tolerate slipshod behavior.

Will reminded Kenny he had gates to hang before lunch.

Not to worry, lad, Kenny said. Me and Ollie are just catching up. It won't be long before I'm on my way.

It was more than an hour. Oliver Doak plugged in his electric forge and set his anvil on its traveling platform. He laid out his nips and rasps. He tied himself into his heavy cowhide apron, and he blasted the

Springsteen at volume. Kenny Braithwaite talked and talked. Will told himself he didn't need to pull rank on Kenny right away. He would work around the old man. He asked Oliver Doak if he wanted to start with a horse that was easy or a horse that was hard.

I'd be honored to start with a horse that needs me, Doak said. We're privileged to do the work we do.

I like setting up horses, Will said.

I can see that, Doak said. There's nothing in a hurry about you.

I know how to fill a day, Will said.

That's not what I meant. The horses don't stir when you go among them. They accept you. Anybody with sense would notice that. The Tatars have a word for a man like that, Oliver Doak said, shading his deep-set gray eyes with one hand. I wish I could remember what the word is. You ride the rodeos?

I've done it some, Will said. Mixed results.

You're a roper, then. Not a bronc rider. Too tall to ride bulls. I'd guess you're a fair hand with a rope.

I do all right, Will said. But I don't feel like I need to be on the road all the time.

Oliver Doak laughed. A contemplative soul, are you? I should have guessed that.

Will brought Doak the sluggish palomino mare they called Sunshine. Everything

162

about the mare was heavy — her shoulders, her horny bare feet, the folds of her crusted eyelids. Sunshine tended to look asleep even when she wasn't.

What can you tell me about her? Doak asked.

I've rode her once, Will said. She has two gears — slow and slower. Mr. Petrie says she's a grade-A pack animal, though. He wants her in some durable shoes.

She'll be the mount you give to the middle-aged gals from New York City, Kenny said, winking. She matches up good with the fake Navajo jewelry they like to wear.

I'm not gonna choose nobody's mount based on jewelry, Will said, irritated. You need to get on out of here and hang those gates. I saw the work charts this morning. Petrie's expecting you to help the new guy on the saw blade this afternoon.

It's a waste of my expertise to have me sawing firewood, Kenny said. He had come to the shoeing shed wearing his flat-brimmed black Larry Mahan hat and a pair of high-heeled pack boots. He was trying to make an impression.

Not my choice, Will said.

I shoed quite a few of these horses on my own last summer, Kenny said.

Maybe that's so, Will said. I wasn't here last summer. Neither was Mr. Doak.

It's a waste of my expertise.

Right now we're not wasting anything except Mr. Doak's time, Will said. Talk to Petrie if you want different duty, but I'm running this corral. We got sixty animals to get through here. You can come help during lunch break if you want. Or after dinner.

But that wasn't what Kenny Braithwaite wanted to hear. I've told Katie, the new cook, I'll help her in the kitchen this evening, he said.

Uh-huh, Will said. He knew what that meant. That meant flirtation and tippling.

Oliver Doak was scrutinizing the palomino mare's large, biscuit-colored feet. He had begun to reset her shoes in his mind. That was his reputation. A competent farrier rushed to fit and hammer. A great farrier left room for musing.

Let's have lunch when the time comes, Oliver Doak said to Kenny while he was bent over the mare's left hind. A nice sandwich in the cool shade.

It was a simple offer. Kenny Braithwaite was smart enough to take it.

Did you hear about the fellow who nicked his thigh artery while he was shoeing? Kenny asked. He was from up in Montana.

The horse pulled off, and the shoeing nail stabbed into his leg as good as a knife. I heard the fellow bled out before he could turn around.

I knew him, Doak said, adjusting the coil on his forge. His name was Joe McGovern. Big Joe. It's a bad-luck story. Not one I care to repeat.

Are you Irish, then? asked Kenny.

Not when I can help it, Oliver Doak said. But I retain my respect for superstitions. You can't work with animals and not keep a little religion in you. It's not possible. I caught a nail in my own hand a few weeks ago. Hurt like hell, I have to say. The point's still in me. Take a look.

He showed them the blue sliver of steel that was visible near one of his large knuckles. Will noticed how the hair on Doak's forearms had been singed into stripes. The tendons in his wrists looked as woven as rawhide pigging strings.

This can be a priestly job, to some degree, Doak said. The spirits sometimes come to our aid.

I'll see you at lunch, then, Kenny said, holding his black hat in front of his belly, imitating a man of ease.

It'll be my pleasure, Oliver Doak said. We'll catch up.

Will was glad to see Kenny Braithwaite's back.

I'm not sure I recall meeting Mr. Braithwaite at the Lazy L 2, Doak said as he was nipping the winter growth off one of Sunshine's bowl-sized hooves. It's a big place. I may have forgotten.

I doubt Kenny ever drew a paycheck there, Will said. He might have. Or he might have just wished it had happened. I don't want to speak bad about him. He is gentle with the horses. But you can't always trust what he says.

Will noticed that one of Shea Petrie's Australian sheepdogs had come to the edge of the shoeing shed. The dog was watching Doak with its cracked marble eyes.

Gentleness is a good feature in a man, Mr. Testerman. I like how you mark his gentleness. We don't always tell the truth about everything, do we? None of us does. I sense that Mr. Braithwaite is a man of cravings. We'll have a good lunch. My wife says I am a first-rate talker.

I just don't want him in your way, Will said. The dog had crept closer. Its haunches were quivering. Will squatted and picked up a fetid scrap of hoof. He tossed it to the dog.

He won't be, Doak said. I'll put him to

166

use. He'll get tired of my Van Morrison before I get tired of him.

Van Morrison?

Oh, Mr. Testerman. Don't tell me you're too young to know about Van Morrison. That's more truth than I can handle this early in the day. I suppose you listen to that sequined Nashville puke.

You're here for three days, Will said, shaking his head. I think it's best if I don't open my mouth and offend you right away.

Oliver Doak laughed again. He had small teeth for a large man, and they were as evenly spaced as the rungs on a ladder. I believe you just made a request for a music tutorial, Doak said. You want some lessons?

I hope to learn what I can from you. I won't lie about that. If I have to listen to some hippie songs to get through the day, I will.

Good. We'll start with more Springsteen and this good mare Sunshine. Don't worry. I'll ease you in.

Yes, sir.

And you're under orders to teach me as well.

Will looked at Oliver Doak. The farrier had his hand on Sunshine's prodigious rump. The hand looked like the hub and spokes of a well-carved wheel resting there.

I don't know anything you haven't heard about, Will said. I grew up in Lost Cabin, Wyoming.

You know plenty, Doak said. I can see it spinning in your eyes. You're as eager as that gnawing dog over there. You're a pursuer.

A pursuer?

A man who wants a certain kind of thing. The Tunisians have a word for that, but it won't come to me. A man who seeks perfection. You can build cities from the empty wind, the Tunisians say, if you possess that kind of desire. They have songs about it.

I can't sing much, Will said.

Neither can I, Oliver Doak said. No perfection with a tune. Unfortunately, I like to sing, so both of us are about to suffer a long day in the ears. What do you say, then? Are you a man who gets what he wants?

Not usually, Will said, his hand shading his face. I think a person who wants too much is asking to be disappointed.

That so?

It has been for me. I'd like to be good at one thing, I guess, he said, thinking of the filly. Just like you are.

I enjoy spending my days with flatterers, Doak said, laughing. Thank you for that.

You want me to bring you another horse?

Not yet. Why don't you tell me about that

leopard-spot Appaloosa over there? The sturdy one.

Hawk?

I knew he belonged to you, Doak said. That wasn't a guess.

He does stand out, Will said. But he's more than his spots. He's real good under saddle.

Is he a pursuer?

Will paused. Maybe. Maybe he is. He don't like the same duty day after day. His feet ain't the easiest to set up, either.

I'll do him next, Doak said, crinkling the skin around his eyes. He looks like an interesting critter. Let's give him a chance to speak for himself.

They heard the heavy bells ringing from the horses' necks on the other side of the river. That's Jasper, he said. We belled Jasper today. And Kiowa. So we can find them in the morning.

That's nice, she said. The way you know how to find them. Is it hard to get out of bed that early?

Not too hard, he said. I been doing it most of my life.

I like my sleep, she said.

I do too, he said. I get it when I can.

Her name was Angela. She was what they

called a cabin girl, one of those who cleaned the cabins and the rooms of the guests each day. It was her first summer at the Black Bell. She was small, with brown, wavy hair, the kind that was hard to control with clips or bands. She was from out East. Pennsylvania, she said. She went to a big university out there.

He thought she was pretty the first time he met her. The cabin girls were usually pretty. That's how Shea Petrie liked them. Petrie believed attractive cabin girls were good for business. The first time Will actually talked to Angela was the night the guests stewed themselves in the sweat lodge and the staff stayed afterward to swim in the river and drink beer. She was a little tipsy. She told him she had come all the way from Pennsylvania to get to know some cowboys.

He had heard that before.

But he didn't take her up on her tipsy offer, if that's what it was, because it was the first week with guests, and he knew he needed to be careful about a lot of things. He needed to be careful about Kenny. They had to work together for the entire summer. And he needed to be careful about the girls — those who were guests and those who were staff. It was best not to raise expectations with the girls.

And he wasn't lonely or anything. Not with the filly and all the other work he had to do.

It's black, she said. I can't get over how black the sky is up here. And how the river seems to talk at night, like it has all these voices in the water. It scared me at first. Woke me up.

You're in one of the sheep wagons near the river?

Yeah, she said, softly. One of the old green ones. It's nice.

The trees are talking to us now, he said, lifting his face toward the scraping of the cottonwoods. The limbs high above them were creaking in the breeze. He reached for her hand. Let's cross, he said.

He was in his boots. She wore strapped sandals, the kind you could wade in. He led her across the gray table of a gravel bar, then stepped into water that went as high as his heels. The river *was* talking. It was telling everything it knew about the mountains and drainages to the west, every gathering thing it knew. A river, his father liked to say, was a goddamn tangled history. He considered the options he had with Angela.

How many horses? she asked.

He thought about it. He liked to be exact.

Eighteen tonight, he said. Right in this meadow, on the other side.

That's all?

There's a Angus cow and her late calf, he said. The cow's lame, so they brought her in from the grazing lease. And there's a old bull out there. He don't bother anybody. He's too old to matter.

A bull?

He's no matter, he told her, pulling on her small hand. Her skin was rough from the work she did. Rough and dry. He could feel that. He eased her up onto another stretch of gravel bar. The stones and pebbles shifted under her feet. She wore a bandanna around her hair, to control it, but the bandanna held no color in the riverbed's diminished light. It was all black and gray for them at that hour.

He thought of what they were about to do. They could lie down together among the stacked bales of hay in the small barn. Or they could sit in the barn using the hay as a kind of chair, with him sitting down and her sitting above him. He thought she'd prefer a kind of shelter; most girls did. He didn't want to go back to the sheep wagon where she bunked. There would be too much talk about that. The girls kept watch on one another, and they loved to talk.

Will?

Yeah.

I feel like . . . I don't want you to think I'm a slut.

I don't think that, he said. He loosened his hold on her hand in case she wanted to take it away. Girls sometimes went up and down when they were thinking things through. He understood that. We can go back, he said.

The trees sawed and whined above them. The cold water of the river murmured.

We don't have to go back, she said. I just want you to know I like you. I'm not that drunk.

I'm not drunk, either, he said. And he wasn't. He had to be up at four the next morning. We can just walk a little ways. I'll show you that bull.

She swung herself inside the bend of his arm. It was a little like dancing, the way she moved herself. They were still on the bleached and tumbled rock of the gravel bar. Her untamable hair brushed against his chin. She grabbed at the collar of his shirt like she wanted to rise up to meet him, like he had become a ladder she suddenly had to climb. He felt one of her knees against his thigh. When they found a kind of clutching balance, he kissed her. She had a girl's mouth, smooth, uncertain. She tasted sweet, like mint gum.

Let's walk a ways, he said, feeling the hot blood rush up from his legs. She clutched at him again, another kiss, then swayed back into her own space just like one of the fir trees he could hear swaying in the dark. He made it a goal to get her as far as the barn. If they fell together in the meadow, they'd both get wet and cold.

Come on, he said, finding her roughened hand again. They needed to cross one more thin braid of the river.

She broke away from him, tense and separate.

What's that? she asked. Her voice squeezed onto a high note.

What's what?

That? And she pointed downriver, her arm as pale as a stripped limb.

He saw it. It was low over the water, sooty and silent. To her it must have looked like a sliver of sky that had broken free and cast itself toward them, a ghost, undeterred.

It's a owl, he said. A big one.

She watched the bird lift and sweep past them, then wheel back down the river. They both did. I . . . I've never seen one, she said. It came so close.

It's hunting, he said. They don't mind

much else when they're hunting.

He reached out for her hand. Her fingers were cold by now, but the center of her hand was hot and waiting. He could smell the deep mud of the riverbank, and the blossoms of the wild roses. He would have to make sure she got through the thorny reach of all the roses.

Will?

Yeah.

But Angela didn't say a word, she didn't answer with her voice. She spoke with her body, tucking it against him again. They were among the shadows of the towering trees now, and he felt the length of her legs and the shape of her breasts beneath her shirt. He wrapped his arms around her and held her tight, and he knew it would work out between them, if only for a little while. His body knew it. So did hers. He felt that knowledge run through his veins, as sure as the current of any river. But he did not kiss her again, not yet. He buried his wind-dried mouth in the spring and wildness of her hair. He tasted the salty sprawl of it. Then he lifted her up past the muddy bank of the river, he raised the whole light weight of her in one motion. He heard the sigh from her lungs as she got her feet under her. He heard the hanging bells toll from the necks of the grazing horses as they eased farther into the night.

It was a terrible day, marked by one fuck-up after another. Some of it was his fault. The day before, he had driven with Lyle and Katie the cook to sample the bars in Red Lodge, Montana. It was their day off. They deserved some bedlam. But they had gotten back late, and Lyle had failed to get out of bed in time to wrangle the fresh string of horses. Katie was hung over enough to forget to add eggs to the pancake batter. When Wade the irrigator teased her about her mistake, she emptied the orange juice pitcher in his lap. Then she left the kitchen.

It didn't help that most of the week's guests were new to the Black Bell and half-afraid of horses. He would never understand that — how suburban people liked the image of riding a fast, muscular animal or standing in a roaring trout stream, but how they were too unsure of their own bodies to achieve the image they wanted. Angela said he ought to try and see it from their perspective. He had grown up with animals and an outdoors that was wild enough to drown you or break you in half. Most people had not. They needed some time to get used to the idea.

Time? Like a whole lifetime, you mean. Some of this bunch don't even know why they're out here, he said. They saw the mountains in a magazine.

You're right, she said.

They're already talking about the damn great shopping they can do in Jackson Hole.

She laughed. I heard that too, she said.

But he kept everything on the up-and-up. He kept his temper behind his lips. That was his job. He sent Kenny Braithwaite out with Sonia, the kids' wrangler, and most of the older guests and the children. They took any easy ride into Huff Gulch where Kenny could tell his long, tricked-out stories about moose and grizzly bear. He assigned himself the family from Atlanta, Georgia, who said they knew how to ride. He thought they might like to see the views from Sheep Horn Ridge.

It rained at the worst possible moment — while the mother was messing with her camera and tripod on Sheep Horn. The sky had been its usual divided self. It was intent on delivering four or five versions of weather all at once, but the thing that got his attention was a squall that began to bear down on them like the prow of a sailing ship. The mother was trying to frame a long-exposure shot of the shifting, spilling sky. She was thinking Ansel Adams. He was thinking bad outcomes. He got a little bossy about the dangers of lightning when he tasted the heavy tang of ozone on the back his tongue.

The wind smacked itself against them and their saddled horses as if it were a leather quirt. He asked everyone to mount up. As he did so, the clouds above them split open, cracking like stones in a fire. You had to say this about the Georgians: They didn't know much, but they were calm. And they didn't mind getting wet.

They were on their way off the ridge, laughing and singing in the rain, not sullen in any way, when the cinch on the boy's saddle broke. It was just one of those things. The boy hadn't done anything and neither had his horse, Pablo. But it was still a kind of fuck-up. Will had come up the mountain alone with the Georgians because they were a small group. There were only four of them. Now there was an incident, and he was shorthanded.

The mother gave him an out.

I can get us back to the ranch, she said. It's right there. We can see it in the valley. I'll go down the way we came.

The rain was falling faster and colder. There would probably be some hail. He mulled it over. The mother was an okay rider, and she was on Nina. Nothing would happen to her. The father was the kind of dazed and quiet man who knew how to listen to his wife. He might be a money-maker at the office, but he had no illusions about his competence elsewhere. He wouldn't be a problem. The children were more of an issue. It was the nightmare scenario of his life that something would happen to a child when he was in charge.

Jordan can come with us, the mother said, pointing to her youngest child, a girl. Marty can walk back with you. It won't hurt him. A little rain never hurt anybody.

Marty was a stalk of a kid. He had dismounted from Pablo as soon as his saddle began to slide, and he had pushed the sleeves of his jacket up past his elbows so he could expose more of his skin to the downpour. Marty had enthusiasm in his eyes. He might be able to deal with Marty.

Do you feel safe doing that? he asked the mother. We got other options.

We might have other options, but this will do fine, the mother said.

All right, he said. Don't worry about the gate at the road. We'll close that. We'll be right behind you.

But they weren't.

He tried to repair the cinch with his

179

Leatherman tool, but he couldn't get the splice to hold the way he wanted. He was working too fast. The rain spouted off his hat brim. The kid, Marty, held his mouth open to the sky and slurped at the rain until he choked. After he choked, he laughed.

We need to make a move, he told the kid. There's a cave around the corner, in that draw. A little shelter.

Can Pablo go in the cave? the kid asked.

No. Not enough room. But we'll hobble Pablo and let him eat some grass. He'll like that.

He loves to eat grass, the kid said. I've been trying to keep him from doing that all morning.

He piled the kid's saddle on top of his own, then gave Pablo's reins to the kid. You walk ahead of me and Hawk, he said. Just follow the path. You'll know the way.

It took them less than five minutes to get to the sandstone overhang that was known as the cave and another five minutes to strip the tack from both horses and turn them out down the slope with hobbles on their hind legs. Hawk didn't care for hobbles. He wouldn't go far. And Pablo wouldn't go anywhere without Hawk.

It's a tiny cave, the kid said. You couldn't live here.

No, but you could camp here. People have done that for a long time. Will shook water from the sleeves of his yellow slicker. Look at how black the rock is, he said. There's been a lot of fires in here.

Like from Boy Scouts?

Maybe. Maybe the Scouts have been in here a few times. I was thinking more about trappers and Indians.

Indians lived here? What about their tepees?

They kept their tepees at their villages, he said. But they did a lot of lightweight camping in their day, especially the hunters. This part of the world is great for hunting.

Were they hunting bears? Should we start a fire?

They probably did hunt bear. And the bears hunted them. But they'd be looking for deer meat in this part of the basin. Deer and elk. Are you cold? Will asked. Is that why you're wanting a fire?

I just like fires, the kid said. But I am a little bit cold.

He showed the kid how to wear his jacket in a way that would keep him warmer. And he showed him how to wrap himself in saddle pads, too. They probably wouldn't build a fire, he said. The storm was passing. It would be a better use of their time to fix the saddle.

Will you let me help? the kid asked.

Sure.

Is Pablo all right in the rain?

Pablo can stand a lot more than an hour of rain, he told the kid. He's better made for it than we are.

He showed the kid how to safely open and close the sharp jackknife he always carried. And he showed him the attachments on the Leatherman. The kid set himself up on Will's right side as they worked to repair the busted cinch. The kid talked about a vacation his family had taken on a yacht in the Bahamas. He talked about playing soccer. He said he already liked the Absaroka Mountains better than either of those things, and he'd only been at the Black Bell Ranch for two days. His mother was a doctor, he said. She did something with babies all around the world, and diseases. His dad traveled a lot for his bank.

Does your sister like it here?

She doesn't know yet, the kid said. She thinks Pablo is prettier than her horse.

Will gave the kid a sly look. She's on Legs, right?

The kid nodded.

Legs is safe and he's not a knucklehead, but he's not very pretty. Your sister has a good eye. Maybe I'll put her on another horse for tomorrow. Think she'd like that?

The kid showed his snaggled kid teeth. I think so, he said, but I can't promise anything. My mom says Jordan likes to be unhappy.

Some people are like that, even when they don't need to be, he said to the kid. Those people miss a good thing sometimes.

He got the cinch sutured with some rawhide strips he always carried. Kenny Braithwaite had taught him that trick, how to keep rawhide in the saddlebag, along with nylon thread. The rain was ending, and there had been no thunder or wind for quite some time. He caught and bridled both horses. They were soaked. He let the kid lead Pablo back up the slope, toward the cave. The kid wasn't strong enough to lift the saddle onto Pablo's back, but he was able to help buckle both cinches.

Are there arrowheads up here? How about snakes?

Yeah, there are arrowheads. Pieces of them, anyway. Want to look for one? We got a minute. Snakes are not a issue. It's too cold for them in these mountains. But you were smart to ask about them. They are a problem in most caves.

Can you find an arrowhead?

Will dropped Pablo's reins. Hawk was already ground-reined. He took his hat off so he would have more room to maneuver, and he knelt to show the kid how to search the loose rock below the overhang. He explained how an Indian might sit there on a rainy day or by a fire at night and knap at a shiny piece of stone to make an arrowhead.

Make your fingers into a kind of a sieve, he said. And keep your eyes peeled.

He settled into a comfortable squat to watch the boy make his search. The cave floor featured a good slope for drainage, and the sight lines out of the canyon were clear, and he thought about all the generations of men who had chosen to stop in that place and all the reasons they might have had.

You ever think about how men in the olden times found these good places? he asked the kid.

The kid lifted his streaked face.

Sorry, he said. I didn't mean to bother you. I was just thinking. Somebody was the first human being here. I wonder who it was.

Is this an arrowhead? the kid asked. He held out a dirty, cupped hand.

Probably not, Will said, rolling the soft piece of sandstone in his fingers. The ones I've seen are a different color. Pink or red or even black. They brought in special stone for their weapons. Hard stuff that would hold a edge. They traded for it.

Like this?

Yeah. More like that. Exactly like that. He examined the shiny black flake the kid handed to him. It was sharp enough to draw blood, even after all these years.

This is not quite a whole arrowhead, he said. It's a piece flaked off from the making of one. Looks like a good piece of obsidian. The Indians had to go all the way over to Yellowstone to get their obsidian.

We're going to Yellowstone, the kid said. To see Old Faithful.

The Indians weren't scared of much, he told the kid. But they were probably afraid of Old Faithful. Think about that when you're up there. They thought all that blowing steam was spirits coming out of the earth.

What do you think?

I think the Indians were smart. But I don't think Old Faithful is a spirit. You can study the issue for yourself when you get there. Let me know.

Should I keep it? the kid asked. He held the flake in the palm of his dirty hand. The flake had a wicked curve to it. It looked like a shark's tooth.

Will knew the rules. They were on federal land, just inside the border of the Shoshone National Forest. You weren't supposed to take artifacts off federal land.

I'll let you decide, he told the kid.

You're sure it's not an arrowhead?

It's not a arrowhead. It came from making a arrowhead, like a leftover. It's a nice thing to think about — people using this place during rough weather just the way we did.

Have you always been a cowboy?

Will laughed and put his hat back onto his head. The kid had bought a silver felt hat for himself in Cody before he got to the ranch, and he had never taken it off, not during the entire ordeal. Not like you mean, he said. I was a boy first. I used to play football like you play soccer. I did all those science and history projects in school.

Then you made up your mind to get the cowboy job? After college?

It was a little bit like that, he said, picking up Hawk's reins. I didn't do much college. But I made up my mind to work at something I liked. Cowboying is part of my job. There's other things, too.

How old are you? the kid asked.

Twenty-three.

I'm nine, the kid said. I think I'll leave the

186

obsess—

Obsidian.

Ob-sid-an. Okay. I think I'll leave it here. In case another Indian wants to use it.

That's a good idea, Will said.

There was an earthquake. His room on the second story of the barn surged forward like a boat propelled by oars. Once, twice, four times. The room surged. But the quake didn't last long. He was nearly asleep. The orange barn cat had just left his bed in that queen-of-Sheba way it had. He had listened to the cat leap down the stairs. Had it known the quake was coming? He'd heard that about animals and birds, how they could sense the breaking of the earth before it began. He decided to check on the horses.

He was naked. The jeans he had hung across the windowsill in his room weren't dry yet. He put them on anyway. And he put on his boots. It wasn't even midnight. He could hear the mutter of voices from behind the bunkhouse where Lyle and Serge and Wade the irrigator were still drinking beer and making plans they'd never live up to. He wasn't surprised they hadn't noticed the quake.

The sodium lights at the corners of the barn made the night look bluer and colder than it was. Cutworm moths hurled themselves at the lights, combative. The moths were everywhere this summer. He found them in his shaving kit. He found them between his folded shirts. The moths that made it above tree line in the Absaroka Mountains would lay eggs there, under the frosty scree. Many of the laying moths would be eaten by bears. He had always thought that was a crazy thing, how gray moths half the size of his little finger flew all the way from Nebraska to become a meal for Wyoming bears.

He walked to the corrals. There was no breeze. The stars were as thick as spilled salt in the sky above him. He wondered if he'd imagined the earthquake. Or if he'd been the only one who felt it at all.

The horses were awake. The three that had been chosen to wrangle the dude string in the morning were standing separate from one another in the big corral. Nina, with her dark, important eyes. Sully the big-bellied dun. High-withered Jake. They stood on all fours, with their heads higher than the level of the fence, as if they were waiting for something. He spoke to them, just a word or two, but that wasn't what they were waiting for. He could hear Nina swishing her long tail through the shadows.

Hawk and the filly were standing close to each other in the small corral, facing in opposite directions, their sides almost touching. Hawk's eyes were closed, and his lower lip drooped, a sure sign of contentment. The filly had her neck extended, and her ears were at full salute toward the river. The small white triangle between her eyes floated in the air like a stalled satellite. She had heard something, she knew it.

He wondered if the elk herd that bedded down in Huff Gulch was bothered by a thing like an earthquake. Maybe not. Maybe the elk felt the earth shake all the time as they moved in and out of Yellowstone Park. There were more than three hundred quakes a year in the park. His mother had told him that. A cow elk could live as long as twenty years. She might remember all sorts of occurrences. She might think she understood earthquakes after she had experienced a few. Maybe a cow elk passed that understanding along to her calves. He didn't know if elk were smart that way or not. Horses, he believed, had deep and bidden memories. Horses took the world in through their bodies. A new thing would be new, and strange, to a smart horse only once.

He didn't go any closer to Hawk or the filly. They were fine. The filly would settle.

He could feel dew beginning to condense along the tops of his bare shoulders. The moisture was heavy on his skin, like a long-held breath. His legs were cold from the wet jeans. He thought about how he'd just felt the earth break a little beneath him. He wondered how that worked. How did the planet he lived on break itself and hold itself together at the same time?

He was grooming the filly outside the main corral. It was a lesson in acceptance. She needed to accept the intricate invasion of the comb running through her mane and tail. She also needed to accept the distractions. When he worked with her around other horses and people, she needed to keep her attention on him.

Two young girls, guests for the week, stopped to watch. They asked if they could pet the filly.

In a minute, he said. We're actually doing a kind of training test here. This horse is young and still in school. Can you wait a minute?

We can wait, the taller girl said.

What's her name? the other girl asked.

I call her filly, mostly, because that's what she is, he said. A filly, a young female horse. Kind of like you two.

But what's her name? the girl asked again.

You can call her Tick if you want. I do that sometimes, he said.

Tick? Like the bug?

Like a clock?

Well, Tick is short for Ticket, which is part of her mother's name.

But she gets her own name, right? The question came from the smaller of the two girls, the one wearing new red boots. I have my own name. Madeline Rose Curtis.

I'm Rachel, the taller one said. R-a-c-h-e-l.

I see your point, he said. I'm William, but everybody calls me Will. I was named for my grandfather. Would you believe me if I told you that sometimes a horse gets its permanent name after people have watched it for a while? It can take time for a horse to find its proper place. That's kind of the case here. This filly is still growing into her perfect name.

And you'll pick it out, the smaller girl asked.

Probably not.

Ticket is what you came up with?

That's all I got for now. Ticket. Or filly.

Do you think horses have their own secret names for each other? the taller girl asked. She wore glasses. Her nose was sunburned from her first day on the ranch.

Do you?

I do, she said. I think horses have lots of secrets. Lots of huge, not-talking secrets. I think she's listening to us right now. She thinks we're silly.

He paused, looking at the aluminum comb he held in his hand. The afternoon was hot and buzzed with the labor of insects. You're probably exactly right about that, he said to the girls. Then he stood aside so they could stroke the filly on her nose. He showed them how to approach her so that she could see what they were doing. The filly was ground-tied, held in place only by the dangle of the lead rope. She had learned that lesson very well.

She's nice, the taller girl said.

She wants to be nice, he said. She has a good heart. I guess she don't think we're completely silly.

Can I ride her? the smaller girl asked.

I can see right now that she would like both of you to ride her when she's old enough, but she's not old enough, he said. I can't ride her, either.

So you just keep her clean?

I keep her clean. I feed her. I teach her lessons, sort of like she's in school, he said.

I'm kind of the person who looks out for her.

But you don't know her secrets, the taller girl said.

I guess I don't, he said. Maybe she's saving them for when she thinks I ought to know them.

I think she's saving them for the magic time, the taller girl said. You have to be ready, you know. The magic time can happen any minute, like a shooting star. Or a pop quiz from your math teacher.

Yeah, said the smaller girl.

Is that so, he said.

You'll only get one chance with the magic time, the taller girl said, pushing at her glasses. That's the way it works.

And I have to be ready, he said.

Both girls nodded.

Okay. Then I promise to be ready. And when she tells me her secrets, should I tell them to you?

Oh, no, the taller girl said. I'll be back in Kansas City, Missouri. You can't send a secret to Missouri.

The smaller girl looked down at her red boots. You can't tell anybody, she said. That's a rule.

He pushed his hat toward the back of his head. A green-bodied deerfly tried to settle

193

on the filly's flank. Her black tail began to broom back and forth, sweeping.

All right, he told them. I have to play by the rules. I have to protect her secrets. That's a mighty tall order. You think I can do it?

Both girls nodded again.

You think the filly believes I'm up to the job?

The girls looked up at him. Their eyes were solemn.

She wants you to know everything, the smaller one said, reaching out to touch the filly's glossy shoulder just as he had shown her. Anybody can see that.

She left a small piece of petrified wood on his pillow. He thought it was a bone. He thought the orange barn cat had brought him a bone the way it sometimes brought him the stiff body of a mouse. It was the middle of the day. He was in a hurry. He had come to his room to get his sunglasses before he took ten guests out on a ride.

The piece of wood was no larger than the face of a watch, veined red with iron, striped gray with the minerals that made it heavier than a stone. He had shown Angela how to find petrified wood among the rocks that lined the river. Angela. She had left it for him.

And he didn't deserve a thing from Angela. He hadn't been with her for two weeks. Their nights together, all the hot urging, had stopped. He had seen her with the college-aged son of one of the guests. The two of them, Angela and the college kid, had gone for a hike. He didn't mind too much. It was her business.

But he had seen Angela watching him the previous night at staff dinner. They had eaten during the same shift. Katie the cook had served the lasagna that everybody liked. And he had told the story about what he had seen that day — how the three-legged coyote that Mr. Ward wouldn't allow anyone to shoot was in the hay meadow, stalking the sandhill cranes and their mud-colored baby.

The guests wanted me to stop it, he told everybody. They wanted me to stop that fool coyote.

Did you? This came from Jenna, one of the cabin girls.

That coyote was jumping into the air on his three legs, and the cranes were jumping and flapping and croaking like they do. Sonia saw it, he said. She was riding drag.

I didn't see it, Sonia said. That woman

from Miami had me resetting her stirrups for the hundredth time. I didn't see shit.

Well, it was a sight. That coyote was hungry. And a bird like a crane don't have much to protect it.

So was there a killing? asked Katie. Did the Miami people see some blood?

I didn't let it get to a killing, he said, shifting in his chair. I should have, but I didn't.

His confession brought hoots and jeers, especially from Wade the irrigator, who didn't know how to ride a horse and thought everyone who visited Wyoming should learn how tough life really was.

Were you afraid to see a Miami lawyer cry? The question came from Wade.

He could see now how they had all stopped eating and were watching him. Angela was looking at him from the far end of the table with those soft, tilted eyes of hers. He knew what he was supposed to say. He was supposed to say he didn't give a goddamn about the rich guests they all worked for. He was supposed to say the Miami people could go to hell.

I trotted into the meadow a ways, he said. When that coyote saw I wasn't one to parlay, he broke off. He ain't that crazy.

And the baby crane is all right? asked Katie.

It is, he said. For another day. And he went back to his dinner. He asked for more lasagna. Angela never said a word to him. She didn't smile or anything. She only gave him a steady look with those angled brown eyes that he liked so much. It was a serious, measuring look.

But she had come to his room when it was empty. And she had left him the piece of wood. He picked it up off his pillow. It had a dry, velvety feel in his hand.

What had she said to him near the end of their time together? She said he had a sweet face. They had been on the bed in this very room, and he hadn't liked the description. He didn't want anyone to think he was sweet.

Okay, she said, I'll find another word. It's a *nice* face. You have your blond hair that you like to wear really short. Your nose isn't very big, for a guy's nose. You have good skin. Your eyes aren't big or little, and they don't have a color that stands out when a girl first looks at you. I don't even know if I can say what the color is, and I've looked at you a hundred times.

Hazel, he said. My mother says it's hazel.

That only works if hazel is a color that changes from time to time. Your eyes change.

I had to put *green* on my driver's license, he said. They made me pick.

So it's a nice face, Angela said, touching him, drawing a line with her warm finger right underneath his mouth. It's a balanced face, one you can grow into. Is your father good-looking?

I don't know. I never thought about it. My brother Chad's the one who's supposed to have the looks.

That's the thing about you, Will. You don't score yourself very high. You like to fly under the radar. But you seem like a person who wants to grow into something. You're skinny but really strong. You're tall. All the girls here think your body is . . . well, they're right about your body because I know the truth.

Are you trying to embarrass me?

No, she said. I do want to seduce you a hundred more times, starting in about two minutes, but I'm trying to make a point. It's what's behind your face that gets to me. I feel like I can see things happening back there.

He took the petrified wood and placed it on the windowsill among the husks of flies and honeybees that had settled there to die. Angela was an attractive girl. She was the kind of girl he was supposed to want for a

198

long time. But he didn't. Not yet. He wondered if he was being held back, or launched forward, by whatever it was that Angela claimed to see behind his regular face.

The card games started to get ugly. They hadn't begun that way. A group of them had played it loose and easy in the bunkhouse for the first few weeks, hands of gin, games of spades and hearts, mostly without the exchange of money. Some of the cabin girls liked to play spades, and they were willing to enter the stink of the bunkhouse for that. Katie the cook tried to teach them to play euchre. But poker became the game of choice for the late hours. All men. Always for money.

It had ever been that way, in his experience. Get more than two men together and enclose them in a room or a tent without women, and somebody would deal the cards. He liked the games. He won more than he lost when there was skill involved. You weren't allowed to graduate from the Testerman family unless you understood the rudiments of cards. But he was also willing to play the games that were made for people who had been drinking: Indian poker, jacks and deuces wild, that sort of thing. If he lost money, he lost money.

Wade was the one who set the bad tone. Wade couldn't stand to lose. It was worse in front of the girls, so Wade got to the point where he wouldn't even take a hand in the casual games. Instead, he tried to make himself into some kind of impresario.

We're going to play tonight, he'd whisper as Will was shoveling manure into a wheelbarrow. You're invited.

Most of the time he went.

And most of the time it was fun enough. Kenny played. Lyle, the college kid Shea Petrie had hired for the grounds staff, played well enough to keep them sharp. Serge was terrible when it came to bluffing, but he had the decency to laugh at himself and his mistakes. Petrie played with them some nights, though he would stay only as long as they stuck to seven-card stud. Now and again a guest would be at the table, some guy who had ingratiated himself with Wade, or the experienced kind of player who knew how to find gambling if it was nearby. The stakes were always low. Tempers flared. But that was part of the appeal.

He did worry about Kenny. Kenny could be a sap when he was drinking. Kenny could be talked into all manner of things if his Irish blood was fizzing, and by the midway point of the summer, Kenny was always drinking and always fizzing. The girls had figured out how to handle him. They just moved his hands away from their bodies and laughed in a way that was supposed to remind Kenny that he prided himself on being a gentleman. But some of the younger guys, especially Wade, were inclined to take advantage.

I'm raising you fifty dollars, Ken, Wade would say. I want to see how much you'll pay to see my cards.

You want to see if I'm a quitter?

That's not it at all. You know everything there is to know about working on this isolated patch of wilderness, even if Mr. Petrie don't give you the time of day. There's no quit in *you.*

I believe you're impugning my reputation, Kenny would slur.

I'm not. I'm raising you fifty dollars in an attempt to send you a kindly message.

And Kenny would hear the cheap, late-night threat in Wade's words, and he'd smile some kind of Gene Autry smile, and he'd call the raise and lose fifty dollars of his money.

Will did not try to stop any of it, not at first. He had his own code about such things. An adult man was not to be interrupted or given unwanted advice unless bodily harm or jail time was likely to be a consequence. He believed in learning the hard way. He had promised Mr. Ward and Shea Petrie he would make sure Kenny caused no hitches with the guests or with the horse part of the operation. He had not promised that Kenny would drive away from the Black Bell Ranch with his pockets full of his summer salary.

Kenny lost the silver belly Stetson he had bought at a thrift shop in Billings. Five days later he won it back.

Kenny lost his hand-tooled belt with the blued steel buckle. Wade was tacky enough to wear the damn thing every day for the next week.

Serge lost a hundred dollars and quarantined himself from the game.

Will took everyone's money on a Tuesday night when the cards ran his way. It was luck, pure and simple. The cards fell the way they fell. Wade said he looked forward to kicking Will's ass during the next go-round, and he wasn't laughing about it. Wade also said he was going to outlaw certain games, especially those that went high-low. Poker was the only thing on the ranch Wade could control. He had signed on for the irrigator job at the Black Bell imagining himself as some kind of ranch foreman. No one had told him he would spend much of his summer chopping and hauling firewood for the guest cabins.

Kenny started it. He said they needed to clean up their acts and play like men.

In Detroit, Kenny said, there are men who play cards like Joe Dumars played basketball. They practice. They come to games dressed for business. They play for long hours, and they don't drink.

We ain't in Detroit, Wade said.

Precisely, Kenny said. And he proposed a night of seven-card stud, no bullshit, no modifications. Five hundred dollars just to sit at the table.

It was better than a bluff. Wade had to say yes. Kenny had him by the short hairs.

But Serge couldn't do five hundred and neither could Lyle the college kid. Will suggested it might be all right if they redefined the price of manhood at two hundred dollars. This made everyone except Wade laugh. They had their five players.

Kenny ran the game. He decided on the antes and he dealt the cards, every time. He also started to drink. It was beer from a can, but the beers went down fast. After two hours, his face was shiny with sweat and he was three hundred dollars in the hole. He was also having a good time.

Will later decided he would have played Kenny's hand just the way Kenny played it — except for the part about the Cadillac. Kenny dealt himself three of a kind. He drove everyone out with his raises except Wade, who leaned over his cards like a starving man protecting his last slice of bread. Wade called and raised. Kenny wanted to meet the raise, so he offered up his Cadillac.

It's worth a thousand dollars, he said. Maybe more. This is what I've been talking about. This is playing cards. Do you want another one from the deck or not?

Wade waved off the chance to improve his hand. Kenny dealt himself one more card. He shrugged to himself like a shrug was part of his style for the evening, then he emptied the beer can that rested near his elbow. Wade had won the hand, easily.

He reached into the pot for the keys to the Cadillac.

If it's worth a thousand dollars, then you own about a third of it, Will said. I'm not sure you get to take the keys.

He put the car in the pot, Wade said.

He matched your raise of two hundred or whatever it was. The car is collateral for what he owes, and he don't owe the whole thing.

He can have the car, Kenny said. His eyes had gone dull and sleepy, but he was still holding his chin high as if deep inside himself he were royally content.

You might be willing to give it to him tonight, while your head is flying, Will said, but I think you'll feel different in the morning. By my count you owe Wade three fifty. That's a lot of money, but it ain't the whole car.

He anted up the car, Wade repeated.

He matched your bet and he lost, Will said. You know the rules as well as I do. It was coming down to what he'd worried about — a pissing match. Serge and Lyle were still at the table, which was set up close to their bunks. They were quiet, but they were watching. They knew a train wreck when they saw one.

He did what he did, Wade said. I can't help it if he's a drunk. You all saw him drop those keys.

Serge leaned back in his metal chair. He opened his mouth like he wanted to say something, but then he shut it. Will wished Wade was something other than stupid. He didn't think much of a man who chewed his arguments down to their worthless nubs.

I saw him offer up the car, Will said. And I heard him say how much it's worth. You know and I know that any mechanic between here and Seattle will say that DeVille is worth lots more than he owes you. I ain't gonna be party to robbery. He owes you three fifty, and he'll pay it.

Kenny interrupted. In Detroit, he said, a man pays his debts. Polack or Wop or Irish. A man can't leave the table until he's settled. Otherwise, he's broken his word.

Wade smiled a greedy smile.

Then here's how it has to go, Will said, standing. He took all the cash he had from his vest pocket, and he counted out three hundred and fifty dollars. He dropped the bills onto the table near Wade. That will have to satisfy you, he said to Wade. And it had better satisfy you, too, Ken. I haven't been to Detroit. I'm not Irish or nothing else. It could be that people like to kill themselves over solvable matters in Detroit. And maybe you think it's fun to ruin yourself when you're drunk. But I know rules, and I'll bet this one works for those dressed-up hoodlums in Michigan. I just bought the chit. Now Kenny owes *me* money.

You're a motherfucker, Wade said.

Maybe. But you ain't gonna put up a fight

about it, are you? You can see as good as I can that these others — and he nodded toward Lyle and Serge — believe I just got you out of your own jam. You believe it, too, somewhere in your black heart. The night's over once Kenny hands me those keys.

What?

He's square with you, but he ain't square with me. He owes me money. I'm not trusting nobody else with that Cadillac.

Serge produced a sneeze of laughter.

Take it, Kenny said, with a kingly wave of his hand.

You just said I couldn't do that, Wade said, standing up as well. You're a lying motherfucker.

No, Will said. I'm just a fellow who trusts hisself more than he trusts you. This game is over. Feel free to thank me in the morning.

Kenny Braithwaite lasted until August. Shea Petrie fired him without apology. Will had covered for Kenny on the mornings Kenny was too hungover to wrangle the horses, but he hadn't been able to hide all the mistakes. There were complaints from the cabin girls. Complaints from the watercolorist who had been hired to teach painting. Complaints from the kitchen staff. There weren't many complaints from the guests. The guests enjoyed Kenny and his big-hat bluster. Kenny was a character. Shea Petrie let it be known he couldn't run a first-rate guest ranch with characters.

Mrs. Lathrop, who is staying in the Antler Cabin, said Kenny smelled strongly of spirits at the square dance, Petrie told Will. That was her word. *Spirits.* It was the last son-of-a-bitching straw for me.

Mrs. Lathrop from the Antler Cabin got on me about the manure stink in the corrals, Will said. She's got the wrong kind of nose to be up here. Why don't you tell me what really flipped your switch.

He's not taking care of himself, Petrie said, scratching at the goatee he was trying to eke onto his chin. Not sleeping. Drinking too much. He just about killed Lyle with the chain saw yesterday.

Will agreed. Kenny was on a slide. Ever since the card game where he had lost the keys to his Cadillac, Braithwaite seemed to take a high-minded pleasure in his own poor decisions.

He don't really want to hurt anybody but hisself, Will said. You fronting him any pay?

No. And I can't believe you think I should, Shea Petrie said. You're the one he's leaving shorthanded.

Will looked at the pair of braided reins he'd been cleaning when Petrie came into the tack room with the news. It'll be a haul, he said. Sonia will have to take on more work.

Sonia's good enough.

Sonia's plenty good, Will said, especially with kids. But she don't really wake up until after lunch. She spends most of her dark hours chasing after Serge.

Well, there's some goddamn news, Petrie said. My staff members are getting laid. Petrie looked at the dozens of saddles on the racks like they were cousins he never wanted to see again. Work it out with Sonia, he said. I'll try to get some of Kenny's forfeited salary sent your way. You'll be earning it.

Will watched Petrie limp his way back to the main lodge. Petrie walked like he had nothing but blisters on the bottom of his left foot. Will told himself for the one hundredth time that he would never take a job managing a guest ranch.

Kenny's side of the story was more ornamental. He talked as if he'd already gathered a crowd at the Silver Dollar Saloon.

My mistake was not working things out with Margit, not patching things up as soon as I got here. Margit developed some poor impressions of me last year, Kenny said. I should have reoriented her.

Petrie says you got careless with a chain saw, Will said.

That might be true, Kenny said. He had come to the corrals dressed in a chambray shirt and pressed jeans. He wore a blue silk kerchief that brought out the bits of color that had not yet been diluted from his eyes. His face was puffy with booze and sleep. I was somewhat distracted with the chain saw, Kenny said.

Petrie reckons you're nothing but distracted, Will said. I'm sorry. I know you like it up here.

I do, Kenny said. It's a good place. A person can blossom here better than in town.

Is that where you'll go?

Cody? I suppose. My horse is in Cody.

Will didn't even try to suppress the smile that came to him. You still owe money to the woman that's got your horse?

I do, Kenny said, lifting his shoulders just a little. She's a big woman. A good cook, especially in the Italian manner. With my romantic talents, I expect to square up that account very soon. Maybe as early as this week.

That so?

It is, Kenny said. I haven't actually lost

my balls, you know. Only when it comes to being diplomatic with Margit. Margit's not keeping my balls.

So you got a place to stay?

I believe I do.

How about money?

Since when are you my father confessor? Kenny asked. But it was clear from the jut of his elbows that he was grateful for the question. The question implied a remaining supply of dignity. I have money, Kenny said. My tips have been good. I hope you know that.

I'd heard, Will said.

You heard right. I have money and a horse and a woman with working parts who may or may not allow me to step into her arms. What else does a man deserve?

And you got your car, Will said.

Ah. The car. Now there's a situation I'd like to bend your ear about.

Will felt the balloon of camaraderie that had been floating inside his belly begin to deflate. The car. The Cadillac. He noted that Kenny was adrift in the heavy scent of slapped-on cologne. It was Lyle's brand, from the brown bottle Lyle left on the counter in the bunkhouse.

I want you to keep the car, my boy. Seeing as you practically own it.

Not even close, Kenny. You'll need a set of wheels. I'd rather call the debt good.

I can't do that. I may appear to be a ruined man to some people around here, he said, looking ostentatiously into the rolling sky, but I don't lie and I don't welsh. The car is yours.

I don't want it, Will said.

They were standing just outside the corrals. Most of the guests were on a brunch picnic. The horses, who had the morning off, had begun to crowd the main gate at the sound of the men's voices. One of the geldings, a piebald with the full, white face of a mime, hung his head over the gate and chocked his long, stained teeth together. The horses knew disagreement when they heard it.

I don't need a car, Will said again.

But you have one, Kenny said. Consider it a sign of the times. You are moving up in the world. I am . . . well, I'll be looking for another back door to knock on soon.

This ain't a discussion I want to get into.

I understand that, Kenny said. But the decision's made. You already have the keys.

You're making me mad, Kenny. You're about to make me beg in the wrong direction, and I don't like it.

Kenny laughed and knocked his boot

heels together as if they needed to be cleared of mud. Will noticed what he hadn't noticed before — the welter of what looked like fresh sores on the back of the old policeman's hands.

Don't worry, he said to Will. You're not getting a bargain. I have a few favors to ask.

The favors were these: a ride into town, a seven-hundred-dollar cash advance on the value of the Cadillac, and a recommendation to a new employer if it ever got to that.

That's one of the things I like about the West, Kenny told him after they had begun to climb their way out of the Sunlight Basin in the two-tone Cadillac. A man doesn't have to resign himself to a permanent reputation. A man just has to be willing to pull up stakes.

You want me to take you to this woman's house? Will asked. He was unhappy. Shea Petrie had given him permission to drive Kenny into town, but he hated how Kenny had trapped him. He didn't want the Cadillac. He didn't want to leave Kenny in front of a house where he might get kicked right off the stoop.

It's best that I approach Diana on my own two feet, Kenny said. Penitent. You aren't Catholic, are you? You might not understand.

213

I got the concept, Will said. The Cadillac accelerated beautifully up the steep grades of Dead Indian Mountain. That was another thing to hate.

I was raised in the Church. I still believe in a few things, Kenny said. Second chances. Fifth chances. Women can be very forgiving at certain times in their lives.

I don't know if my mother would care to hear you say that, Will said.

Kenny gave off a laugh that turned into a bad-sounding cough. It's a good thing I never met your mother, he said.

Neither of them spoke as they reached the crest of the mountain. It was natural to fall silent when there was so much rough country to see. The Beartooth Mountains. The scour of the Clark's Fork Plateau. The bleached plunge of Sunlight Canyon.

Where will you go after you're finished with the dictatorship of Mr. Shea Petrie? Kenny asked.

Go? I'll visit my family for a couple of days, Will said. Then I'll head to California.

California. With that bay showgirl of yours?

Yes. She'll go, too.

She's a handsome animal, Kenny said. I look at her and I think I'm looking at a hip number from the National Stock Show.

Thanks.

But she's no deeper than a pie pan. You know that, don't you?

Will pretended not to hear the provocation. He made like he was adjusting his wide red seat belt across his waist.

I've seen a lot of horses, Kenny said. I've trained them and rode them and sold them up and down the Rockies —

I don't think you've been in Wyoming but about ten years, Will said, interrupting. I been here my whole life. You don't need to talk to me like I'm deaf.

Kenny twisted in his seat. There were dark spots in the whites of his eyes that shouldn't have been there. The corner of one eye was pink and leaking.

You can keep your temper to yourself, Kenny said. I'm offering you advice.

I didn't ask for advice. I said I was going to California.

Hollywood, Kenny said. Los Angeles and Gomorrah. They don't need you in California.

They don't *need* me anywhere. I'm not that ignorant. But I got a job offer, and I'm taking it.

You have a job? Kenny pulled at the knot on his blue kerchief. I didn't know that, he said. You have two jobs. I can't even hold

215

one. You don't blow your own trumpet much, do you?

Been too busy to use any kind of trumpet, Will said. They dropped onto the red-rock eastern slope of the mountain, and he let the Cadillac's chirring V-8 work the switchbacks. He shifted gears with a moodiness he recognized. The car's tires began to shrill.

I heard you had money problems, Kenny said.

Me?

You would think I'd stay out of other people's business, given my history. But I hear things. I know it's a sign of poor upbringing to gossip —

But you're gonna do it anyway.

I'm going to pass this information along, Kenny said. I've been told you've got some big debts because of a girl back home.

There's no girl back home, Will said. Well, there was one, but she took up with another man, which is her right. My mother's been sick, real sick. But I don't owe the bank or nobody else a dime.

You aren't mixed up with Tug Dupree in any way?

Will closed his eyes for longer than he should have on such a winding road. Kenny was irritating him. Kenny was souring everything he talked about. I know Tug from the rodeos, he said. Tug's a good roper and a quiet man with his beer. Him and me bought shares in a couple of foals once, but it didn't work out. I didn't make a dollar. We went our separate ways. Don't tell me you been talking to Tug. I heard he was down in Ruidoso.

Somebody's spreading talk about you, Kenny said, his voice bruised.

But it ain't you?

It ain't *just* me, Kenny said.

Hellfire, Will said. Why don't you tell everybody that I save my money like a widow woman? Why don't you start with your crowd in Cody? Tell them I got no girlfriends and no babies. The sheriff ain't looking for me. Tell them I'm going to California for the weather.

All right, Kenny said. He seemed to be looking at the space between his knees.

It might be better if you just didn't talk about me at all, Will said. I'm no kind of topic.

You think you can just walk right down the street like everything's going to work out for you? Kenny asked, pushing into his voice. You must be a very young man if you think you can make a life out of a bunch of straight lines.

I don't know what that means, Will said,

pushing back. Are you trying to make me mad again?

Kenny looked at him with his spotted eyes. There was something spiderwebbed at the edges of his pupils. I don't know what I'm saying or doing, Kenny said, sighing. I feel like a wore-out old boot. You know that Wade fellow has plans to take you down, don't you? I wish I could be there to watch your back.

Wade? What's he gonna do? Henpeck me to death?

He says he's going to call you out.

He won't, Will said. He don't have the guts. And calling a man out takes some effort. Wade don't understand effort.

Should I thank you again for keeping my car out of the hands of that prime jackass? Kenny asked.

Sure, Will said, relaxing for the first time during the drive. That's one thing we can both be proud of. And he gave Kenny Braithwaite a splinter of a grin.

He left Kenny in the Cadillac while he made the cash withdrawal at the bank. He left the car running, hoping Kenny would just drive the damn thing away. But Kenny didn't do it. He asked to be let off on Sheridan Street, so he could walk to his destination.

Does this Diana live at the Silver Dollar Saloon? Will asked, pointing to the bar across the street from where Kenny had asked him to stop.

Sometimes, Kenny said, opening the passenger door. I first met her in the Dollar.

Is she in there now?

No. My courage is in there now. If you have to ask.

Keep it in the road, Braithwaite, Will said, dropping the Cadillac into gear. He could feel the smooth hum of the car invading his whole body, coming in through his layered clothes. Shea Petrie ain't the last boss in the world, he said, dropping his voice into low notes of connivance. You got plenty to offer.

Kenny looked down at his scabbed hands. He had a garbage bag full of clean clothes hanging from one fist and his black Larry Mahan hat gripped in the other.

Your horse is not as bad as I suggested, Kenny said, his lips hardly moving. I get gloomy sometimes. Don't listen to me serious when I get gloomy.

All right, I won't. You just take care of yourself, okay?

Kenny Braithwaite didn't answer. He flattened his hand into a kind of tired salute, then Will watched him cross the ruckus of Sheridan Street with the memorized gait of

219

a salesman who has just arrived in town to improve his prospects.

He took Angela fishing. It was after they had stopped sleeping together. She was curious about fishing, which was the kind of thing he liked about her. But she had never tried it with a fly rod. Many of the guests tried it. And many of them gave up after one afternoon. Fly-fishing, like riding, looked easier than it was. But the guests who were good at it, the ones who transformed themselves into silent, graceful beings on the water, they made fishing look beautiful to Angela.

He took her to a wide, braided portion of Sunlight Creek where she wouldn't have to listen to Wade or Serge tease her and where the sloped banks and gravel bars made it easy for her to back-cast. He had borrowed a four-weight rod for her. She wanted to practice casting without a leader or a fly, a good idea. He watched her whip the orange fly line back and forth over her right shoulder, and he offered advice only when she asked for it. He was not a great fisherman himself. He did not have much interest in reading water as if it were an endless sacred book. But he could cast a fly because Chad had taught him how. Chad had also taught him how to throw a baseball and how to rope a calf. Chad had said he would be embarrassed to have a brother who couldn't do those things.

I'm never going to be good at this, Angela said. Her hair was free and crazy. She wore cutoff jeans and a melon-colored T-shirt. She looked ripe in the late afternoon sun.

You don't have to be too good, he said. They're trout. They have brains the size of ladybugs. If you tie a grasshopper pattern onto the end of that line, the fish will do the rest.

You're making fun of me, she said.

I'm not. I'm providing technical support. You remember that knot I showed you?

She nodded. She had already proved she was good with knots.

Let's put that to use and have you hook some trout.

It was one of those summer days that seem forged out of pure golden light. The brook trout took the grasshopper almost every time Angela managed to drop it onto the stream. He was the one who slipped the barbless hook from their bony, gasping mouths. He did it as carefully as he could — the way Chad had preached to him — holding the throbbing fish under water while he pinched his fingers around the hook. They were close enough to the glaciers on Copper Mountain for the cold in the water to make his hands ache.

He sat on the gravel bars and watched Angela lay out her line. He gathered some balsamroot and crushed it under her nose to show her how it smelled. And he pointed to what he thought was a wolf track, though he did not launch into his darker feelings about wolves. They had already covered that topic. It was one where they didn't agree.

Angela asked him the names of the flowers that grew around their feet. He did not know most of them, but he did know bee flower, with its hanging-basket blossoms. His mother thought bee flower was darn near perfect. He knew fireweed. He knew aster, and he picked a lavender one for Angela to wear in her crazy hair. He told her he liked the way the air above the creek smelled of cut grass, even though there were no pastures nearby. It was the smell of the Testerman Ranch in early August, when the meadows had been mowed flat and the John Deere tractor was tugging a neighbor's baler in swaths across the saturated land. He missed that.

Angela kept fishing, even when she wasn't having luck. She was quiet as she cast. Her motion with the rod was still slashing and uneven, but she was not discouraged. She was the same in bed, he thought. Focused, unafraid. He thought she would make someone an impressive wife someday, if that was what she wanted. She was not a simple person, but she understood that some things were made to be simple.

He wished he were that direct. He knew that most of the time he lived inside himself and gave priority to his own considerations. Yet there were moments he could not predict, like this one on the glazed waters of a creek with a girl whose body he had tasted, when he was spun out of himself and toward the recognition of another person in a way that was delicious to him, and frightening. He needed to learn from those moments, he thought. He needed to be better. Watching Angela try something that was hard for her made him feel smaller than she was, lesser, and that was all right because what she believed in was greater than anything he was contemplating at the moment, and sometimes it was okay to shrink down below another person, just as sometimes it was okay to fail at something you really loved. What you had to do, he told himself, was remain loyal to your best impulses, no matter what.

Angela fished until the air became granulated with shadow and the first of the nighthawks appeared over the bends of Sunlight Creek. She asked him what kind of birds they were, with their banded wings and their strange, barely audible cries. She said they looked as though they'd been cut and folded from Japanese paper. She said they flew just the way she had dreamed she might fly when she was a very little girl.

Wade had a big mouth. And poor judgment. He didn't even wait until dark to organize his ambush. He tried it at lunch.

There were maybe eight of them still in the staff dining room, finishing their bowls of soup and roast beef sandwiches. Will was at the far corner of the table, where he always sat, close to the back door. Wade came in through the kitchen with his polarized sunglasses covering his eyes. He wasn't supposed to eat until the second shift.

I see you parked that Cadillac over near your horse trailer, Wade said. You really think I'm planning to let you get away with that?

I don't know what you have planned, Will said. Why don't we talk about it later? We're eating in here.

I want to talk about it now. All of these others should hear about how you gypped

Kenny out of his car, Wade said. You conned that sorry old man.

I paid him for the car, Will said. I didn't want to do it, but he was hunting for cash, so I obliged. If you want to talk about buying the Cadillac from me, we can do that, but I don't care to do it now.

You stole that car.

Will stood up from the table. It was his intention to leave the dining room so he and Wade could finish their quarrel elsewhere. He didn't like disturbing the others. But his sudden move caused some of the staff, girls like Jenna and Dee Dee, who worked in the cabins, to think he wanted to fight. They sucked in their breath. Lyle, who was seated close to Will, scooted his chair away from the table. Lyle didn't want to get caught in the cross fire.

Let's take this outside, Will said, pulling his leather work gloves from his back pocket and laying them on the seat of his chair as if to save his place for later. We don't need to be bothering anybody else with our mess. They've heard too much as it is.

They haven't heard the truth, Wade said, his voice taking on the edge of a screech.

Katie the cook had followed Wade into the dining room from the kitchen. She was watching him the way a big sister watches a little brother who has a sharp knife in his hands. Wade, she said, get your fat ass out of my chow hall until it's your turn to eat. Katie was a large woman, solid and unswerving. She spoke to the irrigator with a stretched smile on her face.

I'm not finished, he said. This motherfucker thinks he knows everything. He thinks it means something to have a big cowboy poker stuck up his ass. I don't think he should get to do whatever he wants around here just because Shea Petrie likes him. Shea Petrie can suck my dick.

Jesus, Lyle said. He was chewing on the end of the bandanna he wore knotted around his neck, trying not to laugh.

We'll settle this however you want, Will said. He could feel the extra moisture coming into his mouth the way it usually did before he got into a fight. His chest was full of heat. Wade had finally made him angry. But his head was cool and clear. Just as it should be.

Good, Wade said. I'm glad you've got your balls tied on. And he took two steps forward and threw his dark sunglasses across the room at Will's head.

Oh, no! Katie shouted. Ooooh, no. Not in here. Not on my turf. She grabbed the wet floor mop resting in the corner, and she swung it hard at Wade's exposed back. The handle thumped across his spine.

Fuck me, Wade said, turning. What the fuck?

Then Katie swung at him again, down around his knees, the mop head slapping and slurping. When Wade high-stepped out of range, she picked up the plastic bucket that came with the mop and flung the dirty water that was in it at his face.

You get out of my goddamn sight, she said, her cheeks splotched with temper.

Lyle moved fairly fast. So did Jenna, who liked a good free-for-all. Wade was still wiping the slop water out of his eyes. Lyle and Jenna got on either side of him and began to herd him out the back door. Dee Dee joined them. There was some pushing and shoving. Then Katie added her bulk to the effort. Wade had no intention of taking swings at pissants like Jenna and Dee Dee. He found himself outside next to the dumpster, as wet as the morning laundry, before he could formulate his next insult.

That's how it goes on my work patch, Katie hollered after him. Don't bother coming back here for lunch or dinner today. I don't waste my time feeding permanent fuck wads.

Will looked at his half-eaten lunch. He

decided it would be best if he sat back down and finished it. He picked up his work gloves and slipped them into his pocket.

Well, said Katie, surveying the jostled room and its new puddles of water. That will get a girl's heart going. You all just sit back down for me, will you? Let's get some calm. I got fresh brownies straight out of the oven.

Jesus, Lyle said, glancing toward the back door as if he thought Wade might come charging back through it. I'll take a god-damn brownie.

Katie, you did good, Will said. I'm sorry for the trouble.

That man is nothing but trouble, the cook said, sashaying in from the kitchen with a large china plate. I reckon I should know.

There was a brief pause, then Dee Dee the cabin girl snickered.

You think Wade ran out of here because you've been giving him some summer love? Will asked. He dipped his head between his shoulders as he spoke. He and Katie liked to pick on each other. But he knew there was a decent chance Katie might throw something at him for mentioning her indis-cretions.

I never did the nasty with that person, Will Testerman. I want you and everybody else to hear that from me. Katie's broad face was shining like a stove coil. She loved to tell stories on herself. I like my tequila, Katie said. And I like to get high if the time is right. There might have been some feeling up that went on between Wade and me. But we never did the nasty. That man would fuck a tree hole if he thought about it long enough. But I've got some standards, she said, waving her hands across the stacked plate of brownies. Let's eat to that.

He stayed until Shea Petrie and Margit closed down the ranch. Shea Petrie had an outfitter's license, and he would manage elk hunts out of the main lodge until Christmas. But most of the cabins were shuttered after Labor Day. The staff dwindled. Angela was gone. Sonia, the last of the wranglers, was gone. He paid Serge to drive the Cadillac to his parents' ranch. Wade the irrigator had packed his truck at the end of August, and nobody was sorry to see him go. The work wasn't hard during those last weeks. Guests who came to the Absaroka Mountains in September were different. They didn't bring children. They preferred slow hikes into the mountains to dusty horseback rides. They dressed warmly, and they lifted their noses into the shifting air as if they, too, could scent the great change that was coming.

He had more time with the filly. On frosty mornings he could hear her taunting Hawk, trying to play with him inside the confines of the small corral. The frost got into her blood. She stalked the gelding. She tried to imitate the bearing of a dominant herd mare just to see if Hawk noticed. He noticed. He raised his oversized, graying head until it was as high as the filly's. He shifted the axis of his body so that she could not dart in at his shoulder as a dominant mare would. Hawk was filled with forbearance. His eyes were as heavy lidded as a deacon's. This put the filly off. She clattered and skiffed, her hooves audible on the hard ground of the corral. She huffed and kicked as if there were submissive horses within her realm. Then she settled into a mischievous amble, circling the corral, pretending she wasn't interested just before she began to stalk the gelding again.

The filly tried on attitudes for size, Will thought. She was like a high school girl who colored her hair all different ways and wanted to fight about it. When she got truly revved up, he put her in the pasture with the horses he had selected to stay at the ranch for the last month. He let her try her stuff on Lark, the swaybacked Arabian queen of the bunch, on whom it didn't work so well.

He took her on short rides, him riding Hawk, the filly following on a loose lead rope. He led her along the county road toward the public campground that was empty now except on weekends. He led her back and forth across the river, teaching her to follow Hawk in a disciplined manner. The ravens perched high in the spruce trees, hunched like old men wrapped in buffalo robes, and watched them crisscross the river. He worked the filly on the long line in the Black Bell's good round pen, and he sometimes put a saddle pad on her back for a while, and he sometimes leaned some of his considerable weight across her back. He did not put a saddle on her. He practiced bandaging her legs until she knew how to stand still for that procedure. When Margit Petrie, a large-boned woman with an open, careworn face, asked if she could lead the filly up the lane one morning, he let her do it. The filly needed to respect the authority of other people. And he could see how much Margit wanted to go up the lane. Summer at the Black Bell was a long process of giving way for Margit. Being with the filly, even for a short time, was not about that kind of erosion.

He saddled up Hawk and rode out alone as often as he could. He had that kind of time now. They rode the Big Skyline Trail onto the old Beam homestead and made a short loop toward Damnation Basin. They followed the dry bed of Trail Creek along the historic path of Chief Joseph and his fleeing Nez Percé. They visited the ruins of an ancient sheep trap that Shea Petrie claimed was older than parts of the Bible. They rode along the river to the east and to the west, and he watched the first of the falling aspen leaves spin into the clear river water as if they were golden coins flung from an exuberant hand. He saw moose tracks and elk sign, and he was a nuisance to the fledgling red-tailed hawks that were learning to hunt the frost-burned meadows on their own. The hawks would migrate soon. They would have to. Their parents had already cast them out.

He came upon the carcass of a mule deer that had been gut-shot by a bow hunter. The arrow had worked itself loose, but the days of leaking blood and pus were crusted on the animal's hide like a series of flaking brands. The deer's death had been slow. He flushed clans of warblers and mountain bluebirds from the mustard-yellow willows, and the birds shed their urgent song around him as if it were confetti. He found strange human leftovers in the forest. A pair of red-checkered curtains on a brass rod and the box for a Parcheesi game and a Bakelite radio like the one Sal Tassione had kept at the print shop in the days when he was in charge. The radio still had its plug and cord. He found clothes, mostly women's clothes, caught in snags along the river as if the world upstream was changing every kind of costume it could imagine to prepare for winter.

Shea Petrie's shepherd dog came with him sometimes. The jingle of the dog's tags was the same as the sound of warm money in a man's pocket.

Hawk was the one that discovered the wolf. He smelled it on the skirling breeze, and he wheeled to face it, a soldier readying himself for war. A wolf. A pup, Will thought, though it was as big as a grown Alsatian dog. A black pup with the absorbed expression of an athlete. Confident. Lolling. Quick to learn. It was lying deep in the wind-beaten grass of Trail Creek meadow, taking in the afternoon sun. Will had not seen it, not one hair. Hawk sat back on his hocks, snorting. There was something deep in his equine heritage that did not want to be encircled.

Will kept his balance upon Hawk's bowed back. He kept his own body loose in case Hawk bolted, and he kept the reins short. He watched the pup. Petrie's dog was not with them, which was a good thing. The wolf's eyes looked flat and amber from that distance, flat and dispassionate. It was in no hurry. It was not the first wolf Will had ever seen, but he hoped it was the last one he would have to put up with for a while. There was talk that the whole Sunlight Basin pack would be removed by the federal government before the next summer. That was fine with him. He did not see a purpose for wolves in this part of the mountains.

He rode in the very early morning sometimes. His saddle creaked like an old trapdoor in the autumn cold, and its leathers were unyielding and slick. The saddle fit like a stranger's saddle until he warmed it. But it was a pleasure to nudge Hawk through the shadowed canals of fir and spruce, both of them making noise to alert foraging bears. Hawk's hot breath came out in white clouds that condensed into frost on the buckles of his headstall. Will's own nose went numb, and he had to wipe it dry with a bandanna whenever he could. But it was good to ride atop the hills and see the sun hammer its first hot spikes into the long, dark rail of the valley. He thought of his mother, who was already back at school for another year, and her easy love for mornings. His mother had written him a letter in August. She wanted to tell him about Chad's engagement to Hannah and the wedding they were all planning. Would he be able to come home from wherever he might be for a New Year's wedding?

He thought he could do that.

His mother's letter did not mention his father or Everett or anything about her illness. It was a purely happy letter, written in the careful style of a teacher whose students were just beginning to read cursive writing. A wedding. It was the sort of event his mother would throw herself into.

He had not written any letters himself, but he had placed a few phone calls. Petrie let him use the office telephone. He had called the only number he had for Don Enrique. A different person had answered each time, sometimes in English, sometimes in Spanish, but he had always been able to make his intentions clear. He had been able to speak to Don Enrique himself only once. Yes, yes, there was a place for him at the estancia. Yes, yes, they were training. His men were always training. Business was very good. Horses coming and horses going.

Much tremendous business. He should come. He is welcome any day. Don Enrique has seen how well he rides. Don Enrique would be honored to have him at the estancia.

He remembered the day he met the don. It was a long day of horse sales and horse trades and parties. Frank Galey, a horseman with connections, had invited Will to Jackson Hole to ride some of his sale animals — everything from pleasure mounts to polo ponies. He offered Will a handsome wage.

The day had been a blur except for two things: He had ridden one of Joe Bill Smith's splashy quarter horse studs. Joe Bill Smith had been world champion in calf roping, and doing a favor for Joe Bill was like thanking him for his genius. He had also had an unusual conversation with a watchful, quick-stepping man who introduced himself only as Enrique from California and elsewhere.

You have the very good hands, the man said to Will as he was dismounting from a liver bay mare that Frank Galey hoped to sell for the show ring.

Thank you, Will said.

I prefer this Jackson Hole for the snow,

the man said. I prefer it to ski. Do you ski also?

I've done it some, Will said, puzzled. I've lived near the mountains my whole life.

But today I am here for the horses, the man continued, and the horses are impressing me. You are impressing me also, young cowboy rider. You have much of the presence. The man, who was now surrounded by other well-dressed men and more than one woman, insisted that Will take several copies of his business card.

I would wish for you to try your presence at my game, at my horses, the man said, smiling. Ask Señor Frank Galey about my excellence. He will speak for me. You will please give the call to me when you are ready.

It was more invitation than promise. That was the way rich people operated. They liked their invitations. But if you worked with horses, you had to be able to make a job from the smallest of opportunities.

He helped Shea and Margit close down the ranch. He scrubbed the wooden floors in the cabins. He set out mousetraps. He trailered the rest of the horses back across Dean Indian Mountain, to their winter pasture near Cody. He caulked window-panes and broke down hard-used fishing rods. He told stories from the summer that he thought might make Margit laugh. He split wood for the fireplace in the main lodge so the elk hunters would have plenty of wood as the snow fell and piled itself as high as the eaves. Wade the irrigator had not finished that part of his job. He roped the old bull that had spent the summer across the river, and he drove it into a stock trailer on Petrie's orders. The bull was going the way of Margit's restive pigs.

He took a final ride up Sheep Horn Ridge. He wanted a last look at the valley. There was fresh snow on the beaten hide of the foothills. The snow squeaked beneath Hawk's shod hooves. The sky to the west, beyond Copper Mountain, resembled a tunnel hewn from blue-black stone. Another storm on the way, another white page of snow. He heard the bugle of a bull elk curl above the treed flanks of Huff Gulch. It was a forlorn sound — besotted and lonely.

The Absaroka Mountains were long teeth in a stubborn jaw. He had looked at those mountains every morning of the summer. He had watched the snow melt, then come again onto their sharp peaks. Only the glaciers had remained the same, stark white tears painted onto the inscrutable and distant rock. He wondered how many months it would be before he was again in such hard, and quiet, country.

He rode onto the high, bare ridge of Sheep Horn and sat astride Hawk as sleet burned at his cheeks and the river wrote its fresh silver signature across the valley floor. There was lightning beyond the scrim of sleet. It flickered across the sky like the bright loops of a swinging lariat. The buildings of the Black Bell Ranch were no larger than a scatter of tabletops, a cluster of unfolded chairs. He thought about what it meant to be that small. It meant, he knew, that you had to be prepared. Prosperity was a fleeting thing, a puffed-up human state.

He reined Hawk downhill and felt more sleet sting at the back of his neck as he aimed for the cave where he had stayed with the boy during the rainstorm those many weeks before. He did not enter the cave. He merely rode close to it, along the sandy path that was used by deer and cattle and hikers from the ranch. The cave was a blackened hood, it looked low-ceilinged and slick, yet he knew he could find cover there if he needed it. More souls than he could imagine had passed through the Sunlight Basin over the past thousand years, but it was not a place where anyone had thrived for long. Men had carried their starvation across

these ridges just as they had sometimes carried the heavy weight of meat. That was
what he had told the boy from Georgia, and
what he told the boy was true. Some places
were made for crossing.

■ ■ ■ ■

Part III

■ ■ ■ ■

It was a mistake. He shouldn't have shipped the horses. He should have driven them to California himself. Too much could go wrong when you shipped a horse. He knew that. He had seen it when he worked in California the first time — the eight balls of cocaine scratched open by the drivers, the salt spills of crystal meth, forged papers for horses, the black market for steroids and tranquilizers, the legal troubles of immigrant grooms. Shipping was a gypsy business, a hobo crapshoot. But he had wanted to simplify his arrival at Don Enrique's estancia near Anaheim. If he arrived at the estancia alone, he would look like a focused man. Instead, he worried about the filly and Hawk. He could make the drive from Lost Cabin in two days. The contractor, who loaded his horses at the Petro truck stop outside of Rock Springs, couldn't get to Anaheim any sooner than the end of the week. The contractor had horses to swap out in Grand Junction, Colorado, and Henderson, Nevada. The guy couldn't make money working the beeline to Anaheim. So Will would have to trust that the scags who worked for the contractor knew what they were doing.

Trust was not a principle he had seen much cultivated during his last tour of California.

His brother Chad told him to have a little faith.

You need to relax, Chad said. Spend some of that money you earned at the Black Bell. You should stop in Wendover on your way to California. The girls are practically legal down there. They're clean. And the drinks don't stop coming as long as you can lift your arm to grab them. You'll like it. Wendover don't take the starch out of you like Vegas does.

His father barely spoke to him during the few days he was at home. His mother hugged him every chance she got.

When he got to Wendover, Nevada, he pulled off the highway and tried to have an argument with himself about the merits of a vacation day. It was midafternoon. The sun was high and blasting. It shone on the buildings along the street without filter. A motel called the Outlaw was in front of him, scabbed with whitewash, heralded by an unlit neon sign the color of burnt coffee. The motel parking lot was empty except for an old-model school bus that had been painted crayon blue. He didn't need to be stopping in Wendover. He needed to be praying that his horses were all right. He needed to save his money in case everything he had built up in his head started to go dumbfuck.

The better part of the argument was that he might need to have a little fun. The summer had been a wall crawl. He hadn't been in a real town for a long time.

He drove a little farther from the highway until he found the Red Garter Hotel, a place Chad recommended. He took Kenny Braithwaite's old Cadillac right up to the front door and gave the keys to a dried-out, freckle-covered man who was zipped into a nylon jacket with the Garter's logo on the back. The man complimented Will on his car.

Detroit don't make 'em like this no more, the man said. His voice had a wheeze to it, like an old freezer door. Cryin' shame, that's what it is. The whole country has gone down the rabbit hole. I don't reckon it's ever comin' back up.

Will tipped the freckled man two dollars. You have a good afternoon, he said.

The Red Garter didn't have a room for him. Or that's what they said at the desk. He knew how it worked. He was supposed to wait and gamble. He wasn't even supposed to look at his room once he got into it, or to stay there. He was supposed to put everything there was to him out on the casino floor.

He followed a loudly patterned carpet into the middle of the noise and cigarette smoke that was supposed to be gambling. Video poker. He could do that. Maybe somebody would bring him a beer.

After he'd lost twenty dollars leaving his fingerprints on a poker screen, he signed up for a seat at a real poker table. By the time they announced his name over the mic, he'd had two more cold Budweisers. The play was slow and predictable except for the antics of a kid dressed in a black hooded sweatshirt and robot sunglasses. The kid acted like he was on television. He cussed and fidgeted and left his seat to pace back and forth — all over nothing. The kid had bought five hundred dollars in chips. He had a girlfriend with him, a swivel of a woman who was bordered in mascara and shoes. The old men at the table, all of them dressed like golfers, had the kid for lunch.

Fuck this, the kid said after he lost his money. Fuck every one of you.

Nobody at the table bothered to respond.

Will lasted another thirty minutes. The old men were rocks. They were soldiers. They folded on nearly every hand. If they didn't fold, you were in trouble. And they all knew each another. Retirees. Settled in Nevada for the low taxes and sunshine. They read outsiders as easily as they read the *Wall Street Journal.*

He did everything he could to fill up the day. Nickel slots. Bets on the races at Santa Anita. He walked down to the Nugget and walked back. He looked at girls. He moved from sipping beer to chewing on the ice in a series of whiskey and Cokes. He didn't feel any kind of brightness enter him, or any ease. He thought maybe casinos weren't best appreciated by people traveling alone. Casinos had a dance hall speed to them. A bait-and-switch hustle. It was a jolt better shared with somebody else.

He didn't have to pay for a girl. Women kept finding him. It was probably the El Patron hat, he thought. He had bought it in Riverton. It had tiny silver conches on its band, and its wide, curled brim wasn't shy. Plus, he had taken a shower when he was finally assigned a room. He thought he smelled pretty good. The cocktail waitresses were nice even when they hefted their cleavage toward his face for a tip, but most of them were older. Well over thirty. You could see the lead weight of age in the black center of their eyes. It was the college girls who kept grabbing at his hat and asking him about the buckle on his belt. They were very drunk and moved in packs, like hungry coyotes. They went to school in Utah.

You dance? one of them asked. She had curled eyelashes and glitter smeared onto her skin.

No, he said.

You do anything fun?

Sometimes.

Do me some fun, she said, slurring.

I don't know if I should. I just met you.

Do me some fun, she said. Now. Just put your hand down in there. You'll know when I'm ready.

Her friends dragged her away before she could get herself into more trouble. She was engaged to be married, the friends said. That was why they were here.

Two other girls found him later. He was tired, but he was also well launched on Jack Daniels and Coke. He was in a bar off the main floor. The girl had her hand on his leg before he knew it.

I've been watching you, the girl said. You're all alone.

He didn't even bother to smile.

You look nice, she said.

I am nice, he said. Buy you a drink?

She ordered a cranberry and vodka.

There wasn't much to it. A second girl came to say hello, but she made herself scarce. She was the kind who seemed to be a happy drunk. She wanted to be moving and celebrating. The one who had chosen him was more of a brooding type. Serious. And greedy. She kept working her hand on his leg. She knew what effect she was having, and she stretched it out. Then she stood up. He followed her, all too aware of how he must look. He walked like a tired man in boot heels, with a hard-on. Stupid.

The girl found a corner he wouldn't even have called a corner. She rubbed at him through the front of his jeans. She didn't even want to kiss him except right toward the end, when he got a taste of her face powder and her slippery lipstick. He rocked and grabbed and shot off when he had to, and the girl left with a big, rubbery smile on her face. She gave him a tiny wave good-bye. There were people nearby, coming and going to the buffet, and to the rest rooms.

Nobody seemed to notice them. The girl had gotten just what she wanted.

See you later, the girl said, her fingers waving.

He wondered why she bothered to say that when she knew they would never see each other again.

When he went up to his room, he was glad for its silence. It was done up in red and black and silver, all the colors that might make regular people feel like whores. He didn't feel like a whore. But he did look at his naked body in the big framed mirror in the bathroom, and he saw how the girl had rubbed him raw in a couple of places. He hadn't even felt that. It made him laugh in a certain kind of way, looking at his dick and his balls in a mirror in a Nevada hotel room that smelled like cinnamon sticks at Christmas.

This was the story his mother told him before he left for California. It was a story that scared him, and he had thought about it as he drove toward Salt Lake City, through the steep plunge in the mountains that had been the Mormons' last, long slide before they found their paradise.

I've told you about Margie Zane, his mother said. Margie was raised on a ranch outside Pavilion but spent most of her life in Riverton, working as a secretary. She was one of the people getting chemo when I was getting it. We were on a similar schedule. I know you met her. Tiny woman with a nose like a beak? Always wore bright lipstick?

Will knew who his mother was talking about, though he confessed to himself that he had tried like hell not to memorize the other people they had seen at the clinic and the hospital. It had been all he could handle to be with his mother, trying to look like he knew what he was doing in his care for her when he didn't know anything at all.

Margie's been in a bad way for a while. She passed on last week, his mother said.

I'm sorry.

So am I. But it was her time. She said that. She just wanted to be sure she died at home, and she did. I sat with her for a few hours this summer when I could. She liked company.

I don't know how you can do that, he said. It would be too hard for me. I couldn't stay still.

It's supposed to be hard for you, she said. You're young. Margie didn't even want us to talk to her much over those last couple of weeks. Just sit there. I could read or nap. Simone Riddle told me she would sing part of the time when she took a shift. Simone

251

has a good voice.

Anyway, when I was there last week, I fell asleep for a while. It was in the evening. The hospice nurse had already gone. Margie was awake for the nurse's visit. They talked about the morphine. Then we both fell asleep.

You know how I am with my dreaming, his mother said. I sometimes work my way into very elaborate events. But not this time. I know from my watch that I wasn't out for long, and Margie woke me up. She was talking. That happened a lot in her last days. Most of the time it was hard to understand what she was saying. Sometimes she was way back in her memory, and sometimes she was reliving conversations she'd just had — with me or with the nurse. She has a daughter who lives in Canada, you know. They talked on the phone when Margie was strong enough. The daughter came in last week before Margie died.

So Margie was talking, his mother said, and she was pretty restless about it. I leaned over and shifted her pillows. I was sitting right by the bed. And I made sure the quilt was up high like she liked it. But she got even more restless. I was afraid she was in pain. I was worried. Then I saw him. The room was dark, which was how Margie set it up, but I could see him clearly — a tall man dressed in a suit. He was standing in the doorway. I noticed he had a mustache. That's how I knew he wasn't the morning nurse.

It was one of those times when your insides know things before your brain does. I was never afraid. I knew I didn't need to talk. I didn't need to protect Margie. I got all that. It only took me a second to understand this was between the two of them.

I don't know what I expected, Will, but this was not it. I've thought plenty about dying over the past year, and Margie and I certainly talked about it. She was a believer. Her minister came to see her many times. He led a good funeral. I've put together some of my own theories about how the end might go. Your dad can't stand to hear me talk about it, but I've left him some instructions if it comes to that — which it will someday. I tend to think in terms of light and weightlessness because those were the things I wanted to come into my body when it was the sickest. I imagine flying off somewhere without any weight. I never thought of a tall man in a suit.

He didn't stay in the doorway long, and his eyes, as much as I could see them, were the deepest spaces I've ever looked into, though they were in no way cruel or sad. He wasn't lit up in glory, either. He just looked professional, in a comfortable way. An angel — who would have thought I would ever see one of those? But I'm sure that's what he was. You must think I'm crazy. I wish I could explain to you how obvious the whole thing felt once I got the hang of it. An angel, or some power of that type. He had come to Margie with a question, and he waited at the door of her room while she tried to answer that question. It wasn't easy for her, but it was easy for him. He knew how to wait.

Then he was just gone. I'm not sure he was even there for more than a minute. The neat haircut, the suit — all gone. Margie had stopped struggling. She seemed to fall into a comfortable sleep, though I'd be lying if I told you I didn't take her hand and hold it and wait for her pulse to stop. I held on like that for the rest of my shift.

Margie passed away a few days later, when her daughter was with her. I never said a word to anyone about what I'd seen. It didn't seem right.

But it seems right to tell you, his mother said, looking at him with that brimming in her eyes that made him want to turn away. It's strange, I know. It's a hard story to put into words. You are so worried about me, she said. You're going to California, and I want you to go, and I want you to know that I'm telling you everything. The doctors haven't found anything. I'm as well as I can be. And I think the man, or the angel, or whatever he was, in Margie's doorway wanted me to see him. It didn't have to be like that, did it? But it was. He wanted to show me how it works. He wanted me to see how they come for you. Because he was giving Margie a choice, Will. Think about that for a minute. I have. He came to her with a question of yes or no, but she got to make the decision. She said no — at least for that day. I wanted to share that part with you because I think it makes a difference. There doesn't have to be a big fight at the end. There doesn't have to be a battle. You get a choice. You have to choose to let the man in the suit take you away.

He got off the interstate at a small town near the California border. The temperature was mild. He could feel the heat of the completed day rising from the asphalt of the gas station where he stopped. The heat filled his boots. He had been driving across the pale and shattered desert for hours. He thought he might actually try to find a restaurant where he could eat a sit-down meal. He was in the mood for decent food and air-conditioning. As he was filling the tank on the Cadillac, his eyes were drawn to a misty, yellow arc that rose into the sky behind the gas station. Bright lights. The familiar, edgeless plea of halogen lamps. It had to be a football game.

It wasn't a real game. It was only a Thursday night, he realized, and the cluster of players gathered at the far end of the grass field was too small to be a team. The boys were in pads and knee pants. Unmarked white practice helmets hung from their hands. At the opposite end of the field, a man drove a red industrial mower in and out of the end zone. He was trimming the lush, irrigated grass. He paid no attention to the boys. The boys paid no attention to him. They were concentrating on their play.

Will knew in his gut what the situation was: the boys had organized extra practice on their own. It was not punishment. There was no assistant coach shouting from the sideline. There were no cartons of water bottles, no clipboards. Two of the boys, both clad in sagging orange jerseys, seemed to be in charge. They took snaps from some of the other boys, backpedaled, then threw the ball down the field. Neither of them had a great arm, but they knew what they wanted to do.

It had been a long while since he had played football. He had been decent. Lost Cabin High School was big enough to field only a six-man team, so he had played both offense and defense. He had been on the field for nearly every play for four years, as had his brothers when they were the right age. Defensive back. Receiver. He had even been the kicker for one year, though he hadn't been any good at it. He could remember the faces, and the attitudes, of all the boys he had ever played with. C. J. Corwyn, who had been quarterback before he moved to Evanston so his mother could shack up with a railroader who worked for the Union Pacific. Lester Monk, who had spent time at the Boys' School in Worland for stealing tires. Patrick Messner. Robbie Oldman from the reservation. Cade Cegelski, who'd been killed in a car accident he hadn't caused. Travis Bonham, who had pestered Lacey to go out with him until she'd given in, then gotten her pregnant. Travis might be the one who finally married Lacey, and Will had to admit he didn't like the thought of that. He really didn't. It didn't set right. Lacey was worth something. Travis had always been about flattening things down to a plain, unmoving state. Travis's nature would have worked well on their football team if he hadn't been so slow off the ball, and so surly.

He remembered the grass stains that ran from his wrists to his bloody elbows. The scabs. The spit. He remembered Everett's old cleats. They were much too large for him. He had lashed them to his smaller feet with white athletic tape. The cleats had filled with melted snow and were like two sinking canoes the night they lost to the team from Cokeville.

The boys on the field in front of him were mostly quiet. They used a silent count at the line, and they didn't shout at one another, even if the throw was good. He could see how weary they were. He was watching them through a storm fence that ran along the back of the gas station. He was more than two hundred yards away, but their fatigue was obvious, and familiar. The larger boys had bibs of sweat on their chests and between their shoulder blades.

It was all right, he thought, playing with no crowd in the stands. It might even be better that way.

He turned to go into the gas station. He wanted something cold to drink, and maybe some information about the local restaurants. Behind him, a shout cut into the heavy air. He could hear the words over the buzz of the distant mower. *Yeah. Yes.* No applause. No band music or head wagging from the parents. He liked that. Just the affirmation from one boy to another. A single word, rising into the air.

They weren't ready for him at the estancia. He wasn't surprised. Some of the Texas horse people he knew claimed that everything was slow and disorganized when it came to South Americans. The same was true of Italians, they said. The English were the best to deal with, according to the Texans, assuming you could break through their English snottiness and get them to talk to you at all.

Estancia Flora. It wasn't far from Anaheim, easy to find. The gate was a pair of white rail stanchions decorated with a small sign and heavy clusters of red, full-mouthed flowers. The polo fields were right up front. He would later be told the place had started as a training facility for Thoroughbreds. Don Enrique had torn out one of the racetracks and put in enough sod for two polo pitches.

He eased the Cadillac up the white pebble driveway. None of the horses were out. He could see some low, red-roofed barns, a parked horse van, a brick ranch house that was nearly hidden by a thick grove of fruit trees. Everything was lined with white fences or freshly trimmed hedges. Very neat. He knew that he had been right to plan an arrival without any fanfare. He didn't see another human being until he slipped his car in next to the unmarked van.

The boy made no attempt to greet him. Instead, the boy actually seemed to run away, back into one of the barns, toward what he would come to know as Edwards's office. He guessed that wasn't so unusual. Strangers needed to be announced at a place full of expensive horses. Wariness was proper.

He waited, just as he would have in Wyoming, where it was good manners to stay by your truck or car until the property owner had an opportunity to scope you out.

There was nothing obviously unusual about the estancia. He knew the Flora wasn't Don Enrique's central operation. It might not even have been the don's biggest horse property in California. Foreigners tended to spread out their investments. For tax reasons. And because that was the way important landowners did things in their home countries. Randal Clague, the Passantes' trainer, had once told him horse properties were like mistresses. It wasn't a good idea to put them too close to one another. Will leaned against the hot metal of the Cadillac's hood and listened to the strange and vocal birds of California. Some of them sounded like broken bamboo whistles.

You looking for somebody?

The question came from a smallish man dressed in jeans and a dark T-shirt. His hair was gray at the temples and had been recently wet-combed. A stylish mustache rested in the middle of a creased and sun-browned face. The man's ears lay very close to his head, like those of a terrier. He couldn't have sounded more unfriendly.

My name is Will Testerman, he said. I'm here on invitation from Don Enrique. Maybe he mentioned me.

The man was surprised. He hadn't expected anything to dislodge his guard-dog act.

I met Don Enrique in Jackson Hole, Wyoming, at a sale, Will continued. He saw me ride. He said he needed help training horses.

I don't know anything about that, the man said. He was American, and he sounded like he came from the East. His accent had a kind of sharpness to it.

I talked to him not two weeks ago, Will said. He told me to come on down. You can call him if you want. I'm not trying to disrupt nothing.

Except that he was a disruption. It was the same every time he looked for a new job. Suspicion. Competition. Distrust and orneriness. Nobody liked it when a new rider or trainer showed up at a barn. It made the existing help expendable.

What did you say your name was?

Will Testerman. I've done my share of horse work here and there. I'm hoping to learn about training them for polo.

The man's face remained unmoved. This was Edwards's way, as he would come to recognize it — blank, unhelpful. Edwards knew how to freeze his face. But his hands unmasked him. He curled his hands backward, protective.

I need to call Don Enrique, the man said.

No problem.

He might be hard to get to. He doesn't always answer his phone. I can't just have anybody showing up here. The don's very protective.

I understand, Will said.

So I need to call.

Edwards turned on his heel and left. As

he disappeared into the shadows of the first barn, he shouted something in Spanish. Will couldn't hear what it was. But he could imagine. Edwards, who would turn out to be the manager of the whole place, had asked his employees to keep a sharp eye on the stranger.

He continued to lean against the Cadillac. No wandering. No scrutiny. Nothing that would give anybody a reason to throw him out. He pretended to listen to the birds. There was more than one kind of bird hidden among the shiny leaves of the fruit trees. He could tell that now. One kind was making a sweet sort of song. The other kind was quarreling. What he really wanted to get a sense of was the horses. He could smell them — perspiration, dander, manure, their piss. He could hear the rattle of buckets, and the occasional long-nosed mutter. They were in those shady, red-roofed barns, more than thirty of them.

Gustavo would later claim the boys were watching him. All five of them. Or maybe only four, because Dodo would have been afraid to join in. We watch you like thief, Gustavo said. Will was never sure whether this meant that they thought he was a thief or that they believed they were stealthy enough to rob him themselves. No matter.

He hadn't noticed any of them except toward the very end, when Edwards returned with an irritated aggression to his walk. Will saw one or two small, shaggy heads silhouetted in the afternoon gloom of an inner doorway as Edwards approached. Grooms, he thought. Don Enrique has cut corners and hired boys for grooms.

You must shit gold, Edwards said from the doorway to the first barn. I'm supposed to give you a room. The don will be down to talk to both of us later in the week.

Thank you, Will said.

Don't, Edwards said. I work for the don. I do what he says. But these ideas he gets at parties don't usually work out. I'm not a schoolteacher. You need to know that.

We didn't meet at a party, Will said.

Edwards was walking away by then, stiff backed, his fingers bunched tight into his hands. You know what I mean, he said.

They weren't actually boys. They were teenagers, and Néstor, who had been at the Flora the longest, claimed to be twenty-five, older than Will himself. But they didn't look like full-grown men. They were small boned and skinny and underdeveloped. They wore the kind of clothes American parents might pick out for shy children — loose jeans,

264

cheap canvas sneakers, knit shirts with collars and stripes. Even the ones who were taller, like crazy Gustavo, were so thin, their height didn't register. They were from cities in Argentina, and they claimed to have papers that allowed them to work in America. At least two — Gustavo and the one they called Dodo — had been badly injured at some point. Dodo was blind in one eye. He wore a black patch. Gustavo's triangular face was a disturbing assembly of crude skin grafts. Will had to keep himself from staring the first time he saw Gustavo. He had met all types in the horse business. It wasn't work that required good looks or the ability to talk well, or even talk at all. Barn work was mostly about following orders.

Edwards showed him a room at the end of the second barn. The barn was newly renovated, and the room, though narrow, was freshly Sheetrocked and painted. It featured one window. There was no closet and no carpet, but there was a toilet next door. A twin-sized mattress that had been hard used was splayed across the bare concrete floor. A two-ring hot plate rested in one corner, unplugged.

This is what I got, Edwards said, his arms across his chest. It's better than living with the noisy *hermanos.* Promise me you won't burn the place down.

All right, Will said, hesitant. He was all too aware of Edwards's hostility, the way the other man liked to announce his negative feelings out loud. This is fine, he continued. I can sleep anywhere. I can sleep in my car. What I can't do is get along good here if you don't work with me.

I didn't know you were coming.

Can you stand to have me around? Will asked.

I don't know, Edwards said. I'm not sure what I'm supposed to do with you. I can always use help. But the situation is . . . fluid around here. You're going to find that out. Don Enrique's very particular.

He invited me to come.

You already mentioned that, Edwards said, his mouth going tight like a cable. What you don't know is the details of the business I'm supposed to operate. You might not like them.

You play polo?

Edwards shifted on his feet. He looked like he wanted to hit somebody. Yes, I play polo, he said, loudly. I'm better at it than anyone you've ever met.

Will knew that was true. Edwards was larger than a jockey, but his body gave off the tensile strength of a jockey. He looked like he could stay on a horse that was doing just about anything.

I got more than thirty horses here, Edwards said, most of them green. I got a couple of riders who come over from Santa Barbara once or twice a week. Decent guys. But they don't mess around. They put these babies through the wringer because that's how it's done. Don Enrique and his friends, they are big on bragging about their horses. They like them finished fast.

Sounds like the Arabs, Will said.

You ever work for Arabs? Edwards asked, his dark face burning darker.

No. But I've seen them in some professional situations.

Then that's your first mistake — talking about something you don't really understand. You'd better not do that with the Argentines, I'll tell you that right now.

It don't sound like you want me here, Will said.

I don't. You represent another way for me to get into big fucking trouble. But you're here. The jefe said so. Until he kicks your ass back to Montana or wherever you say you came from, I've got to live with you. You're not afraid of a shovel, are you?

No. I'm not.

Then I want you outside my office in about ten minutes. The heat's starting to ease off. It's time to get some work done.

Edwards stormed away with the nose-first posture of a drill sergeant.

Will went back to the Cadillac to get his duffel bag. He thought it would be smart to keep his saddles locked in the car. If Edwards stayed pissed off, he might have to lock himself in the car, too. Just to keep the peace.

The boys began to trail him as soon as he retrieved his bag. Edwards was out of sight, so they appeared from wherever they had been among the horses and began to follow him the way seagulls followed the hay mower back at home. Curious about the noise. Hungry for tidbits.

Who you? one of them asked. The question was so soft and indistinct, he almost didn't hear it.

My name is Will, he said, turning to the slight, chestnut-haired boy he thought had spoken. I'm here to work for Don Enrique.

Don Enrique, said another boy. *Sí. Sí. Nos paga Don Enrique.*

He likes horses, Will said.

Sí. Hay muchos caballos magníficos aquí.

I hope he's a nice man, Will said. I'd like to learn some of his business. Who are you?

The five boys had bunched up behind him in a formation that reminded Will of weanling calves. They couldn't help themselves, he thought. They were afraid and interested all at once. Not one of them spoke.

He brushed off the rough Spanish he'd picked up in Texas. *Sus nombres?*

The tallest one, the disfigured Gustavo, stepped forward. Gustavo me, he said in a cough of English.

Gustavo, Will repeated.

Ignacio. David. Néstor. And fidgety Dodo, with his eye patch, who seemed nervous even with his friends. Will was quickly able to tell them apart, despite the similarity of their clothes and the massed tangle of their hair.

Can you show me the horses? Will asked, dropping his gray-banded duffel bag into his new room.

The boys shook their heads. No. Only Señor Edwards could show any of the horses.

Are you afraid of the horses? he asked.

No, no. They loved the *caballos*. The *caballos* were fast and beautiful.

So you're afraid of Edwards? he asked, smiling. He realized the stupidity of his question as soon as he uttered it.

No, no. They had much admiration for

269

Señor Edwards, they said. They put their hands in their shallow pockets. They did not mirror his stupid smile.

All right, he said. I guess I'll get to know the horses while I'm shoveling their shit. Should I ask what you fellows think of Don Enrique?

Silence. And a string of beaded, watchful eyes.

We afraid of Don Enrique, Gustavo said, his high-pitched voice very proud. And for him, we work very, very hard. To us, it is same thing.

Edwards lived in the brick house. Will couldn't tell whether he lived there alone or not. A series of cars and trucks came and went via the circular driveway every day. A plumber. A woman who was said to do accounts for Don Enrique. Deliverymen of all kinds. Vehicles were occasionally parked in the driveway overnight. Gustavo said Don Enrique sometimes stayed in the brick house, but only for a single night. Sometimes there were women, yes. Sometimes friends of the don's. Eating and drinking. Loud parties. Gustavo said that was the way of Argentines.

Edwards had relented a little when he saw that Will knew how to break a sweat in a horse barn. But he was sparse with information about himself. He would say only that he had been with the don for five years. He had started in California, spent almost two years in Argentina, a place he claimed to hate, then he'd gotten himself back to America with the opportunity to train premier horses.

You ride for clubs and all that? Will asked on his second day.

I ride for money, Edwards said. That's all it's ever been for me since I was on the team at — He stopped. He was not in the mood to paint a picture of himself. I ride for whoever pays me, he repeated. I train for the pleasure of working with decent animals.

You got some beauties here, Will said. What I've seen of them.

Edwards was noncommittal. They were in his office. Or he was in his office, and Will was standing in the doorway to the office with a rake in his hands. They come and go, Edwards said. I don't have much control over that. There are maybe ten horses here that have done much work with me. Of those, maybe two will make it.

Make it?

Survive the training and the growing up long enough to get into some serious chukkers. It takes years to make a good polo pony. Three, four years just to lay the right base. And you shouldn't even start them until they're four years old, if you're asking me. That's my opinion. Training racehorses is kid's stuff compared to this. Racing is bullshit.

Sounds like it's more along the lines of working with roping horses, Will said.

I don't know anything about ropes, Edwards said. I don't want to know anything about them. Rodeo is bullshit. The only other aspect of horses that's worth a damn is show jumping. And that got ruined by politics.

I've never done the jumping, Will said, feeling itchy in his armpits.

I can tell that, Edwards said, scowling. That's no goddamn surprise.

Gustavo said Edwards was always angry. Like he want to make bomb, Gustavo said. Like he boom-boom inside. Gustavo said Edwards was always working, never taking a break with a glass of wine in his hand, never relaxing with a woman, which was what he clearly needed. Will thought Gustavo was probably right. Edwards was burned out, or close to it.

He did like watching Edwards in the saddle, though. The man had excellent balance and a pair of soft, anticipatory hands.

He rode from the legs, as all the best riders did, and it didn't seem to matter if he was on a gangly, ignorant stud colt or one of the don's precisely muscled mares. Edwards found the center. He rode a horse like he was sailing before a steady wind, just him and the animal, the two of them, gliding.

The mattress was uncomfortable. It was like trying to sleep on a snowmobile seat, a thing he had tried once and only once. The lightbulb that was screwed into the ceiling of his room threw shadows the shape of sickle blades onto the walls. He mostly kept the light off.

What disturbed him most were the sirens. They never seemed to stop. They wailed and pleaded. They yowled through the streets at night and tore through the few dreams his uneasy sleep felt obliged to bring him. Dreams. Of boisterous stock sales where he wanted to bid but had no money. Of drought-racked meadows where he was walking and walking and could find neither a fence line nor a gate.

He dreamed of Annie Atwood during those first days at the estancia. She was always running away from him in the dreams. He thought it was strange that she was running in his new territory, the dry, bare hills of California, and he thought it was strange that he could not quite see her face. He could not see her haunting eyes. She did not speak to him. She ran in silence. But he could see the light-footed speed of her strong legs and the way she paused at the top of each California hill to look back at him, to wait.

There was no good time to break the news to Edwards. But it had to be done. The transport carrying Hawk and the filly could arrive at any time.

I got two horses coming, he said. They belong to me.

It was his third day at Estancia Flora. He was up before dawn to feed horses. They all were.

Edwards looked at him like he'd been asked to empty his wallet.

You what?

My two horses are coming down here on B&T Transport. I believe Don Enrique said I could have my horses here. They've had their vaccinations.

If you're trying to kill me, Edwards said, you're doing a terrific job.

You got room. I'll pay board or work it off. There's empty stalls.

I ought to run you out of here right now,

Edwards said, his face swelling above his mustache. The don doesn't want other horses here, not ever. You don't understand that?

What he said on the phone was —

Those Spanish-speaking fuckers will say anything on the phone. They're impressed by their own good manners. It's what they *do* that matters. You just rolled a cold pair of dice, my friend. I won't have anything to do with your horses, Edwards said. And I want you to remember I said that.

They arrived in the evening. The transport driver had one of the grooms, a sallow man in an L.A. Dodgers jersey, unload Hawk first. There were two other horses on the transport, sprinters headed to the racetrack at Del Mar. Hawk looked fine when he came off. Sleepy. Stiff. He was wearing a light sheet, just as Will had requested, and he was clean except where he had stained his own hind legs with manure.

More than anything else, Hawk wanted fresh grass to eat.

The filly had lost weight, Will was sure of it. He could see her anxiety written into the prominent veins on her face. Her eyes rolled and bulged in their sockets when she got to the door of the transport. The white triangle between her eyes looked like a rocket about to launch. She was being led by the other groom, a woman. He wished they would let him lead the filly off the transport, but they refused. It was against the rules.

The female groom was experienced, but even she was surprised when the filly stopped her descent on the rubber-lined ramp. The filly lifted her head as high as it would go, and she seemed to drink in the air of the estancia. There had been nothing but fuel exhaust and asphalt in her nose for five days, Will thought. At Estancia Flora there was also the scent of exhaust from the road, and the smell of many horses, and the flavors of raked soil and tended grass. The filly made a kind of groaning sound and stooped onto her hocks. The groom dropped the lead line. Will thought the filly was going to rear. Instead, she jumped. It was an awkward jump. The filly resembled a disoriented child dropping from the height of its bunk bed. But she made it to the ground without hurting herself or the groom. Will approached her with his voice, low and familiar. Then he reached toward her with his hands. As he grasped the dangling lead line, she snorted in his direction as though he were something to be sneezed away.

She done good the whole ride until right

then, the groom said. I been with her since Colorado. Timmy picked me up there.

Thank you, he said.

It ain't nothing, the woman said. She wore a pair of painter's pants that were stained and much too large for her body. She had on work boots and a shirt that advertised a truck race. Both of her wrists were strapped with elaborate tattoos. Her face had a hungry look to it, pinched and wanting below the cheeks. Her eyes were all coal and ash. You'll excuse me while I go to the little girls' room, she said. It's my only chance. And she stumbled toward the first barn as though the lower halves of her legs were asleep.

She was sober, Will thought. But she had seen a whole lot more on this trip than the ass end of a few horses.

The trips had been paid for. Will signed papers for the driver, and he paid out reasonable tips to the driver and the grooms. He had cash in his jeans pocket for just that reason. He had been waiting for the transport to arrive, hour after hour. But now that his horses were here, he wasn't exactly sure what he should do with them. He let Hawk graze on the damp grass along the driveway while he held on to the filly. The sallow groom, who had lit a welcome cigarette as soon as he hit the ground, unloaded the equipment that had traveled with the horses. It wasn't much. Some brushes and buckets. Vitamins. Fly ointment.

Some of the birds that lived among the orange trees began to settle into their roosts. They twisted the rusty screws of their voices. There was no sign of Edwards or any of the boys. Will was thankful. The transport driver asked him what people did here.

It's for polo, Will said. That's all they do, I think. Train for polo.

I move polo ponies all the time, the driver said. People pass them along like they're chain letters. Never been here, though. Nice place.

It is nice, Will said. Good horses.

What's it called? the driver asked.

Estancia Flora. The owner is a businessman from Argentina.

The owner is always a businessman, the driver said, laughing. Ain't that right, Martin? That's us. We're goddamned businessmen.

The sallow groom had fired up a second cigarette. He gave a gapped and discolored grin as he sucked hard on the filter, trying to finish before he had to get into the back of the transport.

Polo, huh? the driver said.

Yeah. I don't know much about it. I'm from up in Wyoming. I came down here to learn.

Must be money in it somewhere. Place has got the look of money.

Will nodded. There's money.

And you're here to get some of it, am I right?

Will swung his face away to look at Hawk, who was munching at his grass. It was easier to look at Hawk than at the filly. I guess you could say that, Will said. Not right away. But eventually.

Eventually? The driver, who had the ass-heavy build of many truckers, began to hoist himself back into the squat cab of the transport. Eventually? You must be from Wyoming and not from regular America if that's how you talking about it.

Will chuckled with the driver. It's not all about money, he said.

Yeah, it is, the driver said. Don't fuck with me on that. I've been driving these rigs for a long time. I know what I see. You got to make sure you get to them before they get to you, you hear me? And he laughed again, his unshaved chin blending into his unshaved neck.

Will opened his mouth to respond, but he had no chance. The female groom came striding out of the barn, one hand gripping at her giant unzipped pants, the other raised over her shoulder with its middle finger stuck up into the air.

Fuck that, she said. That pompous prick in there don't want me to use his precious bathroom. I did anyway. But I'll be god-damned if I'll flush.

Let's load up, Jade, the driver said. He was pursing a grin onto his lips. I haven't had enough coffee this morning to survive another wrestling match on your behalf.

I take care of my own self, Jade growled.

On most days, that's a fact, the driver said.

Jade, Will thought, watching the woman belt herself up and begin to lift the transport ramp on her own while the sallow groom looked on. Her hair was dyed so black it looked wet. Of course she would call herself something like Jade.

Both grooms locked the loading ramp into place and jumped into the back of the transport with the remaining horses. They moved like people used to leaving in a hurry.

You remember what I said! the driver shouted as he dropped the transport into gear. I've seen every horse scheme there is. Real estate. Breeding rights. Syndications up the wazoo. This is the U.S. of America.

A smart man gets to them before they get to you.

Before the end, he heard many things about Gustavo. Most of them were true. Some were not. He didn't know how to hammer what he had heard into a decent story.

Gustavo was a clown. Will had learned long ago that when more than two people were brought together to accomplish something, one of them would become the funny one. The woeful one, or the begging one. The one who pretended he had less at stake than the rest. This was Gustavo at the estancia. He was the one who was said to be sloppy with the hoses and the tools. He was the one who acted as though he was nervous with the *potros,* the young horses that needed the calmest kind of care.

In fact, he was a good worker. He made few mistakes. Yet it was impossible to read his damaged face, and this put some distance between him and the others. His cheeks and nose had been refashioned from a wide, yellowish slab of skin taken from some other place on his body — his stomach, Will guessed — and there wasn't any understandable movement in that skin. There were no nerves in it. His nostrils were barely visible. His neck bore the signs of terrible burns, as did both hands. He wore long-sleeved shirts. Néstor said Gustavo had been injured when the stove he operated on the streets of Buenos Aires exploded. It was a common accident, Néstor said. Children and old women were often burned while they cooked the yams or meat they hoped to sell.

Gustavo made up for his masked face by using the rest of his body. He was always pointing and waving, except around the horses. He was always dancing. He liked to leap onto the bony backs of his compatriots as if he were a tiny, ardent monkey and to cling there, screeching. He exhorted his friends with nonsense. They, in turn, teased him mercilessly about his tragic passion for the Buenos Aires soccer club he worshipped to the point of tears. They sang obscene songs about the soccer club. They cursed it. And they loved Gustavo enough to remind him of his accident in their crude and tender ways. *Chico quemado, chico de aceite,* they mocked. You cannot work a stove as well as an old woman. You are more worthless than a priest. Gustavo would run at his friends just as a luckless dog runs at a group of strutting crows. Assholes! he would shout, whirling his scarred hands at the wrists. Sons of whores.

Gustavo had supposedly worked for Don Enrique back in Argentina, the same as the others.

Gustavo lived in a cinder-block room in the first barn with Dodo and Ignacio. The room had once been a feed room. It had no windows. Néstor and David lived on an elevated shelf in a closed shed with the tractor. All the cooking and eating and talking took place in the former feed room. The air there smelled of fried potatoes and peppers.

You are rich man, Gustavo said one day.

I doubt it, Will said.

You have auto, Gustavo said, making a flourish with his speckled fingers. You have keys to auto.

Will didn't like to remember how he had ended up with the Cadillac. The car looked good parked in the estancia's parking lot, but that was about it. I see your point, he said. But the car's old. I don't have much else. I don't own land. Don't you measure a man that way in your country — if he's got land?

Gustavo considered Will for a moment. *Sí,* he said. *No tienes finca grande.* His dirty bangs covered his eyes. He relaxed his face until his hairless jaw hung open. He seemed to be playing stupid.

The *potranca* who came, she is yours?

Yes, Will said.

You bring her to Don Enrique as the gift? No.

Then you are rich man, Gustavo said.

I guess I do all right, Will said, knowing he needed to tread carefully. He didn't want the boys to get the wrong ideas about him. I don't know about polo, he said. I'm ignorant there.

Ah, Gustavo said, his wet mouth hanging open again. Ah.

That's why I come down here. To learn how to make horses for the game.

There was another long pause. Will wondered, not for the first time, if Gustavo was all there in the head.

What you call the *potranca*?

Huh?

What is name for *la potranca bonita*?

She don't have a registered name. She's young. I call her filly, mostly.

Fill-ee? Gustavo seemed unconvinced by the word.

Or Tick. Sometimes I call her that. It's from Ticket, which is part of her dam's name.

Teek-et? Gustavo shook his shaggy head. No, no, he said. No word, no good.

Will wished he had a bridle in his hands. Or even a bucket of feed. Gustavo had caught him in the aisle of the second barn, between tasks. It's just what I call her, he said.

You no know pol-o, Gustavo said, mimicking Will's words and the slow, careful American way he said them.

That's right.

But you learn, Gustavo said. *Sí.* You are *estudiante.* And man of riches. *Así tiene que ser.* Gustavo ended his statement with a quick snap to attention, heels squared together, rebuilt nose aimed high toward the barn roof. His mischievous, greenish eyes were closed. He held the pose for a long time. Will thought the stance must be how soldiers or policemen stood in Argentina. He didn't know. Néstor had said there were a lot of police in Argentina. All he knew was that he was being messed with. He wasn't sure he liked it.

El polo bonito, Gustavo said. Beautiful game. And he let his jaw hang down again, as if it had no bone inside it, while he laughed.

They were lovely animals. Short backed and quick. Deep in the girth, for stamina. Their coats bore the sheen of metal. Most of them were small, under sixteen hands, and they displayed the musculature particular to their business. They didn't have the heavy hind-quarters he was used to in roping and rein-ing horses. Their necks were long and lean, perfect pedestals for their chiseled heads.

A great horse could be better at the game than its rider, Edwards said. A great one could read the ball and the weaknesses of the defenders' horses. It could maneuver you right to the goal.

The made horses, the ones that had proved themselves after years of patient training, were kept in the second barn. That was also where the filly stayed. Néstor was in charge of the made horses. He took them out in sets just after dawn, when the sun was beginning to simmer in the milk-colored sky. Six horses at a time. Will helped Néstor sometimes, both of them mounted on old campaigners. They circled the pitches like two tight gaggles of geese. The dozens of thumping hooves beat out an eager work-ing rhythm.

The green horses, the *potros,* were in the first barn. They still had their manes and forelocks. They would not be shaved until they had proved themselves. There were Thoroughbreds there, and quarter horses, and horses of unknown origin that had been found for Don Enrique by various agents. Some of them had cost a lot of money.

Some were destined to be washouts. Will could see their shortcomings in their movements or their attitudes, even when they were only being led from one place to another by Gustavo or Dodo or David. But they all received excellent care. Baths. And brushing. Individualized diets. Handling every day. They were an investment. Each time he looked at them, he felt what a horseman always feels — saturated joy at the sight of so much possibility. Beneath that joy his hard-earned knowledge of animal failure rolled like a heavy stone.

He had seen the game once or twice in Jackson. But that was all he had seen — the game. When Edwards mounted the liver chestnut mare that was called Captiva, or the gray known only as El Argent, their partnership was a thing he examined with hunger. For Edwards, the horses covered ground in a fluent, rocking canter. Their mouths were as responsive as the wings of birds. The manager regularly put his charges through what he called linear work. Will watched horse and rider slalom smoothly, and expertly, from one end of the pitch to the other, mallet swinging, ball rolling, the horse switching its leads and maintaining the graceful center of gravity that was the gift of all athletes.

They were trained to be calm in the center of chaos. They would go eye-to-eye at speed when they were asked. They would war with one another if they had to. That was how Edwards talked about them when he was at his most intense — as creatures of war. But that was not how the boys spoke of them. The boys spoke of the horses as if they were aunts or brothers or *padrónes* in a great extended family they someday hoped to join.

Ignacio made a small mistake. He parked the mower between barns, and he left the mower deck up. Hawk was still getting used to the estancia. He didn't expect the mower. He jigged right into the sharp edge of the mower deck as Will was directing him into the barn after they had taken a short walk. He cut himself.

Gustavo said that if Edwards knew about the accident, Ignacio would get the big boom. He pantomimed a fist pounding into a face as he spoke. Will didn't really believe Edwards beat the boys with his fists, but he couldn't be sure. He knew better than to mention the incident.

The cut on Hawk's ankle didn't heal like Will thought it should, however. Ignacio was sorry for his mistake, but Will asked him to keep his hands off the Appaloosa. He cleaned the cut twice a day himself, though he did not bandage it. It was best for the wound to dry in open air. Except that California was more humid than he was used to. He worried about infection. He used sulfa powder on the cut, and he got permission from Edwards to give Hawk a shot of the antibiotic Edwards kept locked in the refrigerator in his office. He made up a story about the injury, something that kept the blame on him, which was where Edwards liked it. He wondered what other things Edwards kept locked in the refrigerator. The manager was secretive.

Hawk didn't favor the ankle much. He could put weight on it. But Will knew infection had the power to get ahead of him and of Hawk both. He needed to be careful. Edwards had made it clear that a veterinarian could not come to the estancia without permission from Don Enrique.

The cut bothered him not because it was serious — he had seen worse, much worse — but because it wasn't that serious and, thus, could lead to bad or lazy calculations. He remembered how his neighbors back home, the Bookbinders, had gotten into trouble when a colt Linda Bookbinder was trying to raise had cut itself on a strand of forgotten wire. The Bookbinders were sheep people. They had a patchwork ranch northwest of the Testermans. But they always kept horses, and sometimes goats for milk, and sometimes chickens. The Bookbinders liked to try things. Linda Bookbinder was the boss. She was the oldest daughter, and she stayed in a new model trailer that was set perpendicular to the one-story ranch house where her mother and father still lived. The trailer didn't quite fit the property. Linda didn't fit, either. She lived in the trailer with her friend Bonnie, who worked at the IGA grocery in Lost Cabin. Will didn't really think about the implications of that arrangement until he was in high school. His parents never said anything about it, and neither did the Bookbinders, probably because Bonnie was a good hand with the sheep and had grown up in nearby Farson. Linda Bookbinder had a married sister who lived in Casper and a brother who worked at the binocular factory in Riverton. Neither of them put in much time on the ranch. It was like his father said: You never get the children you ask for. You're damn lucky to get children you can use.

Linda bought the colt at Bent Stallworth's auction on a whim. He was a weanling, nothing but knobby knees and mitten ears.

She asked Will if he would break the colt for her when the time came.

Sure, he said. He was thirteen. He had never trained a horse for anyone outside the family. He was at the Bookbinders', cleaning the eave troughs on the main house because Linda had hired him to do that. Linda liked things tidy. He liked Linda. She was a big woman. She wore her pants belted tight around her middle as though she were afraid her stomach might get away from her somehow. She had a megaphone laugh, and her temper tantrums never lasted long enough to really scare him.

He didn't see Bonnie much. Bonnie worked long hours in town and was thick into the Moose Lodge, which was a thing Linda didn't care for.

Linda and Bonnie also liked to quarrel. His mother told him it was healthy.

They're just being honest, his mother said. It's a good trait. I'd quarrel with your father a lot more if he'd let me drag him into it. Silence isn't always golden if you love somebody enough. You might want to remember that.

He didn't see the colt for many months. Winter came. On warm days, Mr. Bookbinder, a World War II veteran whose back had fully given out on him, would drive all the Bookbinder horses into a stubbled field that Will could see from the main road. The colt was growing. That was all he could determine.

Linda called him in February and asked if he'd come put the colt in a halter. Bonnie has macraméd him something she wants him to wear on his head, Linda said. It looks like a Minnesota Vikings jockstrap. I won't have it. He's an animal. I need you to get over here and treat him like one.

The colt was wild and spark eyed. He'd stand still only for a carrot. He'd been spoiled, but Will knew that was something that could be fixed. Anybody could work a colt out of being spoiled.

Bonnie would move him into our bedroom if she could, Linda said, pulling a striped knit hat down over her ears. The sheep were in pens near the house because it was nearly time to lamb. They filled the gray air with their anxious, stuttering cries. He's not too bad, Will said. He just needs some handling.

Bonnie thinks he's a baby. I'm not much better, Linda said. You might have to save us from ourselves.

But he got busy with the high school rodeo team. Linda didn't call him again until the colt was hurt.

Can you come over here? Linda asked.

We're having a fight about keeping the baby as a stud colt. I'm looking for advice.

The colt was much taller. His hooves needed to be trimmed, and his winter coat made him looked more muscled than he was. He was sand colored, tending toward dun. Will suspected the colt wouldn't be very good-looking when he was full grown. He was already a little frog eyed.

Bonnie shook his hand when she came out of the trailer dressed for work in a red apron and a large plastic name tag. She was like that. She was always saying people's names and shaking their hands.

I think we ought to breed him, Bonnie said. He's got a good nature.

I got no interest in a stud horse, Linda said. They are nothing but trouble.

What happened to his leg? Will asked.

Nothing, Linda said. He got tangled in a roll of fence wire. Got himself right out. I'm treating him with powder.

She won't call the vet, Bonnie said. She's cheaper than my dad, which is really saying something.

I did call the vet, Linda said. He told me to keep it clean. It's not infected or nothing.

The wound wasn't infected, at least not that Will could see. It wasn't weeping or open. It looked more like a fat string of some kind had coiled itself under the skin on the colt's right hind leg.

I'm the one who's cleaning it, Bonnie said. Like I got the time for that.

You can shut up now, Linda said. She was only half smiling.

You think too much about money, Bonnie said.

I think about everything, Linda said, her voice taking on the long notes of a trucker's horn. I think about what it takes to keep this place going until it nearly kills me. We don't need to get into this again. The colt is not a pet. Will here backs me up on that.

Will didn't speak. He turned away from Linda and pretended to examine the colt again.

A stud horse would make money, Bonnie said.

You don't know a damn thing about it. Shut up. Go to work. Go to your little store and bitch about me to Leslie Turnslip the way you do. We're going to cut the balls off this colt and put him to use.

You go to hell, Bonnie said. She was younger than Linda and took the time to wear makeup for her job. Will could see how much her feelings were hurt. Her fingernails were scratching into the palms of her hands.

And her whole back was shaking.

I might do that, Linda said. It would give me some peace from you.

Bonnie drove off to work in her waxed GMC pickup. She was sobbing.

I'm trying to get her to take some responsibility, Linda said, yanking at the weeds that had frozen around the edge of her corral. I've told her this colt is hers, but she don't have good sense about him.

The situation didn't improve. Neither woman could agree to a single course of action. The colt developed an infection in the bone. Bonnie and Linda couldn't get ahead of it, not even with the help of the veterinarians in Riverton. They had to trailer the colt to the veterinary school in Fort Collins, Colorado. They spent a fortune to save a mutt horse that would forever have problems with his hind leg. The outcome gave them plenty to fight about.

She don't have the sense of a tree stump, Linda said to Will about Bonnie when he came over one afternoon to help shovel out the lambing sheds. She's stupid about almost everything, but I keep on loving her. Has anybody talked to you about that, Will Testerman, how love makes you stupid? Your dumb brothers ever talk to you? You love anybody yet?

My parents, he said after a pause. At that time Everett had a girlfriend who seemed to spend most of her time acting like Everett was some kind of deep mystery. Will thought she was obnoxious.

That don't count, Linda said, zipping herself into a set of crusted coveralls. Her face was a stack of deep folds that almost hid her eyes and mouth. He didn't see how she could ever be considered pretty. Her nose and cheeks were too big. He was thirteen and thought all women were destined to look good. He didn't know if Linda cared how she looked or not. She sure didn't talk about it.

You'll love somebody enough to try to live with them someday, Linda said. It'll strangle you. It'll bring you right down to your knees and make you want to cut your nuts off. I'm telling you the truth.

I don't aim to get married, he said.

I'm not talking about marriage, Linda said, squawking into the laugh she used on her ridiculous, ungovernable sheep. I'm talking about love. It'll come onto you like a March blizzard. It'll beat the rhythm right out of your heart if you let it.

Maybe I won't let it.

Ha, Linda squawked. That's the best damn part. It's not an option. Love is like a hospital germ. It don't give you a choice.

It was hot in his room. The window cut into the back wall was so new, it still had the manufacturer's label on its frame. But the window didn't open. Nothing got in or out except the slow yellow smear of the sun. What he couldn't explain was the row of insects trapped between the energy-efficient panes of window glass. Wasps. Mosquitoes. Bumblebees as big as the end his thumb. How had they gotten in there? They were laid out side by side, like bodies in a morgue.

He didn't like the smell of the room when it got hot. The smell was sour and soaked all at once. Acidic. He thought the smell came from the Sheetrock and the way people put up Sheetrock in California.

He slept outside as much as he could. All he needed was a blanket. There was a shaded place at the far end of the second barn. The grass was thick and soft. It sometimes even attracted dew. He could hear the horses better from out there, anyhow, and he liked to be able to hear them in the night, the way they stirred and shifted. The way they spoke. He had to get up very early if he wanted to sleep in that place. He didn't want to have to explain himself to Edwards. He also had to cope with the centipedes. They, too, sought the moisture that came into that corner. And they liked the folds of his blanket.

Gustavo and the boys never complained about the heat. They didn't seem to sweat the way he did, either. They worked hard enough to sweat. Edwards drove them like slaves. They just seemed built for the climate. They were thin skinned and as lean as racing dogs. Gustavo, in particular, kept his hair as long as Edwards would allow because all his soccer heroes wore long hair. The hair also covered his burns. Will could hardly stand the small amount of hair he kept on his own head when he wore a safety helmet to ride, which was one of Edwards's many rules. His head always felt like it was half-boiled. He rinsed it under the water pump several times a day.

Some nights he would lie on his narrow pallet of grass and listen to the lives of the Mexicans who occupied the modular homes on the other side of the estancia's high wooden fence. A television was always on, often more than one, and the televisions led lives of great drama. The voices on the television whispered, or argued, with urgency. There were radios, too. He heard the kind of brassy music that Jorge had played when they were both mucking stalls at the Passantes' place in Texas, and he heard the thumping beats that younger people liked. Children wandered behind the squeezed-together houses and cried. Dogs barked at nothing. He liked it when the women from two of the adjoining houses spoke to one another over their yard fence in the dark, giggling in Spanish, or complaining. He had actually seen the woman who lived in the closest house. She was young and slender and seemed to care for only two children. Her man was away, according to Gustavo. He had a job elsewhere. This meant that Gustavo, ever the huckster, had tried to befriend her.

Estella, Gustavo said. *Muy bonita mujer.* She like me plenty.

She like what you wish to give her, Ignacio said, thrusting his hips. *Pobre mujer.* She must come to me for that.

Gustavo grabbed at his own crotch, which made the others laugh. They did not believe a woman with eyes would ever touch Gustavo.

I know her well, Gustavo said.

She's got a swimming pool, Will said. I've heard her kids playing in the water. I'd like to meet anybody who has a swimming pool.

Ignacio and Néstor looked at him as

though he had proposed armed robbery. He thought they'd misunderstood his English.

Ah, Gustavo said, lifting the eyebrow on the better side of his face. You would talk to her?

Maybe, Will said. It wouldn't mean nothing to talk to her. I'd just be friendly.

But it would mean something. The boys were sure of that. Will felt like he was living in a different country at the estancia. He felt like he was always catching up with the way the Argentines saw things.

Estella have party, Gustavo said, sweetly.

I ain't never heard that. It's pretty quiet over there. Just neighbors. And sometimes kids messing around in the pool.

I give her party, Gustavo said.

Ignacio threw up his dirty hands and left to tend the mower that had broken down again. None of them should be dawdling, Will knew that. But it was the first time they had spoken of a woman who didn't belong to Don Enrique or some stratum of the don's world.

You ask, Gustavo said, pointing a finger at him. You ask if she will talk and dance with us. Tell her I have money. She will see how you rich, rich and white. She will hear your words.

I don't think so, Will said.

300

You promise, Gustavo said. He was on his tiptoes, fluttering like he did.

I didn't promise.

You promise. Viva, Guillermo! Viva! A large smile cracked open beneath the make-believe shape of Gustavo's nose. You are *norteamericano,* he said. We are strongest friends, no? You must give party.

We ain't here to have parties.

You afraid of the womans? Gustavo asked.

I don't think so. I'm more worried about getting into trouble. We can't be bothering the neighbors.

Estella say she has *niño* like me. He far, far away. Estella say he in army. She lonely.

Will didn't see how the woman he'd heard through the fence could be old enough to have a boy in the army. She'd sounded young, but everyone who spoke fast Spanish tended to sound young to him.

We don't need to be bothering Estella, he repeated.

She lonely. We make small party?

Will shook his head. Not a good idea, he said. Edwards will let us know when we can have a party.

Señor Edwards is *mierda grande,* Gustavo said, *mierda grande.* And he spat on the ground. He care for *negocio* only.

Maybe so, Will said. Maybe that's how it

works for him. I don't know. Him and me don't talk much. But I know he expects us to do our jobs.

This job not me, Gustavo said. And he spat again. Señor Edwards and Don Enrique not all of me.

He began to work her at night, when he couldn't sleep. She didn't mind. She was awake when he came to her stall, calm but alert, her ears as full of movement as the fringe on a dress. La Soledad, a black mare Edwards was training for Don Enrique, was awake, too. And she wanted to leave her stall. Always. He liked that about La Soledad, her desire to work.

He went as far away from the barns as he could, toward the gates of the estancia and the road. If the sprinklers were on, he turned them off. There was enough light from the road, and from the neighborhood, for them to do what they needed to do. Groundwork. And more groundwork. He was strapping the filly into a pair of training reins now, teaching her to use her gaits in a very tight series of circles. He also worked with a saddle pad and a racing saddle he found in the estancia's tack room. He got her used to wearing light tack. She never balked. She accepted the hand-warmed

O-ring snaffle bit when he introduced it to her mouth. And she stood quietly when he wrapped her legs in bandages and strapped her ankles into boots. She seemed to like new things.

They did their work while bats scribbled the blue air above them. Sometimes the bats dove very low, dipping between him and the filly as newly hatched insects rose from the grass. Cars were on the road at all hours, glittering lowriders with melodic horns and murmuring engines. Sometimes he heard shouts from the neighborhood, human voices that seemed temporarily lost in their own volume. More often it was cats prowling the fence lines, looking to fight one another.

She appeared to be a different color in the dark, the red variations in her coat shadowing toward the maroon tints of raw muscle, but she was not a different animal. He knew how beautiful she was. It was times like these, when they were in a quiet space that felt very far away, that he allowed himself to speak the truth out loud. Beautiful. The sight of her midnight silhouette made his hands ache.

He knew Edwards would never admit it, but Edwards thought the filly was a beauty, too. Will had spotted the manager looking at the filly in her stall more than once.

When they were finished, he cooled her out by walking her along the far edges of the estancia. He told her stories about California. He talked about the folded, yellow hills and the ocean that was not so far away. He mentioned the elementary school he had seen, how the children there played games with ropes and balls in the sand and how they never needed to wear coats, like kids did in Wyoming. He talked about the bodega where he sometimes bought fresh fruit for himself and for the boys. They were short stories. He didn't know much about this part of California. And he didn't want to make too much noise. He was sure Edwards knew he was out with the filly during the night. For some reason, Edwards had not tried to stop them.

He would take her back to the barn and check to make sure she had water. He would unwrap her legs in the warm stew of her stall. La Soledad watched them from her own stall, the wide blaze on her black face stabbing through the shadows like a knife as she bobbed her head up and down, up and down, eager, hoping. One night he just stayed in the filly's stall. He sat down in the corner and drew his knees up to his chest and decided to stay. He wanted to hear her breathe. It would not be the same as when she was trotting on the long line, when she was exerting herself at his command. These would be her slow and unconsidered breaths. Her way into sleep. It would be all right if he didn't sleep much. He could use the time to think.

At one point, she came and stood closer to him, almost as a dog would. She didn't touch him, and she didn't block his way to the stall door. She watched him for several long minutes, her eyes soft, unalarmed. He noticed that her coat looked almost purple in the barn's version of the dark, purple and rare.

I'd sure like to know what's in your head right now, he said.

He recalled a story his brother Everett loved to tell about his friend Darrin. Darrin had tried to set himself up in the outfitting business. He got permits, bought horses, and pitched an elk-hunting camp in a mountain spot no one else wanted. It was hard going. Darrin and his clients had to push farther and farther into the mountains to even see an elk. One rotten night, with the snow cutting sideways like a full set of saw blades, the entire string of horses got loose. Darrin nearly froze himself solid going after them. Two of the horses were never found.

They were destined to be eaten by bears in the spring, if they lasted that long. Or the wolves would get them. That was the conventional wisdom. But Darrin spread the word about his missing horses. They were still worth money to him.

The end of the story was funny as hell, according to Everett. A Game and Fish pilot found the two horses way the hell deep in the Absaroka Mountains more than a year later when he was flying a game survey. The horses were living, and living just fine, with a group of bull elk. Everett yowled every time he told the story. Some of the elk were trophy size, he said, laughing. Bigger than anything Darrin ever got his clients close to with a rifle. And those stupid horses, Fred and Leroy, thought they fit right in with those gigantic bulls. The Game and Fish pilot just about wrecked his plane when he saw them. Horses living like bulls.

Just goes to show what a horse really thinks, Everett said. A horse wants to be as far away from the human jackass as it can get. They want to be boss. They want to be trophy. They're just looking for their chance.

Is that so? Will asked the filly as he thought about the story. He was sitting upright with his fingers laced across his knees. Are you the one that's gonna decide what happens next?

He didn't know why he had gotten out his lariat. Maybe it was because he missed riding Hawk. He had ridden Hawk only once before his ankle got cut. They had saddled up to take a set of older horses out for some morning work. It hadn't gone so well. Hawk was a cow horse. He was used to the obstinacy of cattle. The *caballos* had their own thoughts about how they wanted to be led in the mornings. They hadn't been impressed with Hawk.

He took the lariat from the trunk of the Cadillac just to feel it in his hands. He was tired. He hadn't been eating or sleeping like he should. He was frustrated. Edwards had given him a little more responsibility, but he had been baiting the situations as well. There was no sign of Don Enrique. That morning, Edwards had asked him to ride a very good horse at the same time that Andre and Stefan, the riders from Santa Barbara, were on the field. Will was supposed to imitate the others as they went through some linear work. Even without a mallet, he'd been a complete fuck-up. The horse had been willing. It was an agile gelding with an ugly ax-blade head and a wonderful mouth. But Will hadn't been able to find a rhythm for the two of them. He kept sitting back, sliding deep into the cantle of the unfamiliar saddle and resorting to cues that would have been better understood by a ranch horse. Edwards finally shouted at him to get the fuck off the pitch. Stefan and Andre rested their gloved hands on the pommels of their saddles. He could see their white smiles above the heavy chin straps of their helmets. They were used to Edwards's temperament.

He stepped onto the long, twilight-blurred driveway of the estancia and made a loop. The night was still. It smelled of exhausted flowers. The three-ply rope felt alive in his hands, flexible and ready. He tossed at nothing. The rope made a slight hissing sound as it passed through the fingers of his left hand. Again. This time he aimed at a particular spot.

Dodo found him first. This was the single problem with Dodo. He was as silent on his feet as he was with his mouth. He was always showing up out of nowhere. The one-eyed boy appeared in his Disneyland sweatshirt and jeans and watched Will draw the rope back toward himself with the expert teamwork of his hands. Will hefted the thirty-foot coil and tapped it slightly against his left thigh. Then he split the coil without looking down and made a stiff, whirling loop. This time, he threw at a low fence post maybe fifteen feet away. He hooked it easily.

Dodo pressed his hands together as though he wanted to applaud. Then he disappeared.

But he was back with the others in a very short time. They thronged around Will as if he was handing out Pepsis or pictures of naked women.

Gaucho, David said, drawing his sternum up toward his chin. *Don Guillermo es el mejor gaucho aquí.*

You capture *las vacas*? Néstor asked.

Yes, I can rope a cow.

And all the *potros*?

Sí, I could catch the *potros* if I had a good mount like Hawk. I'd have to do it one at a time.

The womans, Dodo whispered. *¿Atrapas las mujeres?*

I ain't roping no women, he said, looking at Gustavo for emphasis. This is just for fun. It's something I miss doing.

Learn us, Gustavo said. He seemed quite serious for once. It was late in the evening. They had eaten. They had done all they were supposed to do. The sky over the

309

brush-tangled hills was the color of new denim. He thought it might be a good thing, showing them how to rope. It was something he'd been doing with other people his entire life.

He started with Dodo. Dodo was terrible with his left hand. He didn't know how to use it at all. But Dodo had a good right arm. Will made a loop for him and showed him how to aim for his target. Once he figured out how to work his wrist into his follow-through, Dodo was able to make a pretty good throw.

Gustavo strode down the driveway and posed himself as a target.

Aquí, he said, *aquí.*

Too high, Will said. You need to squat down. And watch your eyes.

He made another loop for Dodo, and Dodo threw it. He did not get the rope over Gustavo.

Otra vez, Dodo whispered. The light in his single eye was like the head of a burning match.

He looped Gustavo on his third throw. Everyone cheered.

He tried to work with them all. Every fourth or fifth attempt, he would make a loop for himself and throw it to remind them what the motion should look like.

310

Gustavo remained the target. When the white loop shushed over his shoulders, Gustavo would shiver like a beaten dog and grin.

We need to set up a bale of hay, Will said finally. We need to get a bale and work up some sort of target on the bale that you all can practice on. That's how I learned. We put a calf's head, a plastic one, on a bale of hay, and I threw until my whole arm ached. All it takes is practice.

What is calf head? Néstor asked.

It don't matter, Will said. We just need a target. I can set something up. And I can leave this rope in my room so you can get at it when you want. But you got to make me some promises.

All of them, even posing Gustavo, were silent and listening.

You can't be messing with the rope when you should be doing something else. I don't want Edwards on my ass.

They nodded, all five of them.

You can't be swinging the rope around the horses, not even if they're in their stalls. That's not a good idea. You got to do this where you won't bother nobody. Not even once.

Okay, said Ignacio.

Okay, Don Gaucho, said Gustavo, grinning. We are not fools, as you think.

Maybe not, Will said, working the rope into a good coil again. But it's hard to have fun around here, in case you haven't noticed. I'd like for us to keep having a little fun.

I am calling her La Potranca de la Estrella Blanca en el Cielo, Gustavo said. He was following Will and the filly as they took a short walk. Nothing fancy. Will was trying to get the filly used to wearing a full set of boots.

La Potranca de la Estrella Blanca en el Cielo, Gustavo said again.

Will didn't know what all the words meant, but he got most of them. That don't fit her, he said. That name is too much mouthful.

She is *una reina.*

Not yet, she ain't. Maybe she can be a queen. I'd like that. She could be one they talk about like that Captiva. But she's got a far piece to go.

Señor Edwards look to her all the time, Gustavo said.

I know, Will said, chafed by the mention of Edwards. Proves he's got taste.

Señor Edwards would give to her a name.

Edwards ain't gonna give this horse nothing. You don't have to worry about that.

Tick, Teek, Tick, Teek. Gustavo mocked him yet again.

It's Ticket, Will said. Like what you hand to somebody at a gate.

Gustavo's jester face was empty.

Like this, Will said. And he reached into the back pocket of his jeans and he pulled free his wallet and opened it. He rooted around until he found what he was looking for. It was a scratch-off card he'd bought at the bodega. You have these in Argentina, right? Like a Lotto card, or a piece of paper you buy to get into someplace. A ticket? It's what you buy at a football arena.

¿Fútbol? Ah, *sí. Sí.* Gustavo held out one of his scar-rilled hands. He took the Lotto card. He squinted at it even though he didn't know how to read.

See what I mean? Will asked.

Sí. Boleto. Esto es un boleto. Ella es tú boleto.

Whatever, Will said. She's named for her mother right now.

Boleto, Gustavo said, his hooded eyes twinkling. Teek-it for *el juego bonito.* Beautiful game.

Will dropped the lead rope so he could check the fit of the filly's boots. He didn't like the way the buckles were anchored on the rear set. The buckles weren't lying flat.

I ever tell you of my face? Gustavo asked.

No, Will said. He didn't really want to talk about Gustavo's face. The rubbery skin grafts still made him uneasy, as much as he liked Gustavo.

It was *mi madre,* Gustavo said. She very angry. She believe I not like my working.

You cooked food with your mother? Will asked. He remembered what the other boys had said about Gustavo's burns — the accident with a stove in Buenos Aires.

Sí, I cooking the foods. Very fast. I make the money very fast. *Rápido.* But not fast enough for *mi madre.* She say I not man, I not *su hijo* ever again. And she put oil to my face.

Will felt cold needles prick across his own cheeks. His stomach churned sour. He knew the story was true. Gustavo had, for once, dispensed with the performing and the bullshit.

I'm sorry to hear that, he said, trying to look at Gustavo's lopsided mouth. A thing like that, there's no reason for it. Not from a mother or anybody.

They feed much foods in *el hospital,* Gustavo said, rubbing his belly. I sleeped many, many days. *La morfina* was with me always, but never *mi madre.* She stays cooking. She make *mi hermanito* to help. I have *muchos hermanitos.* When I am fixed, I come to the *caballos.* Monsignor Don Andreas del San Cristobal brings me for the *caballos.*

A priest got you out of there? Will asked. And then you come all the way to Don Enrique in California?

Es cierto, Gustavo said, grinning and pointing at his ugly, intermittent nose. His lips were stretched as wide as ever. They looked like orange-colored plumber's seals. *Esta cara,* he said, is *mi boleto a* America.

The young woman who did the accounts in the brick house brought him the message. She was a small-boned person and wore a tight, foam-colored dress of the style favored by cocktail waitresses, and her shoes had heels as long as his hand. Her shoes were sandals. They were made of a material that looked like oven foil.

She had written his mother's name and the phone number of his house in Wyoming on a piece of lined paper.

This person call you last night, the young woman said. Her accent was as full as the blossoms on the flowered bushes behind her. Here is your details.

Did you talk to her? Will asked. He steadied himself as he took the paper from her.

No. No talk. Was on my message.

Can I come use your telephone?

The young woman shook her head. Her hair, which was streaked with strands of gold and strands of caramel brown, hung to the top of her ass. Her eyes, which were smiling even if she wasn't, were as black lined as an Egyptian's.

Señor Edwards has telephone, the woman said.

He won't let me use it.

Sí, he will let you use, she said. I have told him to do so.

Edwards stepped out of his air-conditioned office as soon as he saw Will. Will punched the numbers on the phone pad before he could think too much about it.

His mother answered.

They said you called last night, he said. They didn't tell me until right now.

I know how it is with horse people, she said to him. They don't think of much else except what they're doing at the moment. But you got my message.

It didn't say anything, he said, his heart pounding. What's happened?

Nothing's happened, Will. Not really. Or what has happened is happening slowly, in a way I can deal with.

How bad? he asked as soon as he could get his breath back.

Dr. Pradit hasn't finished his work-up. He's got more tests to run. But I've got a spot on one of my lungs. I promised I wouldn't hide anything from you, so I'm not. I've talked with your father. He's angry, of course. He acts like it's all my fault. That's how he is when he's scared. Everett's a little better. He knows how to take things as they come.

Should I be scared?

A little, she said. We should all be scared once in a while, I guess. But I'm not frightened to pieces. And I don't want you to be, either. That's the best gift you could give me right now, keeping your boots on. How are the horses?

He almost couldn't believe she'd asked that.

I guess . . . well, they're good. The filly is good. She's adjusted to the heat. Hawk's got a little nick on one ankle, but he'll be all right. These people ain't the easiest I ever worked with. He made himself stop before he went into full babble.

Are you learning from them?

Yes, ma'am.

And you're being honest with me like I'm

being honest with you?

He paused. He understood immediately that it was important that he not lie to his mother, not right now. I'm learning a few things, he said. What I see down here, though, don't always match my way of doing things. The people ain't always . . . decent. They know a lot. And there's money behind the operation. There's resources. But I haven't even met Don Enrique yet. He's never around. And competition seems to be in front of everything else. There's a lot of talk about status. It's not how I'd run a place if I had one.

He listened across the long distance of the phone signal for his mother's response. It took her a moment to compose one.

That's what I'd wish for you, she said, finally. He thought her voice sounded narrower than usual, more bottlenecked. A place you can run on your own.

Should I come home? he asked.

Yes. But not yet. The wedding will still go on. I've talked to Hannah and Chad. I'm insisting the plans stay the same. So I want you to wait.

I —

Don't cross me on this, son, she said, interrupting. I'm fine. I feel fine. You're not going to miss anything, I promise.

But that was not true. He would miss the hours and days when she wasn't shrouded in her sickness, when there was still a reckless humor in her eyes. He would miss the spontaneity that whirligigged in people who weren't considering their own death. His mother had the heart for that — being spontaneous. He might not see that glad heart again.

You take care of yourself, she said, closing off the call in that teacherly way she had. Keep your head up. I love you.

I love you, too, he said. And then she was gone. And it took only the slimmest, most filamental moment for him to realize that she hadn't said she planned to fight on.

He could hear the neighbor children playing in their pool. They were splashing one another, that's what it sounded like, and they were shrieking. It wasn't late. A line of glossy-headed grackles had settled on the privacy fence between the estancia and the children's house, preening their feathers. The birds hadn't yet gone to their roosts. He remembered his conversation with Gustavo. Maybe it wouldn't be so bad just to introduce himself to the people next door. He had been raised with those kinds of manners. How could it hurt?

He pulled himself up by his arms until he could see into the family's backyard. The aboveground pool took up almost all the space there was. It was the kind that had to be filled with a garden hose.

Hola, he said.

The children didn't hear him. They were too busy having fun.

He lowered himself when his arms got tired. His nose was full of the chlorine smell that came with pool water. He told himself he'd try once more.

This time, when he got his head above the top of the fence, a woman screamed. He was so surprised, he dropped back to the ground. His boot heels hit the dry dirt on his side of the fence so hard that the bones in his knees buzzed. It was just as he'd feared. He'd scared them because of a stupid, miscommunicated idea.

I'm sorry! he shouted through the high fence. *Por favor.* I didn't mean to scare you. I just wanted to say hello.

¡Hola! the two kids said, shrieking. *Hola, hola!* They weren't afraid at all.

Me llamo Will, he said. I work over here at the estancia. I'm a friend of Gustavo's.

Gustavo es cómico, a voice said.

He didn't say anything for a minute. Then he thought he should apologize again. He pulled himself back up the fence.

I am sorry, he said.

The woman, the mother, was there. She was in a green one-piece bathing suit and held a cigarette and was wearing sandals with heels. She looked good.

Gustavo es cómico, she said again. *Siempre hace chistes.*

He's real friendly, Will said. I'll grant you that. And I think he misses his family. We all do.

He had to stop talking for a moment, just to swallow. He hadn't thought about that, how he was probably talking to this woman because he missed his family. There's nothing over here but horses, he continued, embarrassed. Gustavo says you have a son in the military.

The woman nodded, but he wasn't sure she'd understood him. He could see there was an American flag taped to the glass door that led into the tiny house. Maybe her husband was the one in the army. Or maybe she was older than she looked. It didn't matter.

I didn't mean to bother you, he said. I just wanted to make your acquaintance. *Buenas noches.* Have a good time with your kids.

Buenas noches, Will, she said, smiling. She

didn't seem too bothered, which was a relief. She wasn't going to call the cops or complain. Maybe people in California neighborhoods weren't bothered by most things, since they lived so cramped together. Damn if he knew.

Buenas noches, the kids sang out. They were attacking each other with some kind of toy that squirted water. Their black hair was slick and sparkling with wetness. He couldn't see them once he let go of the fence, but he could hear the rowdiness in their high voices. They would go until they dropped. He remembered just what that was like, when play was a giant silver bubble pushing at your insides, just busting to get out. It was a good feeling. Big and fizzing. It was a feeling you were certain about when you were a kid, one you were sure would never go away.

A large crew arrived the next day and began to set up a series of white tents. There were also men who came in a rattling flatbed Ford with push mowers and all the tools for lawn care and gardening. They were Mexicans. They didn't say a word, not to Will or to any of them. More delivery trucks circled into the driveway in front of the brick house. No one had seen Edwards since late that morning.

Don Enrique, Néstor said. He will come.

Is it always like this? Will asked.

Néstor rubbed his hands over his prominent lips. He was wearing the gloves he used when he took the older horses out in their sets. And he had a bill cap on his head, one that advertised a treatment for equine arthritis. He looked thinner to Will than he ever had before. *No sé.* We have welcomed Don Enrique only a few times.

And they never tell you what to expect?

Señor Edwards tells what we should know, Néstor said.

And where is Señor Edwards now, do you think?

Néstor rubbed at his lips, harder. I think he gathering the horses, he said.

More horses? Will asked.

Sí. Always very many more horses, Néstor said.

Edwards had not spoken one word to Will except to say that there might be chukkers before long. Edwards had acted as though it was a casual thing, the hosting of polo matches. Relaxed. There was nothing about what was happening at Estancia Flora that was relaxed, however. It looked like the Mexicans were preparing for a big, big wedding. Will didn't understand how Edwards planned for things. Maybe that was the whole idea. Maybe Edwards wanted to keep him, Will, uninformed, which would put him right alongside the boys and the tent-raising laborers and the anxious *potros,* locked in their stalls.

Stefan and Andre arrived and worked the older horses. They asked Will to accompany them onto the freshly mowed pitches to hand them the mallets they wanted and to shag balls as they practiced their shots. He did what he was asked. He admired the way Andre leaned low off the shoulder of the racing La Soledad. The way he blended with the mare's raging speed. Will and his brothers had tried such stunts as children. They had tried to imitate movie Indians as they gripped the barrels of their running horses with their sturdy boy legs, firing their pretend arrows. He and his brothers had never seen a white ball being shot across a rich man's green table of grass. They couldn't have imagined such a thing.

Will knew what Everett and Chad would say about the white britches that Andre wore. And the very tall, calf-hugging boots. Everett would talk a lot of audible shit about the boots.

Here, Andre shouted to him, wiping the sweat from his slightly furred upper lip. You take her. You shoot.

Will mounted La Soledad without hesitation. He didn't want to look cautious in front of Stefan and Andre. The flat polo saddle was tacky with Andre's perspiration, but the stirrup leathers were the right length. Will tried to get a feel for La Soledad. He'd ridden her before in sets. But not like now. She was hot and roaring. He handed Andre his straw cowboy hat. It was an old hat, and it was great in the California sun, but he was sure it was about to blow right off his head.

You take her against Miramar and Stefan, Andre said, grinning. One, two, three. Go to each ball. It does not matter if you miss. Then he handed Will the mallet. The mallet's safety loop, which went over Will's right wrist, was also damp.

I will lay out the ball, Andre said.

And he did. Will and Stefan cantered their horses away from each other in tidy circles. Then they came at the waiting ball. La Soledad was fast, but her great strength was her maneuverability. She did everything she could to steer the faster Miramar, who was being ridden by Stefan, off the ball.

Will didn't even swing the mallet the first time. He forgot all about it, he was so busy speeding the mare to the mark. Stefan, who had fallen a stride behind, crossed the mallet to his left side and swung at the ball like some kind of sword-helling cavalry officer. He gave the ball a clean strike. He made it look easy. Then they both eased up their horses and cantered them steadily back to the start. Will did swing the second time, awkwardly, and he heard Stefan laugh as the horses thundered in on each other, but it didn't matter, La Soledad followed Stefan's shot, and she bullied Miramar off the angle to the ball, and Will swung again. He accomplished almost nothing — the ball skidded sideways in the grass — but he could hear Andre cheer behind him, and he could feel a kind of satisfaction ripple through La Soledad. The mare turned herself even before he asked her to. They cantered back up the field toward Andre.

Again! Andre shouted, gleeful. She is happy. You are happy. Take the ball again.

So he did. Stefan was more fierce with Miramar on the pass this time, for that was what Miramar needed, more courage, and he directed the younger animal right into La Soledad's bold route. The horses bumped twice. Will was able to read his horse better this time, however. La Soledad wasn't so different from a roping horse, not when it came to anticipating her opponent's move. Miramar got to the white ball first, but there was no shot. Stefan hadn't been able to make one. La Soledad had defended too well.

We must not tire them, Stefan said, quartering Miramar close enough to reach out and shake Will's hand. It is fun, no? And they love it very much. You can feel that, I am sure. There are days Señor Edwards pours all of his dark blood into the horses, and it becomes work for us. But not today, Stefan said. Today was for the fun.

And for seeing if the *norteamericano* will stay in his saddle, Andre added.

Sí, said Stefan, with his sure white smile. We know you ride very well, Señor Gaucho Will. But you are new to the polo.

I don't hardly know how to find the ball when I look for it, Will said.

On a *caballo maduro,* you need only to keep up, Stefan said, nodding at La Soledad.

Will agreed. It's not the first time a horse has been smarter than me, he said.

The riders laughed.

Will Don Enrique ride? Will asked.

Andre looked up at Stefan, who had dropped his stirrups but still sat comfortably in the saddle. They both paused.

Perhaps, Stefan said. They are all his property, and he sometimes likes to play the game himself. We do not know what to expect, so it is best, I believe, to expect nothing.

And you will ride for him?

For him, or for someone else, Stefan said, his voice finding the softer vowels of a guarded tone. We will do as we are told.

A veterinarian arrived with an assistant. Will could not tell if the assistant was Argentine or Venezuelan or what. The assistant spoke very good English, and he knew a great deal about polo ponies. The veterinarian was an older American, and tired. He had the pouchy face of a man who has yet to reconcile himself to the fact that he has been forced to give up cigarettes. The vet moved programmatically around the horses, as if there were little he could learn from them. The assistant did not. The assistant moved with the swift certainty of an accountant.

The vet was a man Néstor had seen before. He told Will that Don Enrique and Edwards used a series of veterinarians, some of them hired from as far away as San Diego. The don, Néstor said, liked to move his business around.

Is he gonna check them all? Will asked. Or just the ones that might get used in the matches?

Néstor shook his head as if he had cold water in his ears. He had no idea. He told Will it was this veterinarian's habit to start in the second barn, where the mature horses were kept. The vet would pull the horses he wanted from the stalls. And he would ask for help if he needed it.

Will wanted to watch the veterinarian work. He especially wanted to watch the assistant. The assistant was the one who looked at a clipboard before he pulled a horse from its stall. And he spoke to established horses, the ones like Captiva and La Soledad, as if they were good friends. But Will got the message that he wouldn't be welcome if he loitered. It was early in the evening by then. A steady breeze from the west had swept the humidity away, and the day had burnished itself with the soft, golden light that he thought was the best of California. Néstor had spoken with the veterinarian's assistant. It was acceptable to take the horses that were awaiting their examinations out in sets. Will joined Néstor.

The old campaigners were in a stir. They saw the tents, and they saw the veterinarian's white truck, with its silver-trimmed cabinets, and they knew there would be polo. Néstor had saddled El Argent, and he had six high-stepping horses gathered in a set, and he was laughing. He was singing loudly in Spanish. Will could hear him even while he saddled the broody old gelding Edwards called Cóndor. Néstor was excited. They all were. Will wondered what would strike him deeper — watching the polo or finally seeing the don once again. He could feel the flutter of a kind of nervousness in the lining of his stomach.

The horses he held whipped away from him like flags whipping away from a flag-pole. But they knew just how far they could take it, their romping. They settled into a controlled jog when he asked them to. He could tell that Cóndor had already decided he would be asked to play the next day. The gelding pressed his strong shoulders forward as he moved. He floated his muscular trot as they led the set across the grass, showing off.

When they got back to the second barn, and all the horses had been wiped down and returned to their stalls, David came from the first barn and asked if Will could help with some of the younger *potros*. The don had decided to offer a couple of unfinished horses for sale. They needed to have their whiskers trimmed, David said. Everyone knew Will was very good with the trimmers.

Will stopped first by the filly's stall. He had worked her on the long line during the night. Now she was watching the machinations of the veterinarian and his cheflike assistant.

You got nothing to worry about, he told her, threading his fingers through the glossy, black hairs of her forelock. They won't be fooling with you.

He left to help David.

There were four horses to trim. Two of them were assigned to Gustavo, and the taller boy crooned to them and made saucy jokes in Spanish to keep them calm. He told Will that he was praying Don Enrique would bring his wife and all of her woman friends to the polo tomorrow. He was praying on his knees. Then there was a leak in one of the pipes in the bathing stall. Will fixed that with a little help from David. Then there was a good dinner laid out for them, a whole long table full of tacos and tamales and sodas brought in from a local restaurant. Everyone had been invited to partake, even the Mexican gardeners, in their gray work clothes and salt-stained hats. When Will returned to the second barn to confer with Néstor, the veterinarian was still there, but the filly was not in her stall.

He thought she must be lying down. But she wasn't. Her stall was empty.

A long black shadow rolled through him, from his heart to the roots of his eyes. He felt something like electricity knife down his forearms. He made himself look again. No. Gone.

Hey, he said to no one in particular. I'm missing my horse.

He walked down the long barn aisle, through the sweet-sour stink of manure and liniment. He interrupted the pouchy veterinarian, who appeared to be fingering the knee capsule of a mare Néstor called La Bruja.

You must have moved my horse, Will said. He knew Néstor and the boys would never touch the filly without permission.

The vet, who had a white T-shirt on under his short-sleeved broadcloth shirt, looked at Will as if he were a granular speck on a television screen. Small, indistinguishable.

The blood bay filly, Will said. She was in the end stall.

Ah, the assistant said, appearing from somewhere near the vet's parked truck. The small one with the white between her eyes, sí. We have examined her. She is very nice.

She belongs to me.

The assistant, who was without his clip-board, looked at the veterinarian. The older man loosened the muscles in his jaw as if a familiar message had just passed between them. Then the vet continued his meticulous probing of La Bruja's knee. He still hadn't spoken a word.

So it is, the assistant said. We are doing our work from notes, from very detailed notes, as that is how Mr. Edwards contacts us about the don's business. Perhaps we have made a mistake. Your lovely horse cannot have gone far, can she? I predict you will see her there. And he pointed toward an area behind the first barn.

Will found the filly in the small fenced pen where Néstor had told him Edwards kept stud horses when they had them. There were two horses with the filly. One was a lanky brown colt he had just trimmed. The filly was wearing her halter. He didn't even look for a lead rope. He hooked one finger in her halter ring and led the filly back to her proper stall. They had to go the long way, around the outside of the barn, since the veterinarian's wide truck blocked the near entrance.

So you have found her! the assistant shouted from his position at the other end of the aisle.

Will didn't bother to answer. He checked the filly over. She was the same as she had ever been. He ran a hand from the warm cave of her throat, all the way down to her sternum. It tickled her when he did that, so he had to scratch her next, right along the line of her shoulder. She tried to lean into him as he scratched, but he wouldn't allow it. He didn't sanction bad habits, not even when it came to affection.

He walked back in the direction of the veterinarian and his assistant.

That horse is not for sale, he told them. I'm sorry about the mix-up.

Is she registered? the veterinarian asked.

Yes, sir.

She looks King Ranch bred. Is she?

There's some of that breeding in her, Will said. You like quarter horses?

I like them all on my good days, the vet said. He had a pair of black-rimmed glasses perched on top of his thinly haired head. He slipped the glasses down onto his nose as he took a closer look at Will. What brings you here? the vet asked.

I'm learning to train for polo, he said. I'm from Wyoming. I haven't been here long.

I can tell that, the vet said, but he didn't laugh when he said it. He didn't seem given to light humor at all.

You are working with Mr. Edwards, the assistant said. You are perhaps a great rider like him?

I'm no great rider, Will said, not when it's this kind of game. But I like the way they train up these polo ponies. They get the best out of them. Really athletic.

The vet and his assistant both nodded.

It is serious business, the assistant said.

Have you put that horse of yours under tack yet? the vet asked.

No, sir. But I'm getting close to that point. And she's not for sale?

She will be, Will said, wanting to sound like it didn't matter to him one way or another. Like he didn't care.

You could get a price for her now, the vet said. He was still peering at Will through his glasses.

I want to take my time with her, he said. She's a development project for me.

You riding for the don? the vet asked.

I only met the don once, Will said. I'm still waiting to see him again. And I can't ride polo for shit. I do everything else that's asked of me here, everything Edwards wants. And I watch things. I guess Edwards don't think I can mess that up.

Has Edwards ridden your horse? the vet asked.

Edwards hasn't touched that filly, Will said. He don't even act like she exists.

Ah, said the veterinarian's assistant, reaching out as if he wished to run a finger along the shape of Will's arm just to make sure Will was really there.

Do you know what will happen when they play the matches? the veterinarian asked. Who will come? What they will do?

Will shook his head. I expect it'll be a kind of crazy time, like any big stock show, he said. I can handle that.

Everything will happen, the vet said. Everything. I've been treating animals in this valley for thirty years, and it still surprises me. There will be the matches. And there will be other . . . activities. Lots of competition and showmanship. Emotions. For people like the don, this is about a certain way of life. It's not a way I completely understand.

Are you warning me? Will asked.

The vet looked into a patch of fading light just above Will's left shoulder. No, not really, he said. Warning you would be foolish. And unnecessary. You're new, but you're not stupid. Or you don't sound stupid.

Thanks for the vote of confidence, Will said.

The old vet turned down the corners of

his heavily etched mouth. Stupid or smart doesn't matter very much, he said, with people who are used to getting their way.

All a boy needs to get himself in trouble is a rope. Or a book of matches. Will's mother must have said that into his ears a thousand times.

Gustavo had borrowed the lariat, but he hadn't taken it to practice his throws. He waited until dark, and he confirmed that Edwards was still away from the estancia, then he used the lariat to get himself over the fence and into the neighbor's swimming pool.

There were so many idiocies about the prank that Will couldn't list them all. He discovered the situation when he heard music through the walls of the barn. There was also cheering of the kind that he associated with ball games, or the beginning of a bar fight. He put aside the saddle he was cleaning and followed the noise.

He would never forget the way the boys looked. They were like urchins who had arrived at the entrance of a peep show, peering through gaps in the fence, half-paralyzed by what they saw. Ignacio and David were actually *on* the fence, perched there. David was punching the air with a closed and happy fist. When Will could see into Estella's backyard, it was as bad as he'd imagined. Estella was there. So was Gustavo, who was floating in her pool with his clothes on. Estella had an open brown bottle of beer in her hand. She was trying to give it to the wallowing Gustavo.

Jesus Christ, Will thought. This was what happened when you never let your employees blow off steam.

Weel, Weel, Weel. Dodo was beside him, hopping from foot to foot as if the ground beneath him were heated with coals. His black eye patch bobbed up and down, up and down. Weel, *está Gustavo en la piscina de la mujer.*

Sí, he said to the boy. I got it. Gustavo went and made a party.

Par-tee! shouted Dodo.

He wanted to do two things. He wanted to suggest to the boys that they shut it down, and shut it down soon. And he wanted to get his lariat. Gustavo, or somebody, had anchored the rope with an ugly set of knots tied to the winch bar of one of the mowers. The rope had been stretched. It had been treated very badly, which made him angry.

Gaucho! shouted Ignacio, who now had a beer in his hand. *¡Hay cerveza! Ven a tomar* *una cerveza.*

I don't think so, Ignacio. I don't need a beer. I'm glad Señora Estella is so generous. But we could have some trouble.

Señor Edwards, *no esta,* Ignacio said. There is no harm.

Edwards will be back. I don't think he'll care for this. We've got a big day tomorrow.

Don Guillermo! *¿Está el gran gaucho?* Where is Don Guillermo?

The questions came through the fence from an exuberant Gustavo, who was paddling himself around the pool in one of the children's inflatable inner tubes.

Will wasn't going to speak to Gustavo. Not a word. Edwards might treat the boys like children, but he wasn't going to stoop that low. They knew what they were getting into. He saw how Néstor, who was the quietest of the five, and the oldest, watched him as he tried to untie his lariat from the mower's winch bar. Néstor had been working like a madman to prepare for the polo matches. He also had a beer bottle in his hand, but it was empty. The way Néstor looked at him, with a moist detachment in his dark eyes, suggested to Will that the beer wasn't Néstor's first of the evening.

You are angry? Néstor asked.

Not me, Will said, yanking his rope free. I

don't blame you all for cutting loose. I just question your timing.

Several of the boys drew close to him as he was trying to recoil his damaged rope. They seemed prepared to calm themselves. Then one of them stole his hat right off his head.

It was Dodo, he was sure of it. The one-eyed boy had the hands of a pickpocket. The straw slope-front hat, which was not his best hat, but which was still crisp and mostly clean, was gone from his head, then it was over the fence, then it was on Gustavo's wet and swaying head in the pool.

That was *not* a good idea, Will said to Dodo. He spoke in a tone he'd never used with any of the boys before. His words stripped the crescent smile from Dodo's dirty face.

I need my hat, he said through the fence.

There was a broad band of laughter, probably from Estella. In fact, it sounded like there was more than one adult woman over there now. And the kids were there, too. And there was the music, much of it trumpets and voices.

I have you hat! Gustavo shouted.

I know you do. I want you to give it back. And I want you to loosen up my rope from whatever it's tied to over there. Then I'm leaving. I don't want to be around for the end of this story.

I have you hat.

Sí. You've got the hat and you've got your party, Gustavo. But I ain't sticking around.

Ignacio and David, who had both climbed back onto the fence, looked at him as if bright flames had begun to flicker from his mouth.

Just untie the rope, Gustavo. That's all I'm asking. I'll leave the rest of it up to you and Señora Estella.

Es sombrero bonito.

Sí. I paid good money for it. He could feel the chastened Dodo crowding behind him, working right behind his knees, trying to re-coil the rope he had already coiled.

You no like party?

Now's not the time, Gustavo. You know that. Maybe Edwards won't blow his stack. But I'm not willing to stake my job on it.

Edwards, he making love to the womans, just as I am doing. Edwards is busy. You, too, should make the busy, Gustavo said, giggling.

Edwards has a way of finding out about things, Will said. I won't bust you. Don't worry. That ain't my style. But you need to keep the noise down over here. Did you think about that?

All of them were quieter now, listening. Ignacio and David were climbing off the fence. Dodo had disappeared into the barn. Will could hear Estella talking, quickly, insistently. Her words were a maelstrom of Spanish.

Estella say you a *maricón.*

That's not what she said. I know enough words to get that much. Tell her I'm not stopping anything she wants to do. It's her house. She's been very nice.

She has *hijo* like me, Gustavo said.

No one, Will thought to himself, has a son exactly like Gustavo. Why don't you ask Estella if she'll help me get my rope, he said. Then I can stop bothering you.

The rope went loose when he tugged on it, and he could hear Estella's children, the young ones, laughing. David brought him his hat. David climbed over the fence with his knotty brown arms and got the hat from Gustavo or whomever and climbed back. One of the children swimming in the pool applauded.

Thank you, Will said to David and to all of them. *Gracias,* Estella. And *gracias* to you, too, Gustavo.

I am still party, Gustavo said.

Suit yourself.

Edwards, he not your friend, Gustavo said.

I reckon not, Will said. Don't worry. I won't say nothing to him. He looked into the unfurling nighttime, where the mower was parked, where Néstor sat with another bottle of beer dangling between his knees. Néstor, who had begun to sag into a morose posture, was the person who most needed to hear him. Néstor did not like unpredictability.

Llevate una cerveza, Gustavo said.

Not for now, Will said. Maybe tomorrow. Maybe after all that polo celebrating is done.

I party now.

Sí, Will said. I got that the first time.

The night washed across him in waves. There were the sounds of diesel rigs arriving at the estancia. The sounds of horses being unloaded, of horses kicking the metal sides of trailers, of people cursing as they worked in the dark. Once, very late, he heard a car speed down the driveway, away from the barns. It wasn't safe to drive like that at the estancia. He wondered what fool had tried it. He didn't know what he was supposed to do to make himself fit into the hours, so he did nothing except lie on the mashed pallet of his bed and listen to thwarted insects batter themselves against the trap of his ceiling. Then he could take it no longer. He rose and brushed his teeth with a mug of lukewarm water and the toothbrush he kept wrapped in plastic to protect it from the flies.

He went into the barn, where the horses that would play that day were as jittery as he was. The filly, too, was on edge, pawing at the wood shavings in her stall, the muscles of her throat going tight when she heard the squeal of an unknown horse. He cleaned her stall with a pitchfork. Then he moved up the aisle and spoke very softly to the other horses. Only El Argent was asleep, with his gray rump facing the gate of his stall, one hip cocked. El Argent had no concerns.

Trailers and vans were parked along the full length of the driveway. The brick house had all its lights on, and he could hear women giving directions in English and Spanish. The caterers.

He went into the first barn, where the shaggy *potros* hung their heads over their stall gates to look at each intruder. He saw no sign of Dodo or Ignacio or Gustavo. The door to the room they shared was closed. He hoped they weren't sleeping it off on Estella's pool deck. That would be cutting it close.

The lights were on in Edwards's office,

but it, too, was empty. He moved outside again and found himself facing a slender, impatient man who wanted to unload his horses. The horses wore heavy foam leg wraps, but they moved nimbly. Their coats flickered in the misty light of false dawn. Their skin smelled to him of ocean air and cedar. The slender man — the owner of the horses — didn't speak to Will. He wanted help, not conversation. Will was only a pair of hands.

He kept at the tasks given to him by bleary-eyed strangers until the sky flushed itself to pink. He had seen Néstor by then, but Néstor had not acknowledged him. When he crossed paths with Dodo as he began to feed some of the horses in the second barn, Dodo cupped his hands over his good eye and passed Will with a peculiar stiffness in his young knees. Dodo had made himself fully blind. He also did not speak a word.

They are ashamed, Will thought. I guess that's not so bad.

But shame wasn't the largest blade that hung over the boys' heads. There was fear, an arsenal of it. He got the truth a few moments later, when Ignacio told him what had happened. Ignacio's pockmarked face was streaked with what might have been tears. He spoke with his head drawn in like a turtle's, between the protrusions of his bony shoulders.

They say no word, no talking, Ignacio said. Gustavo is gone.

What? Will said. His arms were full of saddle pads. Is Gustavo still at Estella's?

Ignacio shook his head. No, no, no. Gustavo come back. He is sleeping. We all is sleeping. And the mans take Gustavo.

What man? Edwards?

Ignacio shook his head again. Will could see the pulse beating in the veins of Ignacio's retracted neck. Not Señor Edwards, the boy said. The mans from Don Enrique. I never see him before, but I heared. . . . The boy stopped, gulping.

Will was confused. The morning was already a blow-up. He tried to ask questions that would calm Ignacio.

So a man came to talk to Gustavo? Was it a policeman? That was the worst Will could think of, Gustavo tangled up with a curious American cop.

No, never *la policía,* Ignacio said.

I don't get what you're telling me.

The mans comes. He *comes,* Ignacio said, snot sliding from his nose. He take you where . . . where the *mozos de cuadra* go if you do bad work for Don Enrique.

Fuck, Will thought. La Migra. Would they do that? Would Edwards and Don Enrique bust their own employee with Immigration?

Have you talked to Néstor?

No, no, no, Ignacio said, his hands spidering. He wiped his nose, his pitted face twisting around the only words he could find. Never the Néstor. You must understand what I am to say. Néstor makes telephone to the mans from Don Enrique. This is job for Néstor. Or they take him also.

Will blew the air that was in his lungs out past his teeth. Had he heard that right? Was Gustavo really gone? Was Néstor some kind of paid-off rat?

I'll go talk to Edwards, he said. This is fucking weird — whatever it is you're saying. And ridiculous. He pushed the load of bleached saddle pads into Ignacio's arms. The boy wiped his face across the bright, clean material, sniffling.

Edwards was wearing white riding pants. They were spotless.

I just got told that somebody came for Gustavo in the night, Will said. Like he's a criminal. Can that be true?

I don't know what you're talking about, Edwards said. Will could see that Edwards had gotten his hair trimmed while he was

347

away from the estancia. There was a rim of pale skin visible behind Edwards's flat and smallish ears. The mustache had also been trimmed. It looked like a hyphen.

You *ought* to know. You're the manager around here when you decide to be.

This would not be a good day to bust my balls, cowboy. Don't try it.

Where's Gustavo?

Edwards walked right past Will with the low-hipped, prowling stride he had. Gustavo's the one with the fucked-up face, right? The long-haired, stupid one? I don't know where he is, Edwards said. I just got back.

Don't pretend you don't know who he is, Will said, his voice warping low.

I pretend a lot of things, Edwards said, turning. Especially today. The kid probably ran off. They do that when they decide the work is too hard.

Gustavo didn't run off.

So you say.

So I know, Will said. I saw him at ten o'clock last night. He was blowing off a little steam with the neighbors. I guess you know *that* from your spy. But he didn't do nothing wrong. None of them did. They deserved their fun. They get treated like dogs most of the time around here, dogs with fingers and hands.

Edwards squeezed his blue eyes half-shut as if Will were falling away from him, or shrinking. I don't know what you're talking about, he repeated. I got polo to play. You've got ponies to handle — all day long. Don Enrique is here with his goddamn extensive entourage. Do yourself a favor, Testerman. If someone asks you to *do* something today, just do it. If someone asks you to stand on your fucking Wyoming head, stand on it.

I ought to quit right now, Will said.

Go ahead, Edwards said. That would be the best news I've had in weeks. But you won't be able to get that sad little Cadillac of yours out of here for about ten hours. You're blocked in. The *carnaval* has begun. So it looks like it's a tragedy for you all the way around.

You got a sick, mean way of doing things, Will said.

I'm a guy who survives, Edwards said. Welcome to the horse business. And since you're complaining, why don't you go help those *hermanos* you love so much get their work done? They're going to need it.

You don't see nothing but the price in things, do you? Will said. We might as well be made of paper to you, or straw.

Take some responsibility, Edwards said, making his eyes as narrow as staples. You chose to come here. You wanted part of this. You came to take something from this place, and when you did that, you gave up the right to have things your way. That's how it's done. You give up your shit to get at the other guy's shit. Pay, or make them pay. If you want to fight with me about some kind of injustice you think you smell around here, we'll do it later. I got fucking great horses to ride. For fucking assholes.

He wrapped legs. He braided and taped tails. He thought about what Edwards had said about Gustavo, and the frozen way he'd said it. Wiry men in untucked polo shirts ambled into the barns and greeted the horses they were scheduled to ride. He watched the strangers come and go, calculating, fretting. Would the next one be Don Enrique? Or the next? There was plenty of help in the barns. Men had come from Don Enrique's other properties, and many of the guests had brought their own grooms. There were a few women serving as grooms, none of them Argentine but all of them as unblinking and world weary as the dark-skinned *mozos* who hissed their curses in Spanish. Néstor seemed to know most of the *mozos*. He spoke to them briefly, with the formality of a bell clerk at a large hotel.

Néstor did not speak to Will. They had nothing to say to each other.

The first match was for amateurs. Will was asked to hold several horses for a team that wore red-striped shirts. He stood close to the field, ready to provide fresh horses between chukkers. But he looked for Gustavo whenever he could. He kept hoping the boy would reappear, jittering into one of the barns in that lanky way he had. Yet he saw no Gustavo. And he couldn't shake the settled menace he had seen in Edwards's eyes. There were only a few people in the white tents, most of them stirring ingredients into their tall paper cups of coffee. No Don Enrique. No irreverent boy with a patchwork face. The amateurs played polo with spirit, but they were unimaginative with their horses, cautious. This didn't surprise him. The amateurs were protecting what they had — a pair of decent horses, an opportunity for bragging rights. The professionals wouldn't be protecting anything. They would be looking to pillage.

When the first match was over, miserable Dodo was ordered onto the field with a pitchfork and wheelbarrow to clean up the manure that had been dropped across the fine green grass. A few small children also spilled onto the field to kick a soccer ball.

They shared the field with a trio of squawking magpies that plucked mercilessly at the earth for beetles.

Will made a tour of the tents as soon as he could. He didn't bother with coffee. There were pastries, too, expensive ones. And large bowls of cut fruit and sliced breads. Two silent men in dark pants and vests were on hand to keep the magpies and sparrows from thieving the food. A few riders lolled in the shade of the tents in their high boots and sunglasses. They were all young and long haired, as physically sleek as pampered cats. Don Enrique, Will decided, must be holding court inside the brick house.

He could go into that house. He could introduce himself and say what he wanted to say, about the work that he was grateful for and the disappearance of Gustavo, which disturbed him greatly. But going into the house would doom whatever results he hoped for. Don Enrique didn't know him. He would remember Will only as the quiet American who had ridden a few sale horses in Jackson, Wyoming. It would be better if he were reacquainted with the don in the kingdom of the barns. There was grace to being a rich man. There was also grace to being a poor man who knew his territory.

As it was, the don found him. The second match was under way. Stefan was on the field in a black shirt, riding a horse Will had never seen. Stefan's face was embossed with an uncomfortable frown. Will was watching Stefan's mount, trying to see what the problem might be, when a large man in a tin-colored suit tapped him on the shoulder. He was needed, the man said. Would he please follow?

No one really *needs* anything today, Will thought. This is all about want.

The don was in an enclosed tent, a smaller one that was set back amid the thickly leaved fruit trees. The air in the tent was warm, and smelled of lemons and the starch used to press tablecloths. There were light-weight plastic chairs jumbled about, and a few food-covered tables. There was a bar and a large television that was tuned to a soccer game that was being played some-where else in the world. The television made no sound, but the men watching the game did. They groaned and hissed. They drew on their plentiful cigarettes with disdain. There were also a few women. They were expensively dressed, slim and gleaming.

They, too, were smoking cigarettes, although they seemed indifferent to the soccer. The don wasn't watching the game. He appeared to be conducting business.

It was funny what stuck in your mind when you met a man or a woman, Will thought. He remembered Don Enrique as a bigger person, plump in the stomach and hands, soft beneath the chin. He hadn't seen the don's uncovered eyes in Jackson. They had both been outside under the bright and unmediated sun on that day, among the polo pitches and stalls that held the horses that were for sale. The man seated in front of him now had light-colored rings around the pupils of his brownish eyes. He didn't seem quite as large. And what struck Will this time was the almost feminine width of the don's pleated trousers and the deeply bitten color of his damp and meaty lips.

Edwards was also in the tent, standing behind Don Enrique at as much height as he could muster. He was wearing a bright-blue jersey sashed with a diagonal band of yellow. He looked as confident as Will had ever seen him, and as instinctive. Edwards's eyes simmered with hunger.

The man in the tin-colored suit made a looping hand gesture. Will was to introduce himself.

It's good to see you again, sir, he said, removing his hat the way his mother had taught him. I've been honored to be working at Estancia Flora.

Mr. Testerman. William. I understand you have labored very hard for my horses.

I've tried, sir. I've got a long way to go.

Mr. Edwards tells me the same, the don said, enhancing the only facial expression Will had ever seen on the man — a handsome, political smile. Mr. Edwards says you are sure with the *caballos* and not so sure with the mallet.

The men within earshot laughed a genial laugh.

Would you like a drink, William, or some food before you speak with me? the don asked. I know you have been up early with the *caballos*. But this is our time. I have much I wish to hear from you.

No, sir, he said. I don't need a drink.

Edwards pinched his tanned face into a smirk. He wanted Will to know he'd made a mistake. You don't turn down a powerful man's offer of hospitality.

Then come and say what you have been doing, the don said, unperturbed. He waved at the chair next to his. The man who was in that chair looked surprised, but he quickly stood, hitched at his tight-fitting

355

jacket, and stepped away.

Will sat.

And how is Señor Galey? the don asked. Has he bought many more good horses?

Frank Galey was the man who had introduced Will to the don. Galey kept polo ponies in Jackson, and cutting horses, and horses for dressage and eventing. He ran things right, and he spent a lot of money doing so.

I don't know, sir. He was hoping to buy one or two big reputation mares to breed. He said it was gonna be tricky.

The don grinned. Frank Galey should have one of my mares, he said. Perhaps the blessed Captiva. What do you say? Shall I sell her?

Will knew the questions were a kind of trap. Or a test. Captiva is a fine animal, about as perfect as I've seen, he said, keeping his voice steady. Frank Galey would be right to make a serious offer for her. I couldn't say if you would be right to take it.

The don tilted his head, amused. He kept his hands in his lap, and Will could see how perfectly cared for those hands were. Mr. Testerman is not always as impulsive as you claim, the don said, speaking to Edwards. You will show us Captiva's perfection today, no? You will decide if I should sell her?

Edwards bowed forward slightly from the shoulders, but he didn't answer.

Soon, Thomas? Am I correct?

The match is scheduled to start in about an hour, Edwards said. The words sounded dry coming from his tongue, dusty.

Then go, the don said. Whisper encouragements to my blessed *yegua*. Ride her well. Mr. Testerman and I will come to watch you.

It was an abrupt dismissal. Edwards had no choice. He left the tent as proudly as he could, leading with the shined toes of his boots and his blue-and-yellow bannered chest.

You would like a drink now? the don asked.

Yes, sir, Will said, calculating. I'd take a Sprite if you have one, or a ginger ale.

Very good, the don said, glancing approvingly at his buffed fingernails. We are relaxing.

He asked Will dozens of questions about operations at Estancia Flora. They were informed questions, detailed, infused with an apparent modesty that Will knew he should not trust. Were the training methods sound? Did Will believe the *potrancos* were handled well? Were they fed appropriately? He took the only tack he knew — he answered honestly, and he didn't provide answers he wasn't sure of. He didn't criticize Edwards in any way. And he didn't embellish. Don Enrique controlled the conversation in his own particular manner, so Will bided his time. He knew he could not afford to bring up Gustavo at the wrong moment.

And you are happy here? the don asked.

I'm honored, Will repeated. He was treading carefully, making sure each word was as solid as a stone. I've seen good horses and good training, he said. You've give me a valuable opportunity. I'm getting what I came for.

We are more . . . *elaborate* than the cowboy American trainers, the don said. This was not a question.

You're different, Will said. Different traditions. But most of the goals are exactly the same.

Yet you do not love Thomas Edwards, the don said.

Edwards and me don't have to like each other, Will said, reminding himself not to drop his eyes to his feet. Respect is all it takes. I respect Edwards. He is very worthy of your horses.

I assure you, Mr. Testerman, that I am certain of that. Thomas has worked for me for many years. He is a great *jinete de polo,* but he is more than that.

Will nodded. He understood the don wanted him to cut out the bullshit.

Do you believe Thomas respects you? the don asked.

No, sir. He don't. I don't blame him. I haven't done much to earn his respect. Not yet.

Does he envy you?

I don't see how he could, sir, Will said, swallowing around a hasty sip of his ginger ale. He could not imagine that Edwards had spent more than thirty seconds thinking about him one way or the other.

You do not know this man, Mr. Testerman. I do. He is a gifted man, and also a distorted one, *retorcido.* This is often true with those who have gifts, no? They are, in a certain way, unbalanced. Thomas Edwards believes I have brought you here, to my modest estancia, to further unbalance him.

Will kept his eyes on the crackling ice that floated in his frosted glass. He didn't know what his face might reveal if he had to witness the smacking movements of the don's ripe lips.

Are you here to unbalance Thomas Edwards? the don asked.

No, sir. I'll leave right now if anybody

thinks that. If you think that.

No, no, Mr. Testerman. William. My desire is not for you to leave. I am merely . . . probing. I am learning who you are. Would you like to know my desire?

I reckon you're hoping everybody will work hard and get along, Will said, speaking past the knotted pressure he suddenly felt against the hinges of his jaw.

Perhaps I hope you will bring out the best in Mr. Edwards, the don said. You have gifts of your own, do you not? You are also *retorcido*?

I guess I don't know what you mean, sir.

You know pleasure from the *caballos*, Mr. Testerman. I saw this very purely in Jackson, Wyoming. Señor Galey speaks of it also. Señor Galey sings your talents. Many people have affection for the horses. In my own family there are these *tipos sentimentales*. Affection can be foolishness. And some see nothing but the body of a horse, its *maquinaria*. You are not like that, Mr. Testerman. You have something of the calmer person in you. I do not know how to express it exactly, but with the animals you do not worry so much about the making of a mistake. Thomas Edwards thinks of nothing but his mistakes.

Flattery was a two-bladed ax. Flattery was

a way to cut you down. Will knew that from his father. So he sat carefully, and he listened.

You want what is the best for each *caballo,* the don said. This is what I see. And I am the same as you. It is that simple. We want what is best. We value the excellence. I am told you have a most beautiful *potranca* here at my estancia. You are most particular with her.

A word could be as certain as a stone. A line of words could become as certain as a line of stones. You could build bridges if you spoke to another man with certainty, or you could throw up walls. This was what he told himself.

I have two horses here, he said. One of them is a young mare. She don't have much value yet because she don't know much.

And you believe knowledge is value, the don said.

I guess I do.

And beauty? What do you say for that? Your mare is quite beautiful, I am told. I would like to know your thoughts on the beauty of a thing — just from one old gaucho to another.

Will saw how the pale rims of the don's eyes had widened with the widening of his questions. The don was joking. He did not consider himself a mere gaucho, not for one second.

Beauty don't have much effect on ability, whether it's humans you're talking about or horses, Will said. All we got to do is go out to the barns, or to your polo pitch, to prove that.

But what is lovely has an effect on *me,* the don said. I must say this to you very clearly. Beauty has a force on the heart. On the viscera. This force must be cultivated every day. I think you will not disagree with me.

Will shook his head. He kept his gaze measured on the don. Though he hadn't lifted a hand from the clutch of his ginger ale glass, he felt as though he had just been asked to sign something, in the blackest of ink, if not in viscera. Don Enrique was attempting to lift something away from him, lift it and turn it and take it away for his very own, and he wasn't even asking.

There was a *mozo,* Will said. I mean, there is a *mozo.* His name is Gustavo. He might have been taken away from here because he made a mistake, and I'd like to say —

The *trabajador* is fine, the don said, abruptly. He looked at Will from beneath the dark lashes that surrounded his fluctuating eyes. He seemed irritated by the interruption, but his manners held. This . . . this Gustavo was part of my sister's household in Buenos Aires, the don continued. Perhaps you have heard of his . . . trials. He was once burned in an accident. It was no one's fault, not really. And I can assure you he is very well just now. He is not what I wish to speak about when we are speaking of the beauty.

Then maybe I can ask it this way, Will said, angry at the dismissal. Maybe I can ask why so many of these boys appear to have had . . . accidents. They got missing eyes, they got —

Why do you speak of damage at this moment, Mr. Testerman? This is not appropriate. We are talking of the *caballos.* We are having good conversations.

I'd just like to know —

We will speak of it no more, William Testerman. That is my word. You will refill your glass, perhaps, and I will take my own drink, and we will step outside to admire the chukkers, and the bold play, and the hardworking *caballos.* That is what the two of us are about, yes? The best of the *caballos.* The presence. The loyalty. We are much alike. You have a certain . . . American way of saying your opinions. Yet I enjoy speaking with you. This is a fortunate thing. You and

I, we see what is around us. We see very many pieces. And we put those pieces together while other men stand and see nothing. They are lazy, those men. They see nothing. So it is our duty to make the many perfections from those men and their pieces. You will know this soon, I believe, the don concluded, reaching once more for Will's callused and tired hand. You will see this very soon.

Dodo was the one who awakened him. Troubled Dodo. Exhausted and guilty Dodo. The rest of them were hungover from the alcohol they had sipped from abandoned glasses. They were all still sleeping except for Dodo, who never drank a drop.

Weel, you must come, he said, his eye patch hovering above Will's throbbing head like a black kite. *Ahora,* Weel. *Ahora.*

He knew from the sound of Dodo's voice that it was bad. He had to swallow the sour history of the don's endlessly offered champagne before he understood how bad it was.

It was the filly. What Dodo needed to show him was how one of Don Enrique's guests was riding the filly.

He didn't believe it at first. Her head was trussed in some other horse's bridle, with the noseband set too high and the headstall buckled short and tight. Her black forelock was crammed under the brow band. She was as red as Wyoming sandstone in the layered morning light, and about that fragile. The bit in her mouth was a heavy curb fitted with a pinching chain. Her mouth was open. Her tongue was lolling to one side, trying to avoid pressure from the yanked reins. She looked like she was going to choke.

The man was drunk. He was in light-colored pants and shiny ankle boots, and he wore a tailored cotton shirt of the kind Will had seen on many of the *padrónes* who had circled Don Enrique the day before. The man was drunk, but not so drunk that he couldn't saddle a horse. He had slapped a saddle with no pad onto the filly. Then he had dropped his considerable Argentine ass into the saddle.

Hey! Will shouted. What the hell are you — ? Hey!

The man did not appear to hear him. He was aiming the filly toward the polo pitches in a flailing, celebratory way.

Will ran after them. He did not want to grab at the reins. He feared for the filly's already bruised mouth. So he tried to get in front of them.

Ho, baby! he shouted. Whoa, there. Ho.

The filly stopped. She could see Will coming from behind. She was writhing under the weight of the stranger. There was froth at the corners of her mouth.

The drunken man did not appear to notice that the filly had stopped. He was riding to some cavalry charge or chukker in his imagination. His glossy feet were out of the stirrups, flapping ineffectually at the filly's heaving sides. His hands were held very far apart, with the reins draped absurdly between them.

You need to get off my horse, Will said to the man. He began to strip the bridle from the filly's head. He didn't care if she got loose. He hoped she would get loose, and go as far away as she could.

¿Quién eres? the man asked, smiling.

It don't matter who I am. I'm the owner of this horse. I'm a guest of Don Enrique's. So are you. You don't get to borrow this horse.

The man said something dreamy and soused in Spanish.

I'm being polite, Will said, his hands trembling even as he laid them on either side of the filly's neck to comfort her. Please dismount, *por favor.* That's what I'm asking.

He does not know you, Néstor said. He says the horse is his. Néstor had arrived from his burrow of sleep to stand behind Will after an apparent pleading by Dodo. The one-eyed Dodo stood even farther back, fidgeting. Néstor was dressed in the secondhand Oakland Raiders jersey he had worn the day before. The jersey was stretched and dirty at the hem.

I don't know him either. And I don't care.

He does not listen to men who . . . he does not listen to ones like us, Néstor said. He was twisting an orange bill cap in his hands. Will could see new, deep lines in the skin along the sides of Néstor's mouth. They looked like scars.

He don't need to listen. He just needs to get off my horse. She's scared to death.

Sí, Néstor said, I understand. I think it best to go to Don Enrique.

That's just what you *would* say, you ass kisser. You snitch. I don't need to go to Don Enrique for this. He ain't awake, anyhow. They went all night. They had their music on until an hour ago. I'll handle this. You can just get the fuck gone.

Néstor focused his bleary eyes on his boots. One thing, he said. He drew a folded piece of paper from his pants pocket. I know you do not like me ever again, but I am told to give you this.

I ain't in the mood for manners, Will said,

grabbing at the paper, stuffing it in his own pocket. He looked up at the drunken man and tried to get his attention. *Por favor, señor. Por favor.* I need you to get down from my horse.

The man looked high into the sky and laughed. He seemed to be galloping farther into his dreams. He reeked of red wine and the smothering perfume preferred by old men.

All right, Will said. *Perdón, señor.* That's all I ask. And he grabbed at the man's linen-covered leg and tugged at it until the man and the saddle he'd barely cinched both slid to the left. After a brief, clinging moment, the man thumped to the ground.

Néstor and Dodo were shocked. Dodo began to run away.

Gustavo would appreciate a move like that, wouldn't he? Will said to Néstor. Gustavo has a good sense of humor. It's too bad he's not here to see mine.

Néstor turned and walked back toward the barns. He moved like a man pushing into a heavy wind.

But the man who had been on the filly didn't seem to mind his new position on the ground. He noticed, but he didn't mind. *Ven aquí,* he said to Will. *Ven aquí.* Help me. I go for the dancing.

That figures, Will said.

He didn't trust himself to speak another word. He uncinched the saddle that hung from the filly and dropped it to the ground. He flung the bridle far away from them both. The filly trotted off the moment she was free. She did not wait for Will or a single thing he might do or say.

Distrust was a sharp splinter in her eye. He could see it, the chasm between what she expected of men and what had suddenly proved to be true. She wasn't hurt, not beyond some chafing at one corner of her mouth. This, he thought, would be the hard part. He needed to go easy with her even though there was no portion of him, not even his heart, that felt easy in any way.

They were alone at the edge of the polo fields. The drunken man had stumbled his way back toward the brick house. The air above the fields still smelled of torn and pounded grass and of the pit where the Argentines had grilled slab after slab of raw meat over a fire that had raised crowns of orange flame into the night.

He tried to tell her a story.

This hasn't started as a good day for either one of us, he said, swallowing. But we can get through it. We just have to go back to our own expectations. We have to get rid of the expectations these other people have for us.

He stood in front of her with his arms held slightly away from his sides. He didn't have a halter or a rope. He knew he didn't need one.

A woman I met down in Texas used to love to tell me how tough certain horses are, he said. She owned Arabians. There's no doubt in my mind that a Arabian horse can be tough. You know what I mean. You met Lark up at the Black Bell Ranch, and old Lark was tough on you.

He was close enough to touch the filly, but he didn't touch her. He kept his arms by his sides.

This Texas woman was a little crazy, he said. And she had some money to spend. I don't know where the money came from, exactly. People in Texas seem to have money like people in Wyoming have Kleenex. It just falls out of their pockets when they need it. But she had money. So she thought she'd go over there to the Middle East and see what she could learn from the Arabs themselves.

He watched her ears. She was still very tense. A big part of her wanted to break away. He could see the struggle in the angle of her head and in the burn of her exquisite eye.

The Arabs don't take to women directly, he said, quietly. They wouldn't meet with her. So this woman had to deal with them through a man from New Zealand. She thought that was insulting. She felt disrespected. But she saw some wonderful horses, barn after barn after barn of them. All of them trained on sand and broke to saddle in the Arab way of doing things. For Arabs, it's mostly about racing. The tribes race against each other all the time, and they gamble like hell over it. But they sometimes bragged about raids and wars, too. This horse, they would say, pointing to some old broodmare, she is the daughter of the daughter of the mare who carried sheik so-and-so across the desert to avenge his brother. And this mare, they would say, can run to heaven and back without a single stop. The Arabs care about their heaven.

He was within reach of her now, just about parallel to her shoulder. He thought of Art Slocum, the crazy vet who had cured the filly when she was lame. Art Slocum. Jesus. He wished he had some of the old man's magic right now.

It all made the Texas woman a little angry, he said. A Arab man won't have nothing do

371

to with a woman in public, but when it comes to fighting, he likes his female horse. Mares are great stalkers. I'll bet you didn't know that, did you? The Arabs claim you can slit the throat of your greatest enemy in his tent when you're riding a mare. What do you think of that?

He almost had her. Her breathing was slower, and she had cocked her left ear toward him, ready for his guidance. He felt a swelling, aching fatigue in his own legs. Guidance? It had been a long twenty-four hours, a sucker punch of a day in ways he couldn't even think about yet. Don Enrique had fed him and filled him with bubbling wines and talked him through the theater show of polo. They had watched Edwards ride Captiva as if he weighed no more than an empty shirt draped across her back. Edwards had scored three goals, and he had carried himself like a prince of the saddle. Will had met people who gave him their hands but not their names. He had been ignored but not allowed to return to the barns until the sun set and darkness gave the talkative Don Enrique the comfort he appeared to crave. Women drifted in with the darkness. Will didn't know if he had ever seen so much that was perfect and so much that was wasteful in a single turn of the clock. He had stumbled to his bare room feeling caught in the wrong set of snares. And now, he didn't know how to end the story he'd just begun. The Texas woman hadn't told him anything else. She had mostly been trying to punch up her reputation as an important person.

Ah, shit, he said, leaning into the filly, bracing against her. The stuff I ought to be telling you is the stuff about me. About us. How there once was this kid from Wyoming who wanted to live in a uncomplicated way and make horses into the best horses they could be. And how this kid, because he was too stupid or too broke or too ignorant about what went on inside of his own head, couldn't ever seem to make that happen. It ought to be simple, right? You do a thing, and you do it right, and it gets done. But this stupid Wyoming person kept reading the situations wrong. He kept getting the people so wrong that it didn't matter if he got the horses right.

He pressed his thrumming forehead against the smooth skin of her withers. She was warm there. No matter what, she always felt warmer — better suited to the world — than he did.

I know what I said to you once, he told her. I said that I would always take care of you. That was a lie. I haven't been able to do a damn thing about other people and their evil behaviors. I haven't been able to stop things that I should have stopped. So here we are, and it's time for me to man up and tell you the truth. That son of a bitch I never seen before just came out here and put a saddle on you. I want to be mad as hell about that — and I am mad. I'm also fucking emptied out. There's a bad piece of paper in my pocket right now. Néstor, that *maricón,* just gave it to me. I don't even have to read it. I already know what it says. It says I have to get back home, and get there now. My mother is sick.

So here we are. We are at a steep turn, filly, and I'm trying to see how we can negotiate the slope. Maybe you can help me. That fat man slapped a saddle on your back like he owned you. But you don't have to act like he owns you, do you? Nobody owns you. I don't care what Don Enrique says about men and all of their pieces. I'm the one who got all sewed up in this mess. I'm the one who can't shake hisself free.

He placed his trembling hands on her, one on her sleek neck, the other on the wood-carver's bow of her ribs. How about that's the promise you pretend to make to me? he said. It can be your turn to lie. You can say to me that nobody and nothing will ever own you. You can say to me that you're gonna stand tall in your pretty little life and always be free.

There was a numb weight in his booted feet. He knew the feeling. It was the weight of shame and poor calculation. Edwards would see the heaviness on him as if it were a visible set of iron chains, and Edwards would have no pity. This was all Will could hope for, that he could at least negotiate with Edwards's lack of pity.

The manager was in his office. He had showered and shaved, despite the early hour. He was dressed in jeans and a collared shirt the color of pine needles. Will thought he would be seeing plenty of that color soon enough, the dark pines of the Rampart Range, the timber that hid his father's wandering cows and calves.

You still drunk? Edwards asked. Don Enrique has told me to keep you happy here, which I have no choice about, but I don't have to play nice with you if you're drunk.

I'm not staying, he said. I'm sober enough to tell you that.

Edwards jerked his chin back. Will's words were rocks from a slingshot.

You're what?

I'm leaving. You and the don set it up just about perfect. I have to admit that I'm closed up in more than one of your boxes. But that don't change what's about to happen. I'm leaving.

You're turning tail? I think that's about the most candy-assed statement I've heard from you yet, cowboy.

There are conditions, Will said.

Conditions? Edwards was standing behind his office desk, his fists knotted against his hips. Will found himself looking at the thicket of polo mallets that leaned against the undecorated wall behind Edwards. Who had thought up the polo mallet? The game would be more true, he thought, if it were still played with murderous wooden clubs.

Sure, Will said. Don Enrique wants me to stay. I believe that part. He'd like to showcase me for a while, for reasons that are mostly in his head. He seems to think I'm some sort of echo for him. And your horses are worth working with — I'll give you that. But you don't want me here. If I leave right now, you get what you want.

And what do you get? Edwards asked, snake-coiling his eyes.

Gustavo, Will said. I get your assurance that Gustavo is cut loose and not beat to death or sent back to Argentina in a shipping container or whatever it is you people do. Maybe I'm exaggerating here. I'm in an exaggerated mood. But I think you know what I mean. I want that boy to have his life back.

He could see slippage in the way Edwards shifted his face down toward his desk. He had guessed right. The man was tempted.

You'd trust me, Edwards said.

I'd have to, Will said. But this is the way for you to get rid of me and for the don to have what he really wants — without all the slow-motion courtship and bullshit. He don't want my cowboy personality. He wants my horse, probably because you've said nice things about her. Good for you. She's not ready. She as breakable as a bowl of glass, and I swore to myself that I would never walk away from her before she was ready. But she and I ain't at the top of the heap here. So I *am* trusting you. You're a empty person. You got a cold center I don't like. But I haven't seen you be ruinous with a horse. She's got a chance with you.

I don't have the power to —

You got all the power you need, Edwards. *Thomas.* So here's how it needs to go. I'm gonna drive out of here in that Cadillac you hate so much. Maybe I'll tell the boys I'm checking the bus station, looking for their friend Gustavo. I'll be gone for a few hours, long enough for you to turn the right wheels. But I'm coming back for my gear. And for my Appaloosa. You touch Hawk, or mess with me having him shipped out of here in any way, and I will kill you. Think about it. You got the upper hand. So does the don. There's nothing in what I'm offering that is gonna set you back.

The heaviness in his body began to heat itself. It wanted to boil itself into pain, to become molten and to flow. But he couldn't let that happen. Not yet.

Do you hear me?

Loud and clear, Edwards said. He had sucked his lips in behind his teeth, stretching his mustache, misaligning it. Will could see how right he'd been. The manager had been craving victory, and victory had just been given to him.

What's your price? Edwards asked. The don will —

There is no price, Will said. When you have time to think about it, you'll probably agree that what's really being bought and sold here ain't my filly.

Welcome to the horse —

I know. I know your motto, he said, his lungs feeling as though they had been welded closed with hot metal. Welcome to the way things really are.

The Cadillac started on the first crank. He rolled down both windows because the floor mats stunk of mold.

He had backed the silver car right up to the trimmed hedge before he saw David in his rearview mirror. David was running after the Cadillac with his skinny arms in the air, waving them like a crazy man.

No leave! the boy shouted. Will braked the Cadillac. David's dish-round face was blotched with exertion. Will could only hope his own face was less readable.

I'm gonna look for Gustavo, he told the boy. I think I might know how to find him. I ain't leaving for good. Not yet.

Gustavo? *¿Puedes encontrar a Gustavo?*

I don't have him yet, but I'm working on it.

The boy looked confused. But Señor Edwards, he say . . .

He say what?

David closed his mouth, despite the fact that he was breathing hard. He seemed to be replaying a past moment in his mind. Señor Edwards say Gustavo *está acabado.* Never come back. But I am maybe wrong. *Estúpido.* You are finding him.

And Señor Edwards is helping me, Will

said, almost winking despite the nausea he felt below his throat. You go tell everybody that. I'll be back as soon as I can.

David waved the car out the driveway before he began his sturdy trot back toward the barns.

It took Will twenty minutes to get to the first place the Yellow Pages had listed as a bus station. He had decided to make his errand as real as possible. And why not? He had nowhere else to go. The bus station was located in a small, crushed can of a building that looked as though it had been torn off the end of a strip mall. It was empty at the moment. The pavement in front was puddled with something that looked like melted strawberry ice cream. A digital schedule claimed the next arrival from San Diego was due in two hours. Will pulled the Cadillac into a marked square of pavement as if the whole lot were filled and he needed to be careful about matters like parking. Would Gustavo, or any of the boys, ever be allowed to get near a bus station? Gustavo had once told Will that Edwards kept their passports and visas locked in his office, in the same place he kept all the precious papers on the horses. Will wondered if Gustavo — if any of them — actually had a passport.

He could almost see the boy there, however, paying for passage to San Francisco or L.A. with his scarred hands, claiming he could get easy work at one of the racetracks near the city. *You not see me in Hollywood, Don Guillermo? The big films, and the womans. You not see me famous, with my handsome face?*

Gustavo would be a joker to the very end.

He sat in the Cadillac for an hour. He did everything he could to keep his head empty of recrimination and grief. It did not help to think of his family — or even his mother — not in any way. He could not imagine Wyoming as a home for the man he had become.

Before he returned to the dim and shrinking whirlpool that was Estancia Flora, he stopped once more. There was a bodega on the boulevard that he had visited from time to time. He had bought food and magazines there for himself. And once or twice he had bought gifts for the boys, items he had guessed at. Fresh tamales for Dodo. Mountain Dew for Néstor. Pecan rolls for Ignacio and David. A jar of the hottest green chili for Gustavo. The bodega was run by a family of Pakistani immigrants. He had seen the daughter of the family, with one parent or the other, in the bodega each time he stopped. The daughter was there now, with her hair covered in a bright-pink scarf and golden bangles on her wrists. She smiled at him, modestly, as he came through the door, and the tentative brace of her smile made him halt in his tracks. He couldn't do it. He couldn't *buy* anything for Dodo or David or Néstor or Ignacio. Not ever again.

But for Gustavo he could do one last joking thing.

He asked the Pakistani girl for a scratch-off Lotto card. He wouldn't be able to play the lottery in Wyoming. Wyoming was not a place that believed in luck. He took the stiff rectangle of cardboard from the girl when she handed it to him, and he made a point of smiling back at her as he paid for it, of being polite. He looked at the ticket's garish colors, the daubs of silver powder that covered the numbers he'd just paid for, his secrets, his chance. He planned to put the card into his wallet. He planned to keep it there for a very long time. A reminder. Then he noticed the shelf of inexpensive luggage that floated above the searing pink of the girl's head scarf, above the shadowy pigeon-holes of cigars and cigarettes.

I'd like to buy a satchel, too, he said, knowing the bigger truth when he saw it. *El boleto.* There would be one more reckoning

that he would have to survive. *El boleto.* The
filly. Gustavo. All the tickets in the world.
There would be one more knife to the guts,
whether he liked it or not. He fought to
keep the words he spoke to the girl calm
and normal behind his teeth.

Sa-shel, the girl said, puzzled.

Yes, he said. One of those bags from up
there, a medium-sized one. Please.

The girl followed the pointing of his
finger, nodded, and stepped onto a small
stool to pull a plastic-wrapped bag into her
arms. It was black.

This? she asked.

Sí, he said, forgetting for a second that
the girl wasn't Mexican or Argentine. How
much?

Nine and ninety-nine, the girl said,
pleased. It is very cheap.

I guess I knew that, he said, speaking to
no one in particular, understanding that he
would never forget that sorry black bag, not
ever in his entire life. Cheap is perfect. I
thought I was a person who put stock in
important things that can't be taken away.
But cheap is who I really am.

The story he would never tell.

He coasted the Cadillac down the dry,
white carpet of the driveway. The sign an-

nouncing Estancia Flora hung crooked from its posts. Some van driver had run into it after the long night of revelries. Two things were clear to Will when he passed the fruit trees that grew higher than the roof of the beige brick house. The estancia's four-horse transport, the one with no markings, was gone. Driven away. This meant that Edwards, conniving bastard that he was, had been true to his word. The stall in the barn that had been the filly's was empty. And Dodo was standing in the turnaround, not next to the turnaround, but *in* it, waiting and waiting, with his small hands practically shredding the lead rope that attached him to the gelding Hawk. The Appaloosa was fine. He was grazing. And his large, spotted rump hung in the midmorning air like a hysterically spotted balloon.

When he parked the car, he felt something steel sharp break away from above his knees and flay its way up through his rigid body. This was the price. It could never be forgotten. It was not to be acknowledged.

Weel, Mr. Weel. *Han llevado tú potranca.* Dodo ran to him with his small mouth popping open like a fish's. Dodo ran right into his arms.

It's all right, Dodo. It's not something I didn't know. But I thank you for thinking of my filly. And for protecting Hawk.

But she is gone. *Le han llevado,* like Gustavo.

I know it looks the same, he said to the boy. But it ain't. How did she — ? But he couldn't finish his question.

Did Edwards do the driving? he asked.

Sí, Señor Edwards. He did not look so angry as sometimes.

I guess not, Will said.

His whole body felt like a sewer pipe, a sucking drain. The parts of him that he recognized as Will Testerman were swirling away. And he wasn't sure they would ever come back, not even if he wanted them to.

Who are you today, Will Testerman? What will you be today?

He knew his dying mother would not ask him that damn question ever again.

He took the empty black bag from the car, and he made himself stand up straight. He reached into his left boot and pulled up the sock that had slipped somewhat off his heel. Then he reached into his right boot and did the same. He walked — he walked with his shoulders square and his breathing like something deep and unblocked that would come from a man and not a hoodwinked child — and he made his way to the tiny cupboard of his room in the barn.

And there it was, on the filthy pond of his mattress. They hadn't even bothered to hide it. So much cash. A heap. A bonfire. Thirty-five or forty thousand of the don's unconsidered dollars. They had left the money tumbling and contorted in a plastic grocery sack. He had not wanted payment, but he had known it would be there. There were men in the world who could not end their days without a sale. And he had a container for the cash. He had just purchased it. He had the perfect suitcase for a plucked and failing man. Right there in his hands.

ACKNOWLEDGMENTS

CWS. RWS. Meade and Andrea Dominick. Katie Dublinski. Gail Hochman. Sue Ibarra. Jim and Sharon Southard. Eileen Beckman, who taught me how to ride a pony. Dr. Dewey Dominick, who wrote down his stories. The young man with the lovely bay filly he hoped to take to California.

Thank you.

There is a small place in Wyoming known as Lost Cabin. My fictional Lost Cabin, however, is its own kind of town.

ABOUT THE AUTHOR

Alyson Hagy lives in Laramie, Wyoming.

The employees of Thorndike Press hope you have enjoyed this Large Print book. All our Thorndike, Wheeler, and Kennebec Large Print titles are designed for easy reading, and all our books are made to last. Other Thorndike Press Large Print books are available at your library, through selected bookstores, or directly from us.

For information about titles, please call:
  (800) 223-1244

or visit our Web site at:
  http://gale.cengage.com/thorndike

To share your comments, please write:
  Publisher
  Thorndike Press
  10 Water St., Suite 310
  Waterville, ME 04901

CPSIA information can be obtained
at www.ICGtesting.com
Printed in the USA
FFOW042136160413